DAVID OWEN was born in Zimbabwe and grew up
in Malawi, Swaziland and South Africa. He lived
in London before migrating to Australia in 1986.
A past editor of *Island* magazine, he writes fiction
and nonfiction. He lives in Hobart, Tasmania.

A PUFFERFISH MYSTERY

How the
Dead See

DAVID OWEN

EER
Edward Everett Root, Publishers, Brighton, 2024.

EER CRIME FICTION
Edward Everett Root, Publishers, Co. Ltd.,
Atlas Chambers, 33 West Street, Brighton, Sussex, BN1 2RE, England.
Full details of our stock-holding overseas agents in America, Australia, China,
Europe and Japan, and how to order our books, are given on our website.
www.eerpublishing.com

edwardeverettroot@yahoo.co.uk

We stand with Ukraine!
EER books are **NOT** available for sale in Russia or Belarus.

First published by Forty Degrees South Pty. Ltd, Hobart, Tasmania 2011.

Cover by Hilton Owen.
'Pufferfish' series logo by Hilton Owen.

British production by Pageset Ltd., High Wycombe, Buckinghamshire.

|

A MYSTERIOUS ISLAND, TASMANIA. TAKE THIS FACT. I'M WEARING a Tasmanian devil tie. I bought it exactly a year ago on a fund-raising day to combat devil cancer, a freakish disease circulating through an inbred population by biting, and still without a cure. Today, I'll just bung money in a tin.

Heineken here. Detective Inspector Franz Heineken, long-time copper of the Tasmanian Police Force and still with a few irons in the fire, though less of the latter in the belly so to speak.

The nickname's Pufferfish. A prickly, toxic bastard, ability to inflate and even explode when severely provoked. Such is my career that I'm happiest down in the murk and decay of our criminal side, of which we have our share here at around forty degrees south.

Tasmania, for those who know nothing about the place, is a large island, about the same size as Sri Lanka or Ireland but nowhere near either. In 1803 red-coated British soldiers and their chained convicts came ashore to this place, then known as Van Diemen's Land and, to preserve themselves, set about eliminating its perceived dangers, namely nine black tribes and a rare striped marsupial carnivore. A difficult birth, you might say, without pain relief, and the bringing forth of a strange child.

I'm at my desk in my office, in the big old building with its majestic views of the port city of Hobart, early on Monday morning. Head down. Depressed? No. Merely reading through southern Tasmania's only major newspaper, the *Mercury*, going strong since 1858 or thereabouts.

Young Detective Constable Faye Addison, seated on the other side of my desk, is tapping stuff into her iPad. Ostensibly we're yacking about what we did at the weekend, so I'm aware that she watched a forgettable Netflix movie called *Unforgettable*, but my attention's been caught by an exclusive that scuba diving 'eco-guerillas' are planning to cut salmon farm nets in the D'Entrecasteaux Channel and Port Esperance.

Rafe, Detective Tredway, my main offsider, strolls in. He's well built and as laid back as a working class Aussie bloke could wish to be, but the one you want in a crisis. It's not unusual for this amiable boofhead to be fashionably late on a Monday, but his face isn't quite the one we cheerio'd last Friday. Drooping off the left side of his bottom lip is a swelling, like a purply-black overripe cherry plum. To go with it, he's sheepish.

'Mate, what *happened?*' Faye scowls in squeamish sympathy.

'Guys, laugh and get over it,' he says. 'I took this one for the team.'

'Meaning? You need half your face lanced, Rafe.'

'Yeah, boss, yeah.' He sits, a wisp of a lisp escaping his fat lip. 'Played cricket Saturday arvo, remember? Against the DDTs, the Deloraine and District Tremblers, and their field's a paddock in winter, so never mind how she's mowed in spring, she's full of these knots of cowshit-fed grass come summertime. And, y'know, I'm fielding at fine leg and go down to stop a miscued hoick by a very ordinary batter, down on one knee, ball whacks a grass topknot and I cop the fucking cherry in the lip!'

'Or you muffed a simple catch, Rafe.'

2

'Jeez boss! Fair dinkum, mate. Plus the canine's wobbly. But I'm not going to the dentist just yet. "Open wide Mr Tredway." That'd split the lump and how painful would *that* be?'

'Is it sore?' Faye asks.

He sits alongside her. 'Nah, not at all. Not even aware of it.'

'Of course you are!'

He ignores her, pretends to. 'Tell you something, though, we won by two runs. How's that?'

'Score any yourself?'

'The vital two, boss.' He laughs comically with a wince out of the undamaged side of his mouth.

'I think it might be a good idea if you take a day or so off, Rafe.'

'No, seriously boss, I'd rather come in here and do fuck all than the same at home.'

OUR BANTER'S INTERRUPTED BY A CALL FROM THE RADIO ROOM.

'Incident at a New Town property, Mr Heineken, involving a firearm, owner a Mr Gavin Bellyard reporting his safe broken into and his German shepherd watchdog shot dead.'

'That's it?'

'Yep, patrol car's there, no sign of perps, Mr Bellyard is physically fine. He's saying he's just back from interstate. But scared. A dangerous gunman in daytime New Town, if you follow.'

'I follow. Okay, we'll go and have a look. Give me an address.'

A robbery in the northern suburbs would normally not be my business, but there have been a spate of incidents involving firearms in the area and the problem's been given a degree of priority.

LIKE ARNOTT'S ASSORTED BISCUITS, NEW TOWN IS A MIXED suburb. Skewed street fronts of tenacious little weatherboards stare defiantly at grand old homes in leafy gardens. On a New Town pavement you're as liable to brush past a swaggering fashionista as a weaving derro, not necessarily distinguishing between the two. New Town, by turns stately, middle class, run down, historic and cosmopolitan, dominates the inner northern suburbs of Hobart folded around the lower slopes of kunanyi aka Mount Wellington.

Bellyard's is a grand old sandstone and red brick with pebble dash home, set well back behind a high wooden fence in a garden of mature trees with a centrepiece oak that would have been planted when the place was built long ago, say when the *Hindenburg* was making flaming headlines. Big purply lavender bushes front each bricked flowerbed off the steps leading up to the front door, which is angled open. My initial impression of whatever illegal act has been committed here is that it was a good place to do it. Quiet posh street, high fence, owner interstate. Back home now though, an elderly Merc in the garage.

The uniform's been looking out for us, and she emerges onto the corpse-grey stone verandah, a wizened elder behind her. I've heard of Gavin Bellyard, because you hear of almost everyone in an island of half a million souls, and I'd heard stout tales of the man, but the image I'd had of this Taswegian from wealthy stock, dating back to British authority figures versus convict rabble, was wrong. Gavin Bellyard, far from being a spring-stepping symbol of old moneyed success, active and fit and strongly supporting the concept of His Honour throwing the book at the criminal classes, is a straw man on tin legs, with decrepit wispy white head hairs and elephantine ears. And he's tiny, though he'd tower over a child. The constable's a big girl in front of him.

'Morning, Deanne. All good?'

'Yep, premises checked, boss. Looks like a professional safe break job. And the dead dog, over there.' She points.

The hound, on a patch of ground swept smoothly bare by the fronds of a willow tree, has stiffened in its death repose, head glued to the ground by a pool of thick black congealed blood. Big droning flies accentuate the deathliness.

'Good morning Mr Bellyard, I'm Detective Inspector Franz Heineken and this is my colleague Detective Rafe Tredway. Sorry about your dog.'

I have a quick look. The animal took a single, neat shot through the top of the head. The exposed side of the muzzle shows plenty of white hair. This was an ancient beast, a long-retired watchdog.

'This is very shocking,' Bellyard says, his voice emotional. 'I've lived here for thirty-two years without any … and the necklace, they must have known somehow. It's worth a fortune!' He gazes passionately out and up at our great mountain, as if it might provide the sympathy lacking in us.

'Let's go inside, Mr Bellyard. Show us the crime scene, and tell us everything you can to assist us in dealing with this.'

Rafe says, 'Would your dog have been barking and maybe alerted the neighbours, Mr Bellyard?'

'Solo was old and arthritic. He probably would have wagged his tail at the bastards. They didn't need to *kill* him.'

The interior of this place confirms its exterior. Old wealth, stuffy, ancient money. The best way to get it out would be backing a van up and loading it with the silverware and furniture that's everywhere, including some rare colonial-era pieces. They, whoever they were, could have driven off with a nice haul. But no, everything by way of furnishings is perfectly in place. So what kind of a break-in was this, eh? One that also required the elimination of a harmless dog?

Silence springs to mind.

We pad along a well-worn Persian carpet in an elegant passageway. The thing about this kind of situation is that there are three of us and one Bellyard, and in that sense we're also violating him on his own heretofore sacred patch. It's true, coming up against criminality can be life changing, because the victim seldom comprehends why a villain chooses to be a villain. Then again, frequently, nor can the villain understand it of himself.

On the dining room table, face up, is a framed painting of a John Glover-style rural Tasmanian midlands scene. The painting had been on an internal wall, hiding the safe. Its small heavy door is wide open, revealing its emptiness.

'I just can't believe this,' Bellyard says. 'Virtually no one knew about that safe. My late wife, of course, my children – they're settled all over the world, now – and a few of my close friends. And that's it!'

Rafe takes a closer look. 'Bloke spun his way in, boss. It's a group two combo lock.'

'What does he mean?' Bellyard says, looking at me.

'Drilling down to bypass the lock is generally the easiest way in, Mr Bellyard. It's quick. But noisy. Here we had an experienced safecracker listening for a click to find the contact area. He then worked out how many wheels make up the lock of your safe. That enabled him to manipulate the wheels to work out the right combination.'

'Got to be Fink Mountgarrett,' Rafe says. 'And he's been sweet talking everyone he's long retired!'

'*Who?*' Bellyard's all indignant huge ears.

'Nobody.' I shake my head. 'You didn't hear that.'

But the wizened old cove's staring hard at Rafe, who seems to be reconsidering the wisdom of his blurt, accurate though it may well prove to be.

6

'Tell me who he is.' Bellyard angrily sucks in his cheeks, his lips, his budgerigar-like chest. 'I want to confront the monster who killed Solo.'

I like it. Never mind the sparklers. I think we can eliminate the old cove as party to an insurance fraud.

'Mr Bellyard, again, my condolences for your dog. The fact is by the look of it the animal's been dead for at least twenty-four hours, probably longer. Where have you been?'

'I came back from Melbourne this morning. I travel there frequently on business, even though I'm long retired. I have property interests that take me to shareholder meetings.'

'When did you fly to Melbourne?'

'Last Friday morning, for the meeting. Then I generally spend the weekend with my daughter and her family at their Sorrento home. Solo is always fine outdoors in warmer weather, he has his kennel and nudges the biscuit feeder and of course he no longer needs to be exer …'

Emotion stills him.

'In that case, Mr Bellyard, the thief or thieves will probably have known they had a few days at their disposal, given you travel regularly.'

'"Have known"?'

'They've been watching you. Either because they've know-ledge of the safe, or just thought your property was worth knocking off.'

'Criminal scum.'

'Indeed, and they pay my stained wages. But I must ask you this, because I don't think this was an opportunistic visit, have any strangers, any unlikely individuals been in your house in recent times? On legitimate business, say?'

He gazes at me anew, initially perplexed, then astounded.

'The rising damp firm!'

We wait. He frowns, and we watch the cogs clicking and grinding as he takes another unwelcome step into the grimy world of cops and crims.

'Where are we now, late February? It was right at the beginning of spring, last September we agreed upon, because the winter rains would establish just where the water was breaching the foundations. That is when they came and, as they said, "patted the house down" for rising damp. A reputable firm, no question. My brother recommended them.'

'So we're talking five plus months ago. Would they have come through this room?'

'Oh, yes. I clearly remember a fellow on his hands and knees doing something to the skirting boards.' Bellyard points down at them.

'So he, or another, could have removed the painting in the course of their business?'

'I suppose so.'

'We'll need the name of this company, Mr Bellyard. And I must ask you to keep out of this room while our forensic people, who'll be here soon, do their work. Now, let's go to the next step and talk about exactly what was stolen.'

'Right. I have photographs of the necklace. In and out of its box.'

'Good man,' Rafe says. 'Anything else in the safe?'

Bellyard leads us through to a neat-looking room with a big old desk, fireplace, pair of leather armchairs.

'Some cash,' he says. 'A wad of zlotys. I travel to Poland once a year, I have an interest in a piggery through my late wife, and so when I get back I put what I've got in my wallet in the safe for the next trip.'

'How much in the wad?'

'About a thousand.'

'A thousand what, Mr Bellyard?'

'Sorry, I'm sorry, you wouldn't know. A wad of zloty bank notes equivalent to about a thousand Australian dollars.' He sifts through one of the desk drawers, brings out a number of manila folders, selects one, opens it for us.

'That's excellent, Mr Bellyard. We'll need these.'

'Of course.'

The necklace has been professionally photographed against a black cloth backdrop, and also in its opened box of fine-grained walnut with ornate brass hinges and locking clasp, the item nestled on a red velvet bed. The jeweller's name is engraved on the inside of the box lid.

My mobile. Radio Room. I swing away, back into the dining room.

'Heineken.'

'G'day, sir. An emergency call has come in reporting the death of a man at a Tinderbox Road property. In his car, pipe from the exhaust into the vehicle.'

'What's that go to do with me?'

'His girlfriend's made the call and she's saying it's murder. She was pretty hysterical. And the deceased apparently is Rory Stillrock.'

'Jesus, the actor?'

'It's the right address, yes.'

Not that Jesus was an actor, though he may have been.

'Get hold of Faye Addison and tell her to be waiting for me out the front of HQ. I'm on my way.'

2

WHERE NEW TOWN IS A SOLID, POPULOUS AND POPULAR INNER city suburb, Tinderbox Road, not forty minutes away further down the river beyond Kingston and Blackmans Bay, winds serenely through the tall bushland of its narrow high-spined peninsula, eventually dipping down to the cutest little beach in the southern hemisphere. The properties are five-acre blocks or more, well wooded and rising up against the spine, or down to the estuary cliff, and they cost a bit. I hadn't actually known that Tasmania's very own Hollywood bad boy, Rory Stillrock, was a Tinderbox Road resident. Not that it really matters now, though I can understand that the privacy afforded by the area might have appealed to him, given the controversies and train wreck of his career.

Faye's waiting on the pavement in Davey Street. Old school that I am, I lean across and flick her door open.

'So what have you got, Faye?'

'Seems a bit messy, boss,' she says. 'The girlfriend, an Emma Lexington, drove to his place this morning, and –'

'Girlfriend but not live-in?'

'Don't know yet, but because he only separated from his wife, was it less than a year ago, maybe that's why? If Emma Lexington doesn't live with him yet.'

10

'Be a little bit out of character, wouldn't it, if this is the same Rory Stillrock who fornicated his way to the top and then all the way down again. Anyway, go on.'

Traffic's banked up at the Anglesea Barracks traffic lights. Come on, come on, we've got a suspicious suicide to attend.

Faye says, 'The girlfriend's apparently driven there, gone in the house, couldn't find him, then gone to the garage, presuming his car wouldn't be there. But it is, it's locked, he's in it, there's a pipe from the exhaust into the back window.'

'Engine running?'

'Don't know. She tries to smash a window, then calls triple zero. It's then she's screaming that he's dead and that he's been murdered, put in the car and murdered. We dispatched a Kingston car. Then she takes it upon herself to jump back in her vehicle and try to race back to Kingston to get help. But she left the road and hit a ditch. It just so happened a couple saw this, they're off-duty ambos, and they're administering to her at the scene. They've called in. They say she's unhurt but in shock.'

'This is on Tinderbox Road?'

'Yeah, by their description it would be about two k's from Stillrock's place, if that.'

'Mhm. How do we see murder in suicide? Let's find out.'

At the top of Davey Street, where two of its four lanes enter the Southern Outlet highway, I whack on the blue and red lights and the Commodore surges us forward.

I use the radio. 'Rafe, forensics arrived?'

'Not yet.'

'Give them a hurry up. What more from Bellyard?'

'Says the necklace is valued at two hundred k, but he reckons it's worth more 'cause of its age.'

'Get its description to the media fast. Talk to Walter.'

'Will do, boss. So what's the story with Rory bloody Stillrock? Amazing the grog and drugs didn't get him before now.'

Faye says, 'Or that he didn't root himself to death.'

'Oh yeah, you got propositioned by the great man did you?'

She laughs. 'Mate, I was in nappies when he made his movies. Besides, I don't do great fallen idols.'

'I'll let that ageist remark go by, Detective Constable.'

She snickers. 'Oops, sorry boss.'

Rafe signs off. He's got work to do. On-selling a diamond necklace of that value won't be easy, not on the Modest Isle at any rate, so the likelihood is the thief will get rid of it on the big island or overseas. Or, if he knows what he's doing, he'll break it up, remake the necklace, set some stones in rings, whatever. In any event, the image of this necklace needs to be splashed across the media. It's a job Chief Superintendent Walter D'Hayt, my immediate superior, enjoys, talking to the media.

Walter and I are not close, in the way that the North and South Poles are not close. It's a longstanding enmity, a constant source of friction that Chief Commissioner Grif Hunt, head of this island's 100-strong police force, could do without. But the three of us live with it. And at least we're alive. Unlike, say, Rory Stillrock, whose demise will rapidly shunt Mr Bellyard's late wife's necklace out of the news. Stillrock, because of what he once was, and through even the merest hint of foul play, is most surely about to become the news, big news.

We zip through Kingston, noted for being one of the faster growing suburbs in Australia, its beach thinly populated now that schools are back in session. And it has a 1000-strong Dutch connection, giving it most favoured suburb status in the Heineken book. The adjacent suburb of Blackmans Bay, with a smaller beach but boasting rights to a blowhole, leads to the beginning of Tinderbox Road at Illawarra Primary School – the little red uniformed children out for morning recess, all over the place like a juvenile rash – and the narrowing road addresses a slight incline.

'Amazing all these houses,' Faye says. 'My mum used to bring me to visit a friend here when I was little, and I just remember it being like the suburb suddenly ends and the bush begins.' She gestures to the sprawling cluster of large modern houses that effortlessly colonised the expansive hill-side sloping towards the beach.

'My friend lived somewhere in there when it was just one farmhouse and paddocks, nothing else. A few dams. Some goats and heaps of free range chooks. Oh and they had a big vegie patch in the corner, right there.' She points at the roadside's edge. 'I remember one day we were in it eating carrots or something, watching the dad bury a goat. He'd had to get it across the paddock to the burial site in a wheelbarrow, it was that big. I still remember him saying it died of cancer, even though my friend told me they put acupuncture needles in its face, around a big black cancer lump, to try to fix the animal. Even now I remember thinking, there's goat cancer?'

And I'm thinking, there's goat acupuncture? But I just say, 'So the needles didn't work on that occasion, but well done to them for trying.'

'Yeah.'

Kingston's Senior Sergeant Jimmy Lewis calls in.

'G'day Franz, I'm at the Stillrock property. It's as the young lady says, deceased male. In a Cadillac Seville. The vehicle's garaged. I've had a quick look around. No other person on the premises and no particular signs of a disturbance, or violence, other than her smashing at the vehicle windows.'

'Suicide note?'

13

'Not that I saw. Fact is, he may have been having a good time, there's empty wine bottles in the lounge room, and they had a fair dip at a bottle of whisky.'

'"They", Jimmy?'

'Well, it'd 've been a big party for one.'

'Okay. Faye Addison's with me. We're first going to talk to the girlfriend Emma Lexington.'

'I stopped and told them you were on the way, Franz. Physically she looks alright, the ambulance people are saying minor whiplash at most. It's the shock though, the double whammy.'

'Well, then, she needs medical treatment,' Faye says. 'Call an ambulance, boss?'

'Let's have a look at her first. Jimmy, we're going through a couple of sharp descending bends, and the Iron Pot's visible at ten o'clock. Old quarry on the right.'

'Got you. They're a couple of minutes away, less.'

'Right, see you at Stillrock's.'

I accelerate along a short straight road. Very calm and rustic out here, tall native trees, dappled sunshine, magpies, ravens, tiny forty-spot pardalotes. But our focus lies dead ahead.

EMMA LEXINGTON'S WHITE BMW CONVERTIBLE IS BARELY OFF the road, but it's angled into a graded dirt gutter. Behind it parked neatly off the road is a Camry station wagon, tailgate up. In that vehicle we see the shape of the young woman, a blanket around her. She's sitting in the back of the wagon, knees up, something behind her head. One ambo is perched on the edge of the boot, the other standing alongside.

'Good on them,' Faye says, as I pull off the road. 'She's lucky it was people like them, trained.'

We cross the road, the ambulance couple coming smartly towards us. I show my card.

'Detective Inspector Franz Heineken, and this is Detective Constable Faye Addison.'

'Ivo and Petra Bjelcic. The young lady's in shock. But physically unharmed, we're sure of that. She's saying there's a dead man in a house back there.'

'Go to her, Faye.'

They're middle-aged, impressively calm, waiting for the next instalment in this unexpected roadside drama.

I say, 'First of all, thank you for attending to her. Second, whatever she's been saying, keep to yourselves please. There's been an incident at a property, and as it's a police matter we'll need to take a statement from you both in due course.'

'Of course.'

'Good. We'll assess the young lady's condition. Perhaps we'll be able to take her with us. If not, we'll get an ambulance. So if you wouldn't mind waiting a bit longer. Did she tell you anything else you think I should know?'

'Um, well, she was saying something about murder, you know?'

'As I say, keep it to yourself. And thanks again for your help. Please, if you wouldn't mind, stay on this side and wave cars on. You know how people like to slow down and look.'

'No problem.'

They back away towards our car, on the other side of the road.

In the short time that she's been with TPF Faye's learnt fast. That the presence of a cop can be a comfort or a threat. In this case, she's immediately sat and placed her hand on Emma Lexington's blanket-covered leg. Making it easier for me to be myself, an ageing, crusty plainclotheser with no immediate

15

signs of having a warm personality. I stand over her blanketed, hunched form. She's twenty-five if that. Stillrock is, was, fifty-nine. I introduce myself.

Her eyes are bluey-green, and her face, looking up at me framed by the hood-like blanket, still seems to have the very last vestiges of the chubbiness of youth. She's an attractive young woman with long, thick, glossy blonde hair.

'What happened, Emma?'

'She killed him. She murdered my Rory. *She killed him!*'

The vehemence of it is quite something, and Faye's gentle hand's instantly a firm grip, preventing Emma Lexington from banging her head against the vehicle's roof as she lunges up. It confirms she's unhurt after her gentle car accident, and that unless, like Stillrock, she's an actor of sublime talent, she believes profoundly in her accusation.

Faye holds her shoulders, calmly eases her back to her former position.

'Take it easy, Emma. You've had a crash. You're pretty upset. We're here to help you.'

And to me, 'Reckon we get that ambulance, boss?'

I say, 'Do you want to go to hospital, Emma?'

She shakes her head, starts sobbing. Through the swinging mess of her blonde hair we hear her mumble something, with his name in it.

'Say again, Emma?'

'I want Rory back, I want to go to my Rory, oh please, *oh please*, he wants me, that's why she –' Emma breaks off, draws in a deep breath and lets rip a murderous yell of rage and anguish. Faye's barely able to prevent her lunging from the vehicle. She embraces her in an awkward but no-nonsense grip, says, a command now, '*Calm down! Emma, calm down!*' And then she waits.

And I wait. Somewhere up there in the dappled sunlight a magpie trills lightly. The Bjelcics, alongside my car, are unmoved. They know what's going on, they deal with all manner of trauma.

Faye says, 'Come on Emma, let's get you on your feet and see how you feel.' Faye pulls away the blanket, like a magician revealing something unexpected and surprising, and she sweetly manhandles her out of the Camry and onto her feet on the tarmac.

Emma Lexington is of medium height and build, simply dressed in summery jeans and T-shirt, both designer, nor cheap are the necklace, rings, bracelets, earrings and wristwatch. Nor, therefore, presumably, the toe-rings and sexy catwalk sandals.

Out of the vehicle, herself again, she stares at me. Her young expression's hard to read, pouty but also overwhelmed with emotion. So I might as well cut to the chase.

'Emma, you've made a serious allegation. Tell me who.'

'Suzy, of course, for Christ's sake!'

'Suzy?'

'His wife! *I'm gunna rip her fucking eyes out!*'

But this peak of high rage just as suddenly dissolves in a wail of tears, and she smashes a fist against her leg.

I can't actually say to her, your time is up, miss hissy fit, because I do have a heart pulsing remotely somewhere within my innards, but Detective Constable Addison and I have work to do, and Emma Lexington is central to it, having reported the deceased and then helpfully named his murderer. Nor do I have all day.

'Emma, do you feel that you can come with us to the property? You may have other information, so it will be important if you can come with us. Come with us to his house and explain what you mean.'

She says to Faye, 'Please look after me. Please?'

'I will.'

Then Emma Lexington turns her gaze to me. As if I'm, I don't know, an undertaker with ghastly bells on, because I'm way more than a mere body removalist. As if, despite being on the right side of the law, I somehow have a sinister purpose. Hers is a long gaze at me, and then she just nods.

3

WE'LL COME TO OUR OWN CONCLUSIONS ABOUT THE DEATH of this man, but I'm happy to take advantage of the unusual circumstances that have placed Emma Lexington in the back of the Commodore. She could, so to speak, contaminate the evidence by trying to plant further suspicions in our minds, but I'm a bit too much of an old mucksifter for that, eh. I have the lights flashing, nudging 100 k's, a dicey proposition along winding Tinderbox Road, and it appears to have the effect of concentrating Ms Lexington's attention on her own survival.

'Emma, I'd like to ask you why you have such a feeling against Suzy. And I suggest you seek legal advice if you decide to make your accusation against her public. Better still, I strongly advise you not to do any such thing, while this is a police matter. You understand that?'

'Of course I bloody do. Look, Rory loved me, okay? Anyone'll tell you that. Suzy walked out on him ages ago. Then, when he said he was going to divorce her she realised she'd lose everything in their agreement, because she was the one who left. So she tried to get back with him. And he's like, no, you walked out. So she's killed him, because they'd drawn up a joint will saying whoever dies, the other gets the lot. Bitch. There is just no way, *no way*, my Rory would do that to himself. He *loved* me! We were so *happy!*'

I watch her brace instinctively for a sharp corner. She's fine. Then she says suddenly, 'Where's my mobile? I gotta call, where's my bloody *mobile?*' She shifts agitatedly.

'In your car, maybe?' Faye suggests. 'Fell out of your pocket when you went in the ditch?'

'Christ! I need to call someone.'

'Who, Emma?'

Her answer is to clam up.

Rory Stillrock's driveway is discreet. The number on the opened gate is small. Unsealed, down through lightly timbered forest towards an exquisite private view of water, the River Derwent becoming estuary, very wide at this point, sparkling deep blue wave-capped water, the eastern shoreline a rim of hazy hot yellow drought. His acreage is big, it'd be twenty at least, where most are five here. As befits wealth above wealth.

The driveway rounds a final bend and before us spreads an impressively large leveled area, resplendent with well-watered grass, bisected by the driveway. Stillrock's home is in the middle of the clearing, a double garage and large work shed to one side. Senior Sergeant Lewis's marked Ford Falcon is parked in front of the house. He's standing equidistant between the house and the garage, one of the double doors of the latter rolled partly up. In the near distance behind him, through a gap in the tree line, more winking blue water and the sturdy rock upon which the Iron Pot lighthouse has welcomed or warned mariners since 1832, when Lieutenant-Governor George Arthur ruled the roost.

The house is not my style, though I've never been much of a stylist. It's a big two-storey type that would have been popular among the well heeled a few decades ago, a minimalist architectural fusion of sharp corners and bold curves, tinted windows set flush in spankingly white walls. A water sculpture

20

that looks more like a lap pool for toddlers glints in the hot sunshine near the open front door.

'Faye, stick around with Emma for the time being.'

I park, some way off from the garage.

'Oh shit, oh shit …' Emma's looking across the lawn at the garage and she starts heaving rapidly, as if in need of an inhaler, and she reaches for the door.

'Wait here, please, with Detective Constable Addison. That's for your wellbeing.'

And I'm out into the sunshine, firmly shutting my door behind me. A little slam as a little reminder.

'Morning, Jimmy.'

'G'day, Franz. He's in the garage on the right. In the Cadillac.'

'Ta.'

The interior of the spacious double garage is warm and dim even with a door partly open. The two-tone Cadillac, maroon top with light golden flanks, looks like an '80s model. I do know he imported the thing to remind himself of what he once was. A powerful Ducati motorbike and an equally powerful Norton are parked neatly together in the other garage. So, something else I didn't know, still a bike man. Going on for a quarter of a century since our fast-talking Sydney-based CIA operative, heroic, wisecracking and womanising in equal measure, thundered around the Harbour City on his big motorbike, sticking it up the Cold War commie spies infesting the place in their trench coats and bad English. And I know this also, that Rory Stillrock, riding on the success of *Crocodile Dundee*, made three Agent Archer movies in quick succession and earned a lot of money fast. Until, as we so charmingly say, it all went pear-shaped.

'Smell it, can't you Franz?'

'Oh yes.'

Stale puke, and the creeping whiff of warm summer death brought on by rigor mortis. The smell's escaping the starred back seat window on this left side of the solid vehicle. Emma obviously went at it with the heavy spanner that's lying on the floor, which she just as clearly grabbed from the set of quality tools hanging on the back wall of the motorbike side. But couldn't smash her way into good old US technology built to withstand a nation of high-speed drivers and car thieves.

The vehicle's locked. So she tried a door, or doors. Fingerprints kick in. Very important. But more significant to me is this, that in my experience at such tragedies, what we observe is that the overwhelming preoccupation with self-inflicted death mostly precludes such a detail. Having made the fateful decision, there is no need to lock yourself in to do the deed. Mhm. A characteristic of death by this method is a change in facial colouration as the blood comes to resemble dilute raspberry cordial, stripped of its oxygen and thinned. Whereas this plot, even in its infancy, thickens.

And what is odder still is that Rory Stillrock's heavy, asymmetrical bulk is slumped awkwardly against the door and its window, in the right side seat, as might be expected, except that the Caddy's a left-hand drive and he's therefore dead in the passenger seat.

Jimmy Lewis says, 'I did look about a bit inside the house for a spare set of keys. No such luck. Like a suicide note, not there, when you might expect one, in an obvious place. So either, or ...' He tails off.

'Executive decision.'

In my handkerchief-wrapped hand I take a monkey wrench from the wall and backhand it viciously, repeatedly, against the starred rear window. You can't be any gentler against an old well-made car. Stuff crunches, flies. I drop the wrench and feel through to the manual lock, open the rear door. It's just after eleven in the morning. I reckon from the smell and stiffness of him he's been dead well over thirty hours. I carefully open the rear door, still using the handkerchief. Step away a moment, suck of fresh air. Nothing like it.

Lanky uniformed Senior Sergeant Lewis is peering dubiously at the corpse through the driver side window of the car.

Says Lewis, 'He'd fall out if we opened his door.'

'Yes, he would.'

I stand alongside Lewis, he looming tall over me and half my age. We must look like a pair of weirdos through the windscreen, staring at this stiffening, pink-skinned, corpulent, shadowy body. Like most of us who inhabit this delicious isle, from time to time I might hear something about this famously wayward Tasmanian, standard water cooler chatter, but I had no idea how overweight and unkempt the man had become. A wave of fatty jowl hangs over the shirt collar, the cheeks are *Godfather* Marlon Brando's plugged with cotton wool, the once handsome head of hair is, was, dirty grey, falling in tatty locks around the ears and neck. And although the arms are crossed over the midriff, the visible paunch is substantial.

The right side of Rory Stillrock's face rests hard against the passenger side window of the vehicle, flattening the cheek and temple, the right eye dragged widely open. There's a small round skin-tone bandage under the left eye, just about on the point of the cheekbone. The window and dashboard are caked with an ugly grey-brown sludge, like voluminous overflow from a sewerage outlet. An involuntary carbon monoxide spew, I reckon, possibly the final act of life, the one ushering in death.

He'd clothed himself in well-lived-in nondescript trousers, a faded and, by the look of it, much loved candy-striped shirt, and a quality black leather jacket. An unusual combination. Dressed for going nowhere then a decision to nip out? Rather than a decision to end it all?

'Seen many suicides, Jimmy? What do you reckon?'

'A few. But y'know, why isn't he in the driver's seat?'

'Good question.'

In the gloomy garage, the angled windscreen of the Cadillac and the splattered vomit spray afford me no decent look at the face. I need to see the face, because they can tell a story. Standing knee-touch to the front grille of the vehicle, I sway a bit this way, that way, trying to judge and understand why he's in the passenger seat. Nothing doing. So I lower myself, slowly, one hand on the flank of the bonnet, knees ageing.

Until I'm level with Rory Stillrock's face. I've been here many times before. Looking at a corpse. This one, a faint crimson stare. Low down, just above the windscreen wiper, he and I make eye contact. I'm looking at an instance of the levator muscles of the upper eyelid, being tiny, contracting first in death, hence the left eye also open, with the flat side of his face against the window dragging the other eye so eerily wide, showing all that surprised white around the staring iris, like actors are taught to do. Through the grey chunder glass the stare is confronting, demanding something of me, but it's also as if he's cleverly keeping absolutely still, wondering how I'll react to this pantomime, this final piece of Rory Stillrock make-believe.

I sense Jimmy behind me, bending down. I step away, he floats into the cop vacuum where I was, down, down he goes until he and Stillrock make their eye contact.

He flinches then rears up as if stung, shouts *Jesus what's he lookin' at?*

'It's how the dead see, Jimmy. Don't worry about it.'

FORENSICS WILL BE HERE SOON, AND WHEN THEY'VE FINISHED
at the scene the body will be transferred to our Forensic Unit at
the hospital for the full suite of tests required for the report for
the Coroner.

For now, though, the first order of business is Emma Lexington. Seeing me approach, she gets out of the car. So therefore
does Faye. They wait. Not much either can say, really, by way of
enquiring after what I've seen.

'Emma, I'm very sorry for you. Now, as you'll understand,
we have processes and procedures to go through here. So this
is what I've decided. Detective Constable Addison will take you
to the city station where you'll need to make a formal statement
about your discovery of the body. It's a legal requirement, Emma,
you understand that?'

'Yes.'

'Good.' And I'm going to ask Senior Sergeant Lewis to go and
look at your car, see if he can get it running. If not, he'll call for
roadside assistance. We'll sort that out for you. And Emma, I
repeat my words of advice.'

'What?'

'If you publicly accuse someone of murder, you're opening
yourself up to potentially very significant problems.'

'She murdered him. You've seen! You're trying to say he wasn't
murdered?'

'Faye, you can take Emma now.'

'Sure, boss.' She gestures towards the front passenger seat.
Emma looks reluctantly at the seat and just as reluctantly at
Faye, who smiles with a thin politeness suggesting their time
together while I was in the death garage wasn't overly cordial.
Then Faye holds up an arm, as if to just as politely usher the
small of Emma's back towards the seat, but in some way the
arm seems to have an ulterior motive, as if it might just rise up

25

and slam dunk Emma's pretty, thick blonde head down and into the vehicle.

Lewis follows them in his TPF Ford, a wretched little convoy making its way towards the tree line. Standing idle in the sunshine for a moment, I admire the field-sized grass area and consider that Stillrock must have used plenty of water to keep it green. There's an in-ground sprinkler system. And he would have obtained frequent driver points on a ride-on mower, unless of course he hired someone. It suggests a degree of orderliness, for what that's worth. A certain contentment with life.

Call to make. Rafe.

'Yeah boss, what's the story?'

'Odd suicide. But, suicide it is for now.'

'Meaning?'

'Got a job for you, Rafe.'

'Let me guess. Next of kin.'

'Yes, sorry. I can't do it now, obviously. Rory Stillrock's married to, I'm presuming, Suzy Stillrock. Find her and go and tell her, that he's deceased apparently by his own hand. Do it now, Rafe, because word's going to fly on this one. If she's not in town or otherwise hereabouts, phone her. As for further next of kin, help me there too. I'm fairly certain there are no offspring.'

'Will do, boss. Hey, guess what, Fink Mountgarrett must have definitely stolen that necklace.'

'Enlighten me.'

'One of the blokes employed by the firm that checked Bellyard's place for rising damp is a second cousin of Fink. Deon Cawler.'

'So –?'

'So he obviously told Fink, "Hey, mate, Tassie's ace safe cracker, got a good one for ya in New Town!"'

'Supposition, Rafe. Let's let the fingerprints come through.'

26

'Mate, allow sensible leverage, let me go and ask Fink about Deon.'

'No.'

'Why not?'

'I've just arrived at a famous dead man's property. Hold your fire. I know you don't like Fink, but I'm telling you to do nothing. Your job is to hang in with forensics at the scene, Rafe, watch them counting that dead dog's teeth if they have to but don't you dare break rank and get personal with Fink Mountgarrett. He is a special Tasmanian criminal. Don't touch him.'

The interior of Rory Stillrock's house is full of life. For starters, there's an unmistakable whiff of morning-after curry and cigar, and the vestibule's strewn with stuff on wall hooks and the floor, walking sticks, wellies, Driza-Bones, thongs, beach towels, binoculars. There's an open plan feel to the seriously spacious interior, with low white walls acting as space dividers and a zigzag staircase dominating the centre of the sprawling sitting room. Off in the distance is a huge kitchen and dining zone. The floors are black stone, once shiny I'm sure, now showing their age. Two expensive leather lounge suites, one mustard-yellow, the other dove-grey, make two distinct sitting areas. Flourishing indoor plants in big stone pots add to the scene.

The kitchen area's clean. Dishes done. No sign of a meal actually having been cooked. That neat, was he? Four generic plastic takeaway tubs in the pedal bin. They're greasy, slippery with their own curry sauces and what looks like a film of dishwashing liquid. What chance prints? Minimal, I reckon.

My recce takes me back to the larger sitting area, the mustard-yellow leather settees making three sides of a rectangle, a low chrome and glass table in the middle of the space so created. On the table, incense sticks in a narrow-necked ceramic object, magazines devoted to movies, art, fashion, last weekend's newspapers, *Mercury*, *The Australian*, *The Age*, and signs of the festivity Lewis alluded to, namely a three-quarters empty bottle of Glenfiddich, a whisky glass, an ashtray with stubbed-out cigars and marijuana roaches in it, their homemade filters the giveaway, two empty bottles of classy red wine, and a big wine goblet on its side, the sediment stain in it like crusty nosebleed.

Before going upstairs, my attention's taken to a strange door at a far end of this living space. Strange because it has red buffed leather padding. What could it lead to? But before investigating that door, not to mention before going upstairs, another attention-grabbing feature of this capacious home area is a fireplace, freestanding in the middle of the room, a smart white flue doing the business, up through the ceiling, the heat of the fireplace able to radiate 360 degrees. A good Tasmanian idea, given our weather. But a bad place in which to burn something so obviously neither wood nor coal, heat beads, nor any of their clever Australian relatives. It's late summer. Yet the remains of a recent-looking fire sit in this fireplace, a one-off fire, dead wood ash in a clean grate, and a lump of shiny black plastic in the mix.

The strange door opens into a theatrette. It's dark. I find a light switch. How dinky can you get? Custom-fitted for its star owner. About a dozen red velvet cinema seats face a screen, looks like three square metres. The tiny projection room seems to be state of the art, and he has a wall rack of movie DVDs and racks of old-style reels. Other than the Agent Archer series he had lead roles in, I think, four movies, and middling to minor roles in at least twice as many others, in Hollywood and here. Yes, there's the Rory Stillrock collection. I wonder how often he entertained friends with them, or maybe watched them alone? Or not at all? There are hundreds of movies in his collection. I can't help myself. I try a seat. Deeply comfortable.

I ascend the stairway, not to heaven but a series of bedrooms leading off the wide and light-filled passageway. Most rooms are dead-looking, no signs of life, of a second person, like a wife or lover. One room seems to be a long-abandoned gymnasium and the second ensuite is virtually bare, as if unused since this house was built. Whereas the master bedroom's a riot of life. Stillrock wasn't overly fussed about bedroom tidiness, and it shows. Clumps of old clothes lie in piles on the wall-to-wall shaggy cream wool carpet, thick and soft. A comfort to his weary damaged pins, no doubt. I know that the Santa Monica bike crash that helped destroy his career mashed both ankles and left him with a limp. Newspapers and books clutter a glass table and lie all around it on the carpet. The vast bed's unmade, if you can call a giant crumpled Smarties-coloured doona unmade. Built-in cupboards line an entire wall. The double doors of one are ajar, interior stuffed with clothes on hangers. No immediate signs of female occupancy. Ah, Puff, use your eyes, mate, over there, a pair of tossed-away pale blue knickers in a corner. Whose?

Back in the corridor, one room to go. It's at the far end, immediately above the theatrette. An office, perhaps. But I won't find out just for the moment, because it's locked. I return to the master bedroom, quick look around in the places you'd expect to find a presumably important key. No such luck. I trot down the stairs, same again. No key. Interesting.

I step outside, wander around to the front of this elegant slice of northern hemisphere minimalism slap bang in a native antipodean forest. A paved path leads to the edge of the lawn, both terminating in the sparse bush that will lead to the cliff face a little way on with a sheer drop to the water. Funny thought, though not in any amusing way, my tiny hideaway Bruny Island shack enjoys this same eastward aspect and would be no more than fifteen minutes further south by runabout, half that in a decent speedboat. Unlike poor bloody Stillrock I plan to continue enjoying my place.

A broad and well-maintained bush path continues on from the paved one. I see the wooden cone of what looks like a gazebo, poking above the treetops. But any thoughts of having a look at it are put aside, as I hear the cavalry in the distance. Back around the house I go. Another marked car, and two Forensic Unit vehicles coming in. Righty-ho, let's get this party started. While still some way off along the driveway, the marked car flashes me. Huh? Then I see. Emerging through the bush behind them, a representative of the fourth tranche of our beloved system of democracy, namely, a shiny white station wagon from one of the commercial TV stations. My oath, corpse flies are quick aren't they? Doesn't matter how they found out. Put a controversial celebrity and a few cops together in a jar and shake well and things happen soon enough.

Dr William Doll, longtime head of FU, gets out of the first vehicle, waves. I reciprocate. He's a good bloke. I'll word him up, then give the media a few crumbs and send them on their way. Walter would very much want me to call him and let him know the media's here. Therefore, I won't call Walter.

I wait near the garage for Doll. As always, he'll do a quick look around before donning his forensic gear and setting the photographer and others to their work. We'll be here most of the day, and then the wait for the pathology report.

'Morning Franz.'

'Hello William, how are things?'

'Good, good. We have a suicide?'

'Well, it looks like suicide, and it smells like suicide.'

I don't want to say any more. I don't want to seem to be remotely influenced by young Emma Lexington's hysterical accusation.

I gesture to the garage. In he goes.

Some Monday.

4

'ALRIGHT TEAM, LET'S GET STUCK INTO THIS,' WALTER SAYS, THE slick and sleek one bright as a button on this warm morning with a promise of thirty-five degrees to come. I'm not a team man, and he knows that, hence his use of the term. Childish, eh? Then again, I haven't been beyond a bit of it myself over the years. No wonder we tax Chief Commissioner Grif Hunt's considerable reserves of patience.

We're in Walter's office, getting seated at his meeting table. Rafe's lip's looking a lot better but still tender and, well, silly. As for Faye, she has a small folder with her, and I can imagine the information that's in it. The four of us are going to talk about the Bellyard burglary, and then up in his office Hunt wants a briefing on the Stillrock death at ten this morning, because of who Stillrock was, because the foul play rumour's out there, and because of the PR value of knowing when and how to feed the media. Which is where Chief Super Walter D'Hayt comes in. The public trust him because he somehow manages to represent both blue and white collar family-man decency, honesty. A good man in a tarnished world, is our Walter, jealously protecting that hard-won trust.

'So, Rafe,' Walter says, when we're all seated, 'Do you want to talk to the Bellyard affair?'

And that's another thing that gets my goat, Walter's shameless use of corporate speak. I hope he asks me to talk to Rory Stillrock, because I'll reply I can't, the poor bastard's dead.

'Yep,' Rafe says. 'First, very little public response to the necklace, even though it's been in the media two days now. So I don't know what we make of that.'

'Early days,' Walter says.

'The dog was shot with a .22LR.'

'Nice and quiet.'

'Exactly so, boss. And muffled in that big garden under that big willow tree, could have been a car backfiring. But that's why they then wouldn't have gone in and drilled. One strange noise the neighbours can ignore, not two. As for the rising damp people, yeah, they're kosher, but Deon Cawler, Fink Mountgarrett's cousin, is the bloke who moved the painting. Well, put it this way, his fingerprints are on it.'

'Cawler's done time?'

'Town and gown classic, he knifed a uni student outside Knoppy's. The pity is we can't talk to him because he went overseas in January, to work in Ireland apparently, though his mum reckons he's doing the big trip of Europe first, so he'll be hanging out in a fleapit in Amsterdam or pigging out on pigs in Spain or something. Not that if he was here and I said, "Hey mate did you tell cuz Fink about that safe?" he'd reply, "Sure I did!" So ...' Rafe shrugs. 'But I'm confident in the connection.'

'It's a tempting one to make,' I agree. 'But for that very reason Mountgarrett will be well on guard.'

'From the moment he would have seen the necklace in the media,' Walter says helpfully, 'reinforced with word that we've contacted Cawler's mother. Nothing else forensics could help us with at the scene, Rafe?'

'Nah. Bloke obviously used gloves. And probably wore a hairnet, 'cause there was nothing to DNA at the scene. We door-knocked the streets, no strange parked car, van, nothing like that.'

'What about footprints?' Faye asks. 'Like under the tree where he shot the dog? If they're the same size as Mountgarrett's …'

Rafe shakes his head. 'Old man willow swept 'em away, and it's been so dry that shoes had nothing to carry inside. The place is mostly all paved and grassed, mate. Then again, Fink probably took his shoes off before he let himself inside. As he has been known to do before.'

'Steady on,' Walter cautions him. 'We need to remind ourselves there's no evidence he's got anything to do with this.'

Rafe licks his sore lip and favours Walter with a mildly puzzled look.

'Slip of the tongue,' he says.

Walter clears his throat.

'Let's hear about him,' I say. 'Faye, you've had the pleasure of doing homework on Mr Adrian "Fink" Mountgarrett of the Huon Valley. Enlighten us.' I sit back, slip a liquorice allsort from its little brown bag in my pocket. This is Faye's turf. While she's the newest of the team, she's like blotting paper soaking up our business. By my calculation Fink would have done his first job before she was born.

She opens her folder, lays an A3-size sheet of photographic paper on the table.

'This is the most recent image I could find of him. Off a Facebook social site.'

We shift forward interestedly. Male fingers revolve it. My turn, last. Oh yes, I remember him. There's no forgetting him.

'He's forty-seven this year,' Faye says. 'This image of him was posted in August last year. From what I've read, it's a fair call to say he's a hard nut.'

The Fink Mountgarrett I'm looking at is arms linked in a happy trio in a nondescript place, looks like the bar of a social sports place. You can almost smell the spilt Cascade Lager and barbecued snags and onions and tomato sauce and muscle liniment in the bowels of some lowly pavilion subject to rising damp, eh.

He's tall, skinny, wiry and tough, elongated bandy legs in faded black jeans, Blunnies, vest, narrow but commanding face, twinkly green eyes. But strangely, because once he wouldn't have been proud Fink without them, the mullet's been severely cut back, and the once wild pale ginger Van Diemen's Land absconder beard is now an almost respectable goatee, albeit aggressively pointed. So this is the Fink Mountgarrett we coppers once antagonistically knew, a changed man.

'He became an apprentice locksmith after he left school aged fifteen,' Faye says, glancing at her neat notes, 'here in Hobart, though he also worked in Launceston and Burnie. He obviously taught himself to become a master safecracker, because when we finally caught up with him he'd done five or six jobs. Though he was only convicted for one, through lack of evidence on the others.'

'Because he's a *cunning* bastard!' Rafe slaps the table with an open hand, grinning as much as his lame lip allows, working some energy into the discussion. 'Fink's a man always at the top of his game. How about this, Faye, two of those jobs were in Melbourne and Adelaide. The joke was that Fink was Tasmania's rep in a national safe cracking comp.'

She just nods, a little unsure of her role here, reads on rather than responding to him, given that Walter's eyeing her keenly to do so.

'So he got five for the Campbell Town job, out in three. That was way back when. And when you made your unfortunate comment about him, boss.'

'I did indeed, Faye.'

'But it was my fault,' Rafe says.

'No need to go over old ground.' Walter nods at Faye to continue. 'What's he been doing since then?'

'No.' I hold up both hands, palms out, like a 1950s B grade movie redskin who doesn't like the white man's version of events. 'Faye needs to know exactly what happened. It's pertinent to the Bellyard case.'

'Why?'

'Walter, because Rafe and I have personal history with this man. She needs to know *our* truth, not just the public record. This is exactly what happened Faye, word perfect −'

Walter starts to hold up a hand, his own version of an unworkable pow-pow, thinks better of it, says, 'Fine, go ahead. It's just that it's the personal nature of this relationship you have with him that *is* history, and by bringing it up you run the risk of dragging all the old conflicts into a burglary which on the face of it has nothing at all to do with Mountgarrett.'

'Faye needs to know.' I'm holding my temper. She's looking down. This is not a good moment for any of us in this room.

'Faye, we should have nailed him for a safe job he did in Battery Point. A man exactly fitting his description was seen on two separate occasions casing the property that was done. We found a cigarette butt where he'd been lurking, and its DNA matched his. We made the mistake of mislaying the butt.'

'I lost it,' Rafe says. 'I'd been a detective for, what was it boss, three months tops, and I just got too excited with it all and next thing this crucial bloody rollie butt in its evidence bag, in *my* possession, mate, it just disappeared.'

'Jeez, how?'

'Well one rumour had it that Fink had a bent officer mate in the force. The fact is, the court wouldn't accept DNA evidence on an item missing from the brief of evidence. So he got off on a technicality.'

'And then I did what you're never going to do in your career, Faye.'

'What's that, boss?' She leans forward a bit as she looks at me, Walter forgotten.

'I'd had a few drinks and then I gave a media conference. After I thought the mikes had been switched off I was asked one more question, and I said the ugly bastard is as guilty as hell and he's corrupting the force. Didn't go down well, Faye. He did the Battery Point job but we stuffed up, and we had to publicly apologise for slandering Mr Adrian Mountgarrett, innocent Tasmanian citizen. And that's why I still don't often front the cameras.'

'– Right.'

'The decision on what to do now,' Walter says, 'becomes critical. This can't look like a vendetta. Unless we can dig up more than the link with the cousin, it will be played out as a vendetta. And why has he apparently waited almost six months to do the job?'

'Precisely because of the cousin. To put time between the rising damp job and the theft. And because he'll assume we've Buckley's of finding that cousin in Europe.'

'That's a fair call, Franz. We also need to consider how he's been putting himself out and about as the great reformed man, the ex-crim settled down with his lovely wife-to-be. Isn't that so?'

'Definitely,' Faye says.

Rafe shakes his head, sighs. 'Don't get sucked in guys! Fink's a smart cove. He and Lily have been an item for years, they've been neighbours along the Huon River since long before he went inside, years and years. Yeah, maybe she's told him to keep

36

straight, but he's building it all up precisely to, y'know, insulate himself. Like from us when we go asking him about the Bellyard job. I reckon he's done it as his last big one.' Rafe folds his arms, sits back.

Faye says, 'I couldn't find much on Lily Huskisson. Only that people used to call her Lily of the Valley and that she was a well-known sex worker down that way and plied her trade in Hobart too.'

'She did, Faye, and she has her own history, and it may come into play, but for now I think we need to agree that we visit Fink Mountgarrett. Yes, Walter?'

'Agreed. But we set clear guidelines, Franz. He's only ever had that one conviction, all those years ago. Treat your discussion with him in that way, because if he goes bleating to the media about unfair allegations we'll be in a no-win situation. Believe me.'

'I know how to talk to individuals like him. And Lily Huskisson. I'm sure he'll be grateful for the opportunity to eliminate himself from our enquiries.'

'When do you plan to visit him?'

'Later today. The three of us.'

By way of response Walter looks at his watch, rises briskly. 'Upstairs in twenty, all. Hope you're well briefed. Hunt's got a packed diary this week.'

It's called pulling rank. Walter's everything he thinks a public servant should be, blissfully ignorant of what one shouldn't be. Or perhaps it's just me, the toxic ageing prickly one, eh. Maybe it's my sourness at work and it really should be me to be well and truly tested in my profession. Starting with these two cases.

5

TIME TO BOLT A HARSH BLACK IN MY OFFICE AND DO SOME thought gathering. No such luck. I'm barely at the percolator when a lively double rap on my almost closed door admits Hedda. She breezes in like a zephyr, tall, athletic and fit, the elegantly kinked nose. She's welcome to interrupt me any time.

'Hello, Puff, my man, how are we?' She pecks me on the cheek. She just about has to do it sideways down, she's that tall, me standard male height.

'Good enough, Andover. You?'

'Fine.' She drops a lurid-looking paperback novel on my desk. 'Got it at Melbourne Airport on the way to Canberra.'

'Any good?'

'Ripsnorter. Balltearer.'

'Ta. I'll give it a go at the shack, which doesn't look like anytime soon, unfortunately. How was Canberra?'

'Overwhelmingly exciting. Mate, I am conferenced-out. I never thought three days of "Narcotics in a Cyber World" could be so dull, self-important keynote speakers included. But the restaurants are fucking great.'

'Language, Detective Sergeant. I can tell you that suddenly it's been a bit busy here.'

'Don't I know it. The usually staid *Canberra Times* splashed our Rory Stillrock all over itself. It was unbecoming, Franz, and I had to say, no, we Vandemonians are horrified that a wasted, oversexed ex-film star topped himself in murky circs. Did he?'

'Yes and no.'

'Come to my place for tea tonight. Show and tell all.'

'Done deal, but I may be late. While you were away, drug detective, what's come up is the small matter of an expensive necklace gone missing, and funnily enough Fink Mountgarrett's name was mentioned in despatches.'

'You're kidding! I thought he retired long ago.'

She's genuinely surprised. She knows all about him, both in his own right and because she had a run-in with one of his close lieutenants, a little-known customer by the name of Titch Maguire, a shifty bloke with a low profile, the run-in involving a commercial quantity of super-strength marijuana. It was one of Hedda's first jobs as a drug cop relocated from Sydney. Maguire got twenty-four months, walked after ten. She wasn't happy. It wasn't so much the sentence as the fact that local kids were about to be wrecked by an essentially manageable weed turned nasty superbug.

GRIF HUNT, AS STEADY A HAND ON A COPPER TILLER AS YOU could wish for, has worn the heavy brass of the TPF for many years now, with barely a slip. Naturally, he has factional enemies, and there are those who just dislike him – he's a blunt decision maker – but all up the troops fall in behind Tasmanian Police Force Chief Commissioner Griffith Charles Mallory Hunt APM. Not least because he's strong on putting them first, and so has taken his share of political flack for what sometimes appear to be policy decisions ignoring the wishes of the democratically elected government of the day. It helps that he's native born, but equally it helps that much of his formative career was spent on the big island, making important whole-of-police decisions in the Sunshine State and then absorbing the reality that Tassie's really just a sparsely populated place north-west of Macquarie Island.

That he's a bulky, undemonstrative, taciturn sort of Chief Commissioner adds to his non-allure and all-round image of being a sensible character. There are those who think he's privately troubled. That's not Grif, that's guff. Nor can it be put down to the genealogical possibility that he's an undeclared Tasmanian Aborigine, a sensitive issue. Many, many years ago, in Queensland, Grif Hunt and I had cause to be in one another's debt, and even now, and despite the significant inequality of our respective ranks, we're equals of a kind. Strange old world, eh? But the fact is, at the end of the day, when all is said and done, when the playing field has been levelled, the i's dotted, the t's crossed, and the cows safely home and milked, he and I respect one another.

Gathered in Hunt's conference room are the selfsame four desperadoes who were in Walter's half an hour ago, and Hunt's PA, Priscilla, the minute taker. We wait. Up here on the top floor, with its sensational views of harbour, estuary, Southern Ocean, Wilkes Land, we wait. It's not usual for Grif Hunt to be late. Priscilla says nothing. So we wait.

Then he walks in. If it's possible that he's less scrutable than normal, it's this morning. To me, that's trouble. He sits, doesn't say hello, we get the barest of nods.

He's straight into it, saying, 'Is there any good reason why the death of this man is being publicly touted as suspicious?'

'No good reason,' Walter replies quickly. 'The media somehow heard about the young woman's hysterical rant.'

I say, 'Interesting that a lawyer shut her up quick smart.'

Walter shoots me a look.

'To this point,' he continues, 'the substantive evidence is Stillrock died by his own hand. Franz has those details.'

'I ask,' Hunt says, 'because he was apparently about to sign a lucrative deal for a feature film screenplay set entirely in Tasmania. He was about to sign it with a major Hollywood studio, brokered by FilmTVTas. State government money well spent for a change, and a beaming Premier and Arts Minister, just the ticket with an election around the corner. Tragic death is sadly acceptable in these circumstances, but murder's a different matter, it's political suicide, excuse the lousy metaphor. So whatever you have to say, it had better be good, Franz. Even if it's bad.'

I nod. Lean forward, rest my folded arms on the table.

'There are five key players in this man's life and death. His wife Suzy, his lover Emma Lexington, his business manager cum agent Craig Fine, his stepmother and longtime patron Joanna Arundel, and Robin Meuchasse, the Tasmanian-born film actor with whom Stillrock, I think we all know, literally had a love-hate relationship. Let me cut to the chase, Grif, and try to answer your question first. I've spoken to Craig Fine. He gave no indication that the screenplay you refer to was ever a done deal. Did the Minister tell you it was?'

'He did, yes.'

'I'm surprised. What I know about Rory Stillrock confirms that he was well past his creative best. Perhaps he gulled the Minister. It would no doubt have been a useful election booster, getting up on an artsy platform with the famous Stillrock and announcing a great FTVT break into Hollywood. The Minister would also have been aware that it would take years to actually get production rolling, never mind the niceties of nailing down all the finances in the first place.'

'Could be. Make further enquiries, Franz. Now, tell me about what you definitely know to this point.'

'All that's definite is it's not a clear-cut suicide.'

'Great.' Hunt sighs, reaches, pours himself a slug of water, and slurps. 'Go ahead.'

'The pathology report will be available tomorrow. Until then, here's what we've got. He died of carbon monoxide poisoning in his Cadillac. My estimate is sometime during the Saturday evening. The pipe carrying the gas had been fed into the vehicle through a rear window. The vehicle was locked, the key obviously in the ignition. Stillrock was in the front passenger seat.'

'Odd.'

'It is. There were no signs of a struggle. Emma Lexington's fingerprints are on all four door handles. She says she tried each one to get to him. There are various other prints on the external bodywork and windows of the vehicle. There are no prints other than Stillrock's on either the steering wheel or the ignition key or the pipe that fed the gas. There were two empty Mars Bar chocolate wrappers, one in his lap, the other in his left hand. The pathology report will presumably confirm he ate them.

'Forensics found a gold Cartier lady's wristwatch in the back of the car, on the floor. It was mixed up in a ball of fug, so may have been there for some time. It certainly wasn't ticking.

'In the house is evidence that Stillrock, seemingly alone, drank a significant quantity of alcohol, had a party with himself, on the evening and possibly during the day before he died.'

'Alone?'

'One wine glass, one whisky tumbler. No second used glass or glasses in the kitchen or anywhere else, although there were plenty in the dishwasher, clean, unfortunately. There were four curry takeaway containers in a pedal bin. They could have come

42

from any of the dozens of Indian restaurants and takeaways that have sprung up in recent years. No prints.'

Hunt nods again, says, 'Four means two, doesn't it? He surely didn't eat all that alone. '

'You'd think not. In the fireplace is clear evidence of a single fire, not last winter's, the purpose seemingly to destroy something. Forensics are confident based on a visual that it's a cassette for an old style VCR, which makes sense because he has a theatrette and in it's a library of hundreds of movies, including older cassettes.'

'Destruction of evidence?' Walter asks.

'Or coincidence, nothing to do with his death. We'll get a date on that fire, and hopefully greater detail on the burnt object, though if it was a cassette there's unlikely to be imagery, it's a ball of black plastic. There's one message on Stillrock's landline telephone. It was made early on the morning of the day he died. Faye?'

Faye quotes from a page in her folder. ' "It's me. You aren't answering your mobile. When and where do you want this drink?" '

'That's it?'

'Yes, sir.'

Hunt raises his eyebrows. On I go.

'The voice is almost certainly that of Robin Meuchasse. I haven't been able to talk to him because he flew out of Tasmania early on the Sunday morning after Stillrock's death, destination Fiji, apparently.'

'I just found out he's there,' Rafe says. 'Well, a bloke in his name took a connector from Sydney to Suva. I'm checking on guest lists. It takes a while, they're on kava time.'

No smiles.

I continue on my unmerry way. 'There's a gazebo on Still-rock's property, in a bush clearing along the path towards the cliff. There were two empty bottles of Portuguese rosé and two glasses on the table in the gazebo, and an ashtray with five cigarette butts in it. Again, recently consumed in my opinion. Though that too will be forensically determined. I did ask William for an asap on them. And as it happens, though this is peripheral, behind the gazebo's a possum-proof patch of marijuana plants. Four mature specimens. Private use, you'd have to say. And so healthy looking you'd swear he was looking forward to them.'

I stop, sit back.

Silence.

'The path. report, when tomorrow, Franz?'

'William promised no later than midday.'

'Right.' Hunt kneads his forehead with a stiffened finger, purses his lips, eyes each of us in slow turn.

'The girlfriend screams murder at you,' he says carefully. 'She blames the wife. She gives you a motive, money, his estate.'

'Correct. Although she hasn't publicly accused Suzy Stillrock, or made any kind of public statement.'

'The girlfriend went inside the house?'

'Yes, before she found him in the garage. She said she'd not seen him, not been at the property, for two days.'

'Neatly removing herself from the scene at the critical time.'

'There is that.'

'And what about this Robin Meuchasse character? He and Stillrock had a recent public spat, did they not?'

'They did. Concerning a revelation in a newly published book that while he was still living in Hollywood Stillrock actively sought to prevent Meuchasse landing a leading role in a feature film.'

'Charming. And then what about the wife, Suzy, and this wealthy stepmother, Joanna, and the, what, agent? What's his role? Who is he?'

Priscilla says, 'His business manager cum agent Craig Fine, sir. Fine and Associates of Harrington Street.'

'Thanks.' Hunt has another go at his water, looks at me, not happy. 'Any more, Franz?'

'Rafe spoke to Suzy Stillrock, and to his stepmother Joanna Arundel. They both seemed devastated by his death. In much the same way that young Emma Lexington appeared devastated by his death. I can't say the same for Craig Fine. Interestingly, according to Fine, Rory and Robin Meuchasse were at kinder and through junior and senior school together, until Rory was expelled.'

'Why was he expelled?'

'Sexual misconduct. Obviously that was a very long time ago. The fact is, because no media has dared link a name to the foul play rumour, and Emma herself has clammed up, suicide's the logical outcome. That's to say, who killed Stillrock if not himself?'

'Okay,' Hunt says. 'Nothing from us for the media, please, nothing at all. And we meet here again immediately you've crunched that pathology report. Thanks everyone.'

LOGIC HAS DICTATED THAT RAFE CONCENTRATE ON THE BELL-yard theft, Faye on the Stillrock death. Even so it is she who, with typical energy, has brought herself up to speed on all things Stillrockian, pulling together his life story from magazine and newspaper articles dating back many years. In my office she briefs Rafe and me.

'Rory Stillrock was born and raised in Hobart. His mum died when he was ten and that had a huge effect on him, not least because he'd been a mummy's boy. He was an extrovert but he hated sport and stuff like that. When he was twelve his dad

45

remarried. This was to Joanna Arundel, who was divorced with a young daughter. Reading between the lines, I reckon the dad did it not so much for love but to try to get someone to offload Rory on, who was a wild kid, the kind we'd recognise as destined for the youth detention cycle. The difference was that Rory's father, and Joanna herself, were both wealthy. And it seems that Joanna, using money and her own energy and influence, took up the challenge of what to do with Rory.'

Rafe says, 'Wild how? Stealing, vandalism?'

'Those and smoking and drinking and having sex with girls and boys, and getting sent home from school on a fairly regular basis. Like, he was an uncontrollable, precocious, spoilt brat.'

'Attention deficit disorder?'

'Probably, boss, but back then, in the psych books, likely there was no such condition. Well, they called it being highly strung. And in Tassie then there weren't decent structures in place to work with problem children. Then the dad up and left them all for another woman in Queensland. Joanna divorced him and kept custody of Rory. I don't know much about the younger daughter, Rory's stepsister, but she got married and lives overseas.'

'Did he keep in touch with her?'

'Not that I could find out. Anyway, Joanna had a psychiatrist look at him. I found the report buried in a Health Department archive. It's short and basically said he was a boy of quote, manic energy and impulsive behaviour, resulting from a quote, traumatised childhood, with other effects being, quote, rapid speech delivery and a struggle to tell right from wrong, unquote. Thorazine was recommended as a neuroleptic drug. No indication he was given it.'

'Poor kid.'

'Well, Joanna at least knew what she was up against. At some point she then had her brilliant idea. Rory's now about fourteen, just expelled from one private school and she's desperately trying to get him into another. She decides to harness this energy and obsession with being the centre of attention by putting him on the stage. She introduces him to acting. And guess what, he takes to it like a duck to water. Suddenly he's up on the boards with make-up on, prancing around like a dill, and everyone's watching him and clapping.'

'Clever.'

'I reckon. And add Joanna's money, seems she decided there and then she'd buy him into success. For example she flew a top speech therapist to Hobart to moderate his delivery. She was like, "Your destiny is to become a famous actor and my role is to make it happen."'

'Her words?'

'No, Rory's in an interview, years ago. When he was breaking through. He said she was the only one who really understood him, knew how to control him.'

'Okay, so tell us about that.'

'He got into NIDA, the National Institute of Dramatic Art, in Sydney. From there bit parts in TV soaps, bit parts in local movies, stage work. Joanna then set him up in an LA apartment, so that he could fly between there and Sydney as and when. And he got quite a few minor roles in US productions. But then all of a sudden it was like Hollywood discovered, wow, here's this utterly weird Australian actor with magnetic big screen presence.'

'So we're looking at a loopy prick who got lucky.'

'No, Rafe, we're looking at a tragic individual for Christ's sake!'

'Mate, chill pill time. Nothing special about Lord Stillrock.'

I say, 'Well done, Joanna.'

'Yeah boss, great timing. Stillrock was just perfect for the Agent Archer role. They made the three franchise movies over an intense six-year period. It was Stillrock's luck to ride the slipstream of the *Crocodile Dundee* phenomenon, as the Sydney-based CIA agent with a chattery mid-Pacific accent racing around against iconic Aussie backdrops.'

'He never was a Paul Hogan, though, mate,' Rafe says.

'He didn't need to be, because he'd already been sprinkled with Errol Flynn's stardust.'

'I remember seeing one of the Agent Archer films.'

Rafe and Faye look at me. Pufferfish in a movie house?

'It wasn't very good,' I add.

'No, boss, and no one involved in making them pretended otherwise. Agent Archer sorted out the KGB heavies without taking them or himself too seriously.'

'They were a load of shit,' Rafe says. 'But quite funny.'

Faye laughs. 'Make your mind up, mate! Anyway, then it all went wrong. There were three related things. First, the movie studio he was with was bought out by another, which decided to kill off the Agent Archer series. Like, the Berlin Wall had fallen, the Soviet Union was nearly history. But Stillrock was enraged. He apparently thought there was something personal in it. Next, he's accused of trying to rape a senior executive of the studio that's rejected him. He denied it. But this was a woman saying he forced himself on her, a Hollywood veteran respected for her work, happily married, way older than him, so there was never going to be any contest in the public mind about who to believe. Two days later he has the high speed bike accident, breaking both ankles, skinned from chin to knees. There was a suggestion it was no accident, that Rory Stillrock tried to kill himself.'

'Did he?'

'He never spoke publicly about it, boss. Nor about the rape allegation. And it was after that he went right off the rails. The drugs, the alcohol, the controversial porn movie *Hot Lusty Night*.'

'What inspired him to make it?'

'Dunno for sure, though he did try and joke about it, he said in one interview quote, I could no longer ride my Norton Dominator so I rode a porn star unquote.'

Rafe, laughing, says, 'Bad career move, not a bad joke. With me, Addison?'

She says, 'And that was basically Stillrock's Hollywood career. The goss was he would have drank and drugged and fornicated himself into an early grave if Suzy hadn't come along. She persuaded him to marry her, she got him dried out and eventually he decided to return to Tassie and become a brilliant screenplay writer.'

'Which he didn't quite manage.'

'I guess not. And in recent times he'd become quite a recluse.' Faye closes her folder.

We digest the oddity of it all. A complex life extinguished. The strange thing is that if young Emma Lexington hadn't screamed murder we might not have so forensically examined the death scene and surrounds. After all, Stillrock was clearly a troubled and tormented soul. And if it turns out to be true that his Tasmanian Government-touted screenplay deal was a dud, that may well have proved a tipping point. A motive for suicide, high emotional stress, for which perhaps he had a track record. The final forensic and autopsy reports will be interesting.

Rafe stands, puts a hand in the small of his back, stretches.

'Still pushing out those cricket kinks?'

'I told you, it was a shit day in the field, boss. Hey guys, I'm going down to the canteen. I feel like a doughnut.'

'You look like one too.'

'Piss off, junior.'

'I'll come down with you,' Faye says. 'I feel like a sweet tart.'

Rafe doesn't take the bait.

49

Back in my office I stand at the window, looking down at the interior courtyard, a featureless baking hot suntrap of steel benches and tables. I wouldn't mind being at my Bruny Island shack right now. Reading Hedda's lurid paperback in the shade of the ancient she-oak. A swim out to the sacred rock, back for lunch. Even better if with her. Reverie over. Phone call. Doll.

'William, how are you?'

'Good thank you, Franz. Your results are almost all in. I'll be able to deliver first thing tomorrow morning. Knowing your situation re this one, I ordered my team to extract its collective digit.'

'Hunt will be well pleased. Do you want spit-roasted alpaca or lobster parboiled in champagne?'

'Under the circumstances I should think neither would taste nice.'

'Ah. So the results are …?'

'In a word, Franz? Compelling.'

6

THE HUON VALLEY IS ABOUT TWENTY K'S FROM HOBART, SOUTH-west beyond Kingston. The highway climbs winding steeply to the great saddle at Lower Longley, and there suddenly the Valley and its mountains spread endlessly, a grand vision of deep green folds and far-off peaks managing to be both majestic and peaceful, like some fairytale kingdom of eternal good. Once upon a time, maybe. Wishful thinking now. Hard living white settlers cut their way into the Valley back in the 1820s and they had a tough time getting through all that forest to the river. What happened to the Indigenous owners? And the region's had its fair share of economic depression. Still, for all that, you'd never call this place Daggy Valley, nor for that matter its major town Huonville, along the dark and regal Huon River, Hoonville, despite the temptation.

The folk of the Valley bend to their tasks assiduously. Their produce gave the name Apple Isle and they do much more besides, look at all those stone fruit varieties, vegetables, wine, the fishing industry, cows with great views.

And where the Huon River glides into the D'Entrecasteaux Channel past Dover and Port Esperance, there are three charmingly named islets, Faith, Hope and Charity, one of which according to folklore did a roaring trade in the old days as a brothel and pub.

Rafe as ever is driving, I'm contemplating things, Faye in the back, we'd stopped talking soon after the Summerleas Road intersection. There can be too much talk. I'm comfortable with silence in close company, always have been, and there's this too, we're public servants soon to engage at taxpayers' expense in a delicate issue. We don't need Walter lecturing us on how to handle this, because he won't be with us when we do handle it.

Huonville's leisurely town centre is mostly on the eastern side of the river, and now there's a choice of roads, one on the left bank and one on the right bank, each following the broadening body of water in its journey towards the sea. It means that the river divides the valley community, but this is geographical, not ideological, or so I have been told.

We arrive at Huonville, private homes each side of the main road morphing into shops, cafés, real estate agencies, banks, supermarkets, the affable red brick Grand Hotel and bridge humanising the river, which today, projecting its silence, looks like warm liquorice, an impressive, glistening, greeny-black.

Rafe turns left at the bridge. This road on the east bank of the Huon River will take us through the hamlet of Woodstock, and then to the planet's one and only township of Cygnet, except that we're not going that far. And the river here has a famously unknown feature. It is Egg Island, plumply occupying a long and wide swathe of the river, the island named for swan eggs, which fed the pioneers who chopped the wood way back when.

Before too long Rafe slows to a crawl. 'Here we are, boss. We're at their place. But mate, I'm not driving up that shit track into the back of that filthy old ute.'

'No, don't do that. We'll walk up.'

In front of us, some way back from the road on a gentle incline, Fink's house. Old white weatherboard, well kept as befits a man good with his hands. Got a deck. Got recycled car seats on it.

Got persons on them. You wouldn't credit it. Fink Mountgarrett. Titch Maguire. Lily Huskisson. Hers must be the adjacent tired weatherboard, a faded green little house, paint scabbing from the wood, needs plenty of t. l. c., clutter outside, clutter in dusty windows.

Rafe pulls politely off the road, ours an anonymous late model Holden Commodore. Mind you, it's a shiny beast, the windows are one hundred per cent reflective, plus three aerials. Hello, Fink!

We walk up the rutted dirt driveway, past the battered ute in the back of which are a chainsaw, a pair of splitters and a can of two-stroke.

On the deck, a tan and ash-grey blue heeler barks angrily at us.

Unmoved, green beer cans in hand, but distinctly paused in their merriment, the three of them look down on us. They don't rise for pigs, and in a way I don't blame them. If I was someone else and I saw a bastard cop like me invading my personal space, uninvited, my beer'd turn to soap and I'd not be inclined to leap up and salute.

'Hello, Fink. Well, we haven't seen each other in a while.'

Up at their deck level, but not on it and only waist high to them, I lean forward and proffer my card.

'How are you, mate?' He's about to not take it, then sits forward, does, sort of looks at it, nods. I don't like what I see in Fink Mountgarrett's expression, which is yep, it's the one they call Pufferfish, the Dutch fuckwit. And behind him the detective who could do with a glassing, and hey, who's the nice little chick, surely not a cop, surely not their shag?

Not such a friendly welcome. Patriarchal on his busted old sedan back seat, which must have been on this deck for many years of summer sunshine, being faded earwax-yellow, Fink, his arms widespread, does look good. A champion of his ilk. A man of substance. Trim body, clipped facial hair. Also a man of substances, of which the most immediate is beer. One legitimate reason he mightn't have stood for us is eternal hatred of the cops. Another is that on this day, right now, he's well pissed, well on the turps.

Ditto Titch Maguire, who'd clipped the dog on its muzzle to shut its low growl and raised hackles, the hound trained, it would seem, to react negatively to the scent of the nation's finest. And Lily Huskisson has had a few as well. And now they have three plainclothes cops in their faces.

The boards of the deck are liberally festooned with crumpled green VB cans. That they've been on the piss is not the argument.

'And you'll remember Detective Rafe Tredway, and this is Detective Constable Faye Addison. May we step up?'

'Good to see ya, Tredders my man!'

Fink means that like he means well of a footy opponent whom he fully intends to flatten at the first bounce. It's a distinctly Australian thing that even after thirty years, I, a Dutchman, can't quite get. But on this occasion I do feel the hairs moving on my sweaty forearms. There's aggro up on the can-strewn deck. The boys are in shorts and vests, Lily, in the middle, sitting cross-legged, wearing a mini skirt and top half of a bikini. She's petite, dark-featured, attractive, somewhere in her forties, jet-black hair to her waist. Titch Maguire's stocky, got a big head, rough buzz cut, five-day growth, a thin scar running from under the left eye across to the ear. I know from his file that he's a sawmiller by trade. Must be his day off, eh.

'Up you come,' Fink says amiably.

Lily says, 'Yeah, get in the shade. Don't suppose youse want a beer?' She laughs, and so do we, stepping up onto the deck.

Fink has clearly been thinking about this visit. No point in feigning surprise. Rather, get on the front foot. Fair enough. He's been at the V8s for hours, has Fink. His eyes are small, expression leery.

'Let me guess,' he says directly to me, 'A diamond necklace. Sorry. You've come to the wrong address. Not me, wrong bloke.'

'Not sure Deon Cawley agrees with that.'

That's about as much as I can squeeze out of the connection, but it has an effect, because Fink doesn't know what I might know.

Lily frowns at him. He shifts abruptly. 'Don't know what you're talking about, mate,' he says.

'Guess where your cousin Deon is, Fink?' I reply. Squeeze a bit more from Deon the juiceless lemon.

'What's going on, darl?' Lily says to him. She looks concerned, her merriment gone.

'Dunno. Didn't he go overseas? Why you asking me?'

'When last did you speak to Deon?'

'Aw, shit, months ago? Dunno to be honest. Last year, mate, I don't bloody remember!'

'Have a harder guess,' Rafe says to him. 'Your memory's not that shot, is it? Uncle Alzheimer visiting the Finkster already?'

Fink by his expression wants to tell Rafe where to go, but he doesn't. He ignores him, says to me, 'No idea. Last year. Why?'

Another thing about Fink I can't find fault with is that he's a man of pride. He's done the hard yards, he's done time, he's a success at what he is, and now he's apparently nailed his life partner who by all accounts was a favourite in the Valley and significantly beyond.

Who's in charge? We're the irresistible force of law and order, the ugly in-laws of the outlaws, with all sorts of powers, but it's his private property. Our case is weak, there's no evidence to link

Fink Mountgarrett to the crime of theft perpetrated against Mr Bellyard.

'Look, I don't like any of this.' Lily stands. She's upset, her large dark eyes flicking from her man to me, to Rafe, Faye, back to him. And for all of us, silent Titch Maguire might as well not exist. He does look plastered to his seat, bleary-eyed and moulded to the sun-cracked plastic.

'It's all okay Lily, babe.' Fink flings an arm back for a handgrip on the backrest of his seat. 'They're just the cops, gotta do their grubby work. Right, boys?' He grins lopsidedly, now folds his arms. He's pissed alright, but it's a stubborn posture. I take this into account. He's got form longer than a Chappell Island snake, but this isn't the moment to work him over. Give me a sober Fink Mountgarrett, not this unsteady basket case.

'No, it's not all okay,' Rafe says, stepping forward. 'Mate, we're not here to spoil the party, but we haven't come along for nothing. We have to talk to whoever may give us information about the theft. That's reasonable, isn't it?'

'Like you say,' Faye adds, 'We have to do our grubby work.'

Rafe then gestures to the open front door, says, 'Mind if I take a leak, mate? Long journey from Hobart.'

This might be considered an underhand tactic, but it serves a logical investigative purpose. Fink's response will go some way towards telling us if he has nothing to hide. Or something to hide, like diamonds, or money with a funny name, or a .22LR handgun. And besides, it's un-Australian for one bloke to prevent another straining the potatoes, eh.

Fink rears up awkwardly, way too fast for his condition and straight at Rafe, but because he's unbalanced and Rafe's in his path, not for a physical confrontation. Or so it seems. Rafe's instinctively braced himself, he's a big hard-muscled bloke who won't take a step back, and then it's happening too fast for us to stop. They seem to butt heads, like billy goats, over in a flash, bright red blood splashing from Rafe's face onto his white shirt. Lily screams. Titch Maguire rears gruntingly up, Faye stiff-arms him back down because she's seen my gun drawn and pointing at Fink, who puts his arms out, says, 'Bloody accident! He fuckin' went for me!'

'Shut up, Fink. Turn around and put your hands together behind your back. Rafe, cuff him.'

Lily shouts, *'He's clean! He's done nothing!'*

Blood-spitting Rafe snaps on the bracelets. Harshly. He's not talking because I bet that cricket ball lip has been split wide open and it must be hurting like buggery.

Now there is process. And there will be controversy. An officer of the TPF has been assaulted. Lily comes up to me, close. She's scared, tearful, very upset.

'He didn't mean it! Please let him go, he's done nothing, stole nothing, I've cleaned him up!'

'Step away from me, Lily.' I don't like having my gun out at the best of times, and it's pointed at the floor now. 'Step away!'

She does, retreats with great care, not taking her eyes off me.

'Sit down, Lily.'

She sits.

Faye has her gun out. Titch Maguire's in silent self-preservation mode, he's not moving, not keen to say a word, just gripping his agitated dog by its collar.

Rafe, holding his handkerchief to his lip, hawks and spits a shiny wad of bloody phlegm on the deck, right in front of Fink, says, 'Can I take that piss, now, champ?'

'Fuck off.'

'Fink, *don't!*' Lily says, 'Don't make it worse.' And to me she says, 'It was an accident! He stumbled!'

I'm not buying into that just at the moment.

'My bloody tooth,' Rafe says. In the red phlegm patch on the floorboard a tooth is clearly visible. Faye bends, takes out a small plastic evidence bag, puts the tooth in it. She shows it to Lily. 'That's a tooth, Lily?'

She nods.

And to Titch Faye says, 'That's a tooth?'

'Yeah.'

An item of evidence for us. Maybe. And now I want some semblance of calm.

I say, 'Adrian Mountgarrett, I'm arresting you for assaulting Detective Tredway. Anything you say may be used in evidence. Do you understand that?'

He's silent a bit, then sighs deeply, nods.

That's the calm I want.

'Faye, call for a paddy wagon, please. Mr Mountgarrett's to be taken to remand at Davey Square.'

'Sure, boss.' She holsters her gun, takes her radio off her belt, hops off the deck and walks talking towards Lily's unkempt little house.

To Lily and Titch I say, 'The purpose of our visit has no connection to either of you, so you're free to go. Unless you want to say something, Mr Maguire?'

'No, mate.'

A deep voice goes with the dirty facial growth, the dark smudges under the shifty beer-veined eyes, the thin eye-to-ear scar we know about.

'Off you go, then.'

He gets up, affecting not to appear unsteady. Doesn't work.

'Got a car, mate?' Rafe's words are slurry through his hand-kerchief. 'You might be over the limit?'

'No.' Titch shakes his head. 'I live across the river. Got me runabout.'

'Eh, mate, you can't drive a boat over the limit either. Didn't know that?'

'I'll drive you,' Lily says firmly. 'I had two cans all afternoon.'

'Good on you, babe,' Fink says. 'I'll be fine. Been in this place before with these people, can look after meself.'

'Oh, Fink.' She hugs him, starts crying.

'Off you go,' he says.

She doesn't want to let him go.

'Go on, Lily, that's a good girl. Come and visit me tomorrow. Go on.' And he gently moves, so that she breaks away. He's sobering up fast, there are problems ahead for him and so the first order of business is to shield the missus from it. Chivalry in our hardened Fink. You wouldn't automatically have thought so.

'See you, mate,' Fink says to Titch.

Titch steps up to him, gives him a brief bloke hug, says, 'You'll be right, mate. We're behind you on this, by Jesus, we saw what went on. They provoked –'

'Uh-uh.' And Fink bumps him off too. Titch chose the wrong time to open his maw, allowing us a preview of what will presumably be central to Fink's defence. Not that his defence will necessarily count for much, now that we in Tasmania have begun trialling mandatory sentencing for serious assault on cops and emergency workers. For starters, what does serious mean? Hence the c-word, controversy. And Fink is going to be the first to experience it.

We watch Lily and Titch walk next door past Faye to her place, get into her banged-up Daihatsu, drive off towards Huonville. I look across the river, over Egg Island, at the Franklin side. So they'll be driving in a big loop. What a shit way to end your piss-up arvo.

I call Walter, apprise him of the facts, of what went on. I'm of the opinion that Fink's behaviour was sufficiently suspicious to obtain a warrant to search his house. We'd be remiss in our duty not to take that angle, now. Walter doesn't particularly like what he's hearing, but he doesn't have much choice. His most senior major crime cop wants a warrant. And I'll get it.

'Car's on the way, boss,' Faye says, and to Fink, 'Why don't we go inside, Mr Mountgarrett, and I'll help you put some clothes and your toothbrush and stuff in a case.'

He sighs again, shakes his head. 'Okay. Thanks.' Then he looks at Rafe, a direct look, says, 'I'm sorry. But you know I didn't mean it.'

Rafe answers just as directly. 'You head-butted me, Fink, that's why you've got the bracelets on and we're going to go through your place until we find something.'

'Good luck, dickhead.'

HUNT'S OFFICE, NEXT DAY. HE'S PISSED OFF. SELF AND FAYE under the spotlight. Rafe's on sick leave, he didn't want it, but I ordered two days, minimum, and a dentist to fix the gob damage.

'You've some explaining to do, Franz,' Hunt says.

Walter's in full Krakatoa D'Hayt mode.

'How the hell could you possibly have let this happen, Franz?' He's monumentally outraged for the cameras, hot volcanic matter spewing from every orifice.

What do I say? I can, and will, explain. But I can't take this jointly from them. Even though they don't like each other, they're together against me on this one.

'My explanation, Grif, is simple. Mountgarrett stole the rocks and didn't want to let Rafe into his house. If he had nothing to hide, then there ought to have been no problem. Instead he was aggressive, toey, from the moment we arrived.'

Walter shakes his head angrily, wags a finger. 'From what you said to me when you called in, Franz, Mountgarrett had smashed his forehead into Rafe's face. Now we hear that he just *may* have actually stumbled, because he was drunk, and *accidentally* re-opened a cut from a *cricket ball?*

'I did not use the word "accidentally"! It was no bloody accident!'

'Faye?' Hunt says, 'Is that what happened? Mountgarrett stumbled into Rafe?'

'No, sir. He rose aggressively and went straight for him. There was aggressive intent on his part, even if not to actually do the head-butt, he definitely seemed to go for Rafe, who stood his ground, obviously. And they clashed heads. Mountgarrett was the aggressor because he didn't want Rafe going into his house.'

'So he did *not* stumble into him? It was an intentional hit?'

'Sir, maybe his boot slipped on a beer can or something, and of course he was drunk, but in my opinion he went for Rafe.'

'And you say as well that the tooth may have been wobbly from the cricket ball? There's a lot of may-have-beens in all of this.' Hunt jerks his chin, by way of wanting my explanation about the tooth.

I'd advised Rafe and Faye of two things. First, that the incident on Fink's deck was always going to be contested, their word against ours, three versus three. But in the matter of the tooth, there would have been every chance Rafe told his cricket mates afterwards in the sheds or the pub that it was wobbly. To pretend otherwise might aid our case because it would be a significant head-butt to eject a healthily rooted tooth, but if we were caught telling a porkie we'd do ourselves no good at all, bringing the 'accident' scenario strongly back into play. Loose tooth popped out, lying cops.

Hunt sits back, has a think. We wait.

'We're going to have to be very careful with our strategy on this,' he says. 'The fact that the search of his house turned up nothing to associate him with the Bellyard theft is no help to us. And yet your version of the clash at his house with Rafe I feel obliged to support, and to recommend that Mountgarrett be prosecuted under the new mandatory sentencing arrangement. He assaulted a police officer, while under the influence, all of which makes his apparent non-involvement in the theft irrelevant. Walter?'

'I agree. That sort of behaviour is totally unacceptable and if Mountgarrett is the guinea pig for mandatory sentencing, so be it. But I still want to strongly record my anger at you Franz, for putting Rafe up against Mountgarrett, given their history.'

'Walter, it's my history too. You're now suggesting I shouldn't have talked to him?'

'At the very least Rafe should be taken off the Bellyard case. Just keep him away from the bloody mess he's created.'

'Pun intended?' I can't help myself.

'I'll consider that,' Hunt says. 'It may be prudent.'

The pun or the mess? But what I say is, 'The incident shook Rafe up. And there's the dentist.'

Then I keep quiet. Stripping him of the Bellyard investigation is a ridiculous idea. But just occasionally silence is the way to go. Like the judicious silence displayed by Mr Titch Maguire, who made every effort to appear to have been part of the furniture, back there on Fink's deck, while it was all sunnily unfolding. That did not escape my notice.

7

MANY LONG YEARS AGO, I WAS A DOUR YOUNG COP OF DUTCH birth who somehow contrived to marry an exciting Taswegian lass who proudly traced her Van Diemen's Land convict ancestors back to the 1840s. We parted ways, but with a daughter, Nora, the issue. We had her late, and almost never did have her because of two miscarriages. It was a sad, hard parting, not the first choice of either of us. Nora's mother through her family has significant rural property interests on the mainland. Put another way, she has some claim to tens of thousands of hectares of Australia. Whereas I own one modest new two-bedroom house overlooking, across a cluttered valley, a tip.

Nora is a young adult. She doesn't get on with her mother, though I'd like her to, if only for a possible future inheritance for herself. She recently ended a relationship with a bloke in Fremantle, who called himself a sculptor, and returned to Tasmania. She's sharing a student house in Sandy Bay and studying history. And short of money. Good thing I'm such a wealthy cop, eh. And now, before I front up to Hunt yet again, this time with more details on the Stillrock death, Nora's about to test this theory of cop wealth. Once upon a time she would have been sent up to my office with a visitor's tag around her neck. Not any more, not even family, unless there's a mighty important reason for it. And visiting your detective old man for the purpose of extracting money from him isn't considered remotely that, though an unemployed student might beg to differ.

I've checked all but one email, and still mystified how come so much spam can get through a government server, when my mobile buzzes. So summonsed, I fish my wallet out of my jacket which is hanging behind the door, to the lift, down to the foyer.

'G'day, Dad!' Nora gives me a peck on the cheek. 'How are you?'

'Good, and you?'

'Yeah. Hey, what the hell's going on over *there?*'

It would barely have registered with me, had she not drawn my attention to a barefoot man in a suit, one arm of which hangs raggedly torn, the man standing rigidly to attention, being spoken to by two uniforms.

'A gentleman of the road known as Colonel Custard. He's a military commander and visits us from time to time. Checking up on the troops, you understand. We humour him, keep an eye on his welfare.'

'Poor bugger.'

'Well, in his opinion he's important and he's cocooned away in his private world. He's probably happier than you and me put together.'

'Mate! Anyway, look Dad, y'know I hate to ask, it's just that, I dunno, relocating's cost way more than I thought, and youth allowance is just a joke.'

'I'm sure it is. But I'll ask anyway, exactly how much do you need and why?'

'Don't be such a cop!' She grins, but more than half means it. 'Like, the bed in my room must've had some really obese person in it before 'cause it sags *hugely* in the middle, and the cupboard's got this kind of vaguely *rancid* smell? Apparently someone kept a ferret in it. And you remember I told you my car's overheating? I worked out what it is. The coolant reservoir's leaking, probably badly cracked actually.'

My turn to smile. 'Got a new fellow already, Nora? That was quick.'

'Ah, no! Jeez don't think like a chauvinist, but yeah, he's just some bloke who looked under my hood … So anyway, I dunno, what do you think, five hundred maybe?'

I take out my wallet. Three hundreds and a fifty. I thought three would be plenty. I've got a card that only accesses my savings account. I hand it to her.

'Here, use this. Five hundred only. Then bring it straight back, please. But I'll be in a meeting, so give it to the officer at the –'

'Hey, leave the kid alone, she's innocent.'

I swing about. Hedda.

'Hi Nora,' she says brightly.

They've only met twice, and then briefly.

'Hi, Hedda, how are you?'

'Good, mate, good. Fleecing pop, are ya?'

'Well, you know …'

'Sting him for all you can, girl!'

'Hey, steady on, I've my retirement to think about. But I've got to run. Hunt.'

Nora doesn't really know the import of the word, but Hedda does.

'Anything I can do, Franz?'

'Yes, either escort my daughter to the nearest ATM or get her to bring that card back to you. And then make sure you give it back to me. I'm off.'

And I leave them. It's a simple transaction, in which they can get to know one another a little better. Being the two women in the life of Pufferfish. I trust and love them both, not that a small rectangle of plastic is the most gallant way of showing it.

'THIS IS WHAT HAPPENED TO RORY STILLROCK.'

Hunt's office. Him, Walter, me, his note-taking PA Priscilla.

'At approximately eleven pm on the Saturday night, in the passenger seat of his Cadillac, he began inhaling carbon monoxide fumes, fed into the vehicle by a PVC tube running from the vehicle's exhaust pipe. Those fumes killed him. They are deeply through his trachea and lungs. Residual traces of alcohol and marijuana in his system, together with evidence in the house, indicate dangerously high levels of consumption that evening. It's likely he was in an alcohol-induced sleep when the motor engine was engaged to introduce the fumes into the vehicle.'

'So he didn't kill himself. Didn't sit in the passenger seat, lean across and engage the vehicle?'

'In my opinion, no. And although there's a scattering of his fingerprints on the pipe, they're faint and the patterning is unusual. As if the fingers were passively applied to the pipe.'

Hunt frowns, purses his generous lips, looks down at the fine King Billy pine tabletop that his elbows have dented for the best part of a decade now. Then up at me.

'Three things, Franz. First, we need unequivocal, rolled gold evidence that Stillrock didn't commit suicide. You have just about provided that, given he was probably too drunk to set that pipe up, lock himself in the vehicle and kill himself. But not quite enough evidence. And second and third, if murder, *who* and *why?*'

'That's where this investigation is going to be tricky. But I'm convinced Rory Stillrock was driven by another person on the night in his vehicle, until he fell sleep. On a pretext, say, of a

66

late night excursion. For a takeaway, perhaps. The chocolates, at least. He ate them.'

'A takeaway? Two meals?'

'It's consistent with his bulk. He was overweight. The fact is he was far too drunk to drive himself. Someone took him for a drive, to put him to sleep. Then killed him.'

'No absolute proof, though, Franz.'

'A mess,' Walter says. 'We seem to have at least three individuals with something against him. What do the French say? He was an *enfant terrible*, something like that.'

It's a passable, if gurgly, French accent. I laugh, can't help it.

'Walter, he was an *enfant silly bloody sausage*, and now he's dead. These autopsy results recast the death and will help frame my assessment of the people I talk to. At this stage, I believe that either a professional killer is responsible and knew how to minimise traces, or that his killer is close to him, making the traces obvious but therefore difficult to link to foul play.'

'What do we have in terms of DNA?'

'Multiple persons, and its logical that most of those close to him would have a forensic presence in the vehicle and on the property. There are prints, hairs, clothing that's not his. His wife, obviously the girlfriend Emma Lexington. His stepmother, maybe the agent. The odd one out is Robin Meuchasse, who Stillrock seems to have despised. Meuchasse has got form. Years ago he was involved in a brawl in a Sydney nightclub. He was given a suspended sentence. So his prints are on ACIC. And on a wine glass and cigarette butts that were in the gazebo, and also on the rear window and left side panel of the Cadillac.'

'Which tells us?'

'That Robin is the voice on Stillrock's answerphone, regarding where and when to meet and have a drink. That drink was almost certainly in the gazebo on Stillrock's property on the day

Stillrock was murdered. I say this because that phone message was left early on the morning of Stillrock's death, and Meuchasse left Tasmania the next morning and is now in Fiji. But there are two other puzzles. One is that a long single strand of dyed red hair was found on Stillrock's leather jacket. His wife Suzy has long dyed red hair. Yet they apparently separated almost a year ago. The other puzzle is the burnt object in the fireplace. It was a video cassette, a common brand manufactured in Hong Kong during the 1980s. A fragment of tape remains, a portion of a single frame. It shows what appears to be a yellowish background, a wall or some such.'

'The cassette was from his collection, presumably?'

'You'd think so. But a visitor could have arrived with it. The fire was set near enough to the time of his death to suggest a link with it. Just an armful of kindling or one or two small logs were burnt in that fireplace. So it was deliberately made to burn the cassette, or was conveniently burning when Stillrock or another put the cassette in it. But why light a fire on a warm summer evening?'

'Why indeed?'

'Two other details from the autopsy. First, he threw up a death stew of chicken korma and Mars Bar. We know he ate the curry in the house, and there were the two chocolate wrappers on his person in the vehicle. I take this as strong evidence of him having been driven somewhere. Second, he had a dicky heart. And he knew it, because last year his GP advised him to cut out the grog and smokes and take up exercise, as a matter of urgency. Not that he did.'

'Okay Franz,' Hunt says, 'On your way and all the best with it, but take care how you handle these people from hereon in. No way can this detonate in our faces, there's no need, and I'm relying on you to ensure that. As I see it, Rory Stillrock was a difficult individual with personal problems, who just happened to be famous.'

'Colonel Custard might want to claim that honour for the Eternal and Glorious People's Republic of Van Diemen's Land.'

They chuckle.

'And remember,' Walter says, 'the official position for the time being is that the forensic report is inconclusive and so does not invite speculation about foul play.'

'I'll remember.'

'Franz, one other thing.'

'Yes, Grif?'

'Remove Tredway from the Bellyard case.'

'Effective immediately,' Walter adds, in best kick-your-enemy-while-he's-down style.

'As you wish.'

I HAVE THREE APPOINTMENTS. BUT FIRST, WE HAVE UNFINISHED business at the Tinderbox Road home of the undearly departed Rory Stillrock. It's late morning, Rafe's with me, Faye at HQ still trawling for information on the parties close to Stillrock, anything she can find, in or out of the public domain and no matter how trivial. The more you know in advance about a stranger you need to talk to, the better, in this business.

The gate to Stillrock's property is bolted and the waterproof TPF notice prohibiting entry is just big enough to deter stickybeaks. Rafe hops out, opens up. Plump sulphur-crested white cockatoos scattered in big trees over us screech intermittently. You'd swear they're swearing, as they root bugs from the bark.

'Dinky-di spot,' Rafe says, this being his introduction to the place. 'And mate, that's a big enough ground for a drop-in pitch and a Twenty20 game.'

'Don't get ideas. And don't mention cricket. There's surely a reason why that upstairs room was locked, and with no key in sight, given what a slackard he seemed to have been, a man who spent so much of his time exposing himself to others.'

'Good word, exposing.'

'There could be a clue in that.'

We step out into mild warmth. A cooling southerly's coming off the water. The double garage is locked, as is the house. Both Suzy and Emma had kicked up a fuss about not being allowed entry. That's the way it is, sorry.

I unlock the front door, in we go, you can already feel the interior's not been inhabited for a while.

'Nice,' Rafe says, looking around.

'This way.' I'm about to take the stairway when I notice something odd. Alongside the mustard-yellow seating where Stillrock, apparently alone, drank all the wine and whisky and enjoyed the cigars. The big stone pot plant alongside the seat opposite where he'd sat. Its bromeliad has keeled over. My first assumption is that one of the forensic people accidentally gave it a whack, because they swarmed over this area. But no, as I go close it's obvious there's another cause. The flowers are shriveled, the stem withered.

'Rafe, come here.'

He emerges from the theatrette. 'Fuck me, boss, imagine having your own movie house. Why didn't I become an actor instead of a dumb upholder of the right? Jeez, mate, the seats are comfortable, you should try one.'

'Look at that.' I'm pointing at the plant.

'Karked it,' is his matter of fact analysis, then he looks around at its thriving companions in their nice big stone homes on the black floor, says, 'The shit's going on here?'

I genuflect, but not for a god. I take a generous pinch of damp soil in my fingers, sniff it. Hold the sample up for Rafe to do same.

70

'Christ!' he says. 'Glad this plant wasn't behind a wheel, 'cause it died of alcohol poisoning.'

'Someone's poured their booze into that soil during the course of the evening. Lots of it.'

'What a dumb mistake.'

'True, but if you've decided to murder someone, and how to set it all up, notions of a dead plant sometime after the event don't enter into it.'

'Beg to differ, mate, the killer has used gloves or well and truly wiped their prints off everything, bottles, car keys, gas pipe ...'

'As they should have done. The plant wasn't supposed to die, that's all. The person was concentrating too hard on the deed to be done to think of such a trivial matter. Rafe, you know very well how the mistake slips under the radar. That's why it becomes the mistake.'

'Yeah, yeah, mate, no need to bang on about it.'

'Let's go upstairs and see what's in the locked room.'

Up we go. Rafe, big torso and rugby-style neck, has a swift barging look in each of the open rooms. I've a master key. Open Rory Stillrock's locked room, which is indeed his study. The room's big, nice view over the trees to the estuary. A large desk, computer, filing cabinet, a couch and easy chairs, a bookshelf, a writing desk. And on both desks, piles of bound and unbound A4 paper sheets. Rory Stillrock's failed screenplays, no doubt. So this was the room where he tried to reinvent himself, make a new Stillrock, a creative genius operating out of remote Tasmania.

'I reckon this room is all locked up because he didn't want anyone to read them,' Rafe says, picking up a ringbound script. 'Especially if they're shit. So let's see what this says ... This one, boss, is called "Maelstrom". What the fuck is that supposed to mean?'

Rafe flicks through the thick script, muttering. I take myself around the room, looking.

Rafe laughs, says, 'Listen to this, boss. "Tex roils the cigar between his lips, expression calculating, the squint in his eye to keep out smoke or his sinister intent in." And then Tex says, "Lou, you're gonna have to do a lot more to convince me." And Lou replies, "Give me twenty-four hours, that's all I ask. You owe it me, Tex."'

I've tuned out. In the bottom drawer of the large desk is a metal security box, about the size of a shoebox. Helpfully, its key is in the lock, and in fact it's unlocked. I open it. A custom-made cassette box, with slots to hold ten. There are six cassettes. One of them is *Hot Lusty Night*.

'Rafe, shut up. Why aren't these in the theatrette?'

I put the box on the desk, take out a cassette, using just the tip of thumb and forefinger. Black, no label identifying what it is. I slot it back, close the box, hand it to Rafe.

'Some viewing for you back at HQ. There's surely a reason they're under double lock and key, or were intended to be. Depending on their contents, have them checked for prints.'

'Sure.'

'Now let's go carefully through this room. You do the bookshelf, I'll concentrate on the desk.'

'Computer hard drive to HQ?'

'Oh yes. And the pot plant. Your arms are going to be seriously weighed down, Detective.'

AUSTRALIAN POSTCODE 7004, BATTERY POINT, TASMANIA, is one of the nation's more sought-after waterfront enclaves. A paradox it is that the exclusive little suburb began life as a Van Diemen's Land slum of whalers, reprobates and prostitutes cheek by jowl in a dense cluster of rickety wooden cottages at the river's edge, attracting the moniker Assault and Battery Point.

My business parks me outside an immaculately restored and kept nineteenth-century cottage of whitewashed brick, shiny green front door and window frames, neatly tiled roof, white picket fence enclosing a tiny garden of geraniums, bright green grass, and on the low-eaved verandah a pair of bonsai trees in chubby ceramic pots. I ring the bell. A tinkle within. Will a hobbit open the door?

Suzy Stillrock is anything but. Her tallness is accentuated by a long white shoulder-strap dress. Her dyed red hair is long and dead straight, as if ironed. She's attractive. Botox, yes, though at her age I'd prefer a couple of nature's lines.

'Mrs Stillrock?'

'You must be the detective, Mr Heineken.'

Her voice is husky, her words modulated, her American accent leavened by her years in the lucky country. A slinky chocolate-brown Burmese cat wraps itself around her leg.

'I am.' I hand her my card.

'I guess you want to come in.'

'I'd appreciate that, yes.'

She turns. I follow her sandalled whiteness, a somnambulism to her tread. She's not exactly in widow's weeds, but then Battery Point isn't clinging to a rustic Greek island hillside. She leads me into an intimately small lounge room that is perfectly neat, and smells of stale cigarette smoke. She sits on a hard-backed wooden chair, vaguely gestures to what's left. I don't like the look of either the low well-worn couch or the two leather chairs, any of which would fold me in like a clam feeding, so I take a twin to hers from the adjacent kitchen, place it opposite her, sit. And so, peculiarly, we face each other, Yank and Dutchman displaced in Your Natural State.

'My condolences,' I say.

Suzy Stillrock nods. 'It hurts. It hurts so much.'

Her eyes are dull, bagged, she looks wrung out.

'I can imagine,' I say.

She drags her eyes away from me, looks down at the gleaming waxed floorboards. The cat hops nimbly onto her lap.

'Down please, Salvador.' She pushes it gently off her lap. That cat looks at me as if I'm responsible. I've always admired cat intelligence.

'I have some questions I need to ask you, Mrs Stillrock.'

'Suzy.'

'Suzy. I'm sure you understand why.'

'Oh yeah, oh yeah. I up and left him, then I, y'know, gassed him before he could divorce me. Oh yeah ...' She tails off momentarily, refocuses on me. Sits forward, leans on her elbows, her long hair drifting. 'She should be *so* ashamed, Mr Heineken. I brought my dear Rory back from hell. I *loved* him. How can you think anything else?'

'I have no thoughts, just questions at this stage.'

'Right, right! You're a blank page!'

She emits a guttural, bitter chuckle and sits back again, twisting her hands among themselves, long fingers in animated conversation.

'Better for you that I am, don't you think, Suzy?'

The hands come apart, she smiles, nodding, snaps two fingers.

'Yeah,' she says. 'That's the best news I've had all day.'

'Who's suggesting you killed him?'

'Emma Lexington, of course. She rang me to inform me I'd done it. Can you imagine anything more disgusting and hurtful. Oh, *my* ...' She shakes her head, sighs, eyes clouding over again. She blinks slowly. Valium. I expect she popped a few in anticipation of this discussion.

'Suzy, if I could just clarify a few matters. When did you move out of the Tinderbox Road property?'

'Oh, say coming on a year ago? But, y'know, Rory and me had a marriage like a yo-yo. We took time off from each other throughout our marriage.'

'When were you married?'

'You mean what year did I rescue him?' A small smile. 'Took *many* years, endless years, to rescue him.'

'How many times did you separate?'

'Uh-uh, lose that word. Time out, not separation. They're not the same thing. Three, four?'

'So, about every four years. For how long each time?'

'Enough to feel it. Then we'd get back again. And be happy.' She bites her lip.

'Were you planning to get back together this time?'

'Oh yeah, you bet.' She nods her head and keeps nodding, hair swaying.

'You spoke about it?'

'We'd phone and talk.'

'When last did you get together? In each other's company?'

She looks through a window, on the outer ledge of which is a box of happy pansies.

'We had a discussion on the morning of New Year's Eve. I drove out to see him.'

I'm thinking of that long strand of her hair caught up in the zip of the leather jacket.

'It was an amicable visit?'

'Pretty much.' She smiles. 'We shouted at each other.'

'That's amicable?'

'We went for a ride on his Dominator motorbike, Mr Heineken. When you're clinging onto your man under helmets way over the speed limit, you tend to raise your voice.'

'Okay. Well, what about Emma Lexington? What exactly was her relationship with Rory?'

'Excuse my French. His slut-fuck. She parted her legs for him the moment she could. I'd hardly been gone. The stupid girl's an A-list chaser and poor goddamn Rory fell for it. He always liked attention. The guy wasn't getting any younger, overweight, the limp, but she, y'know, treated him like some to-die-for in his prime. He fell for the attention. He was stoned and drinking a lot again, and she took total advantage of that. Silly bitch can't cook though, and he just loves his food. So what the fuck was she gonna do about that huh! Join Drysdale cookery classes?' She laughs sarcastically.

'Rory cooked a lot?'

'Not if he could help it.'

Which makes me think again about the curry.

'You say he was drinking again. So he'd tried to stop?'

'Yeah. He went to his GP last winter to get prescription drugs for the flu and the GP persuaded him to have a full medical. Result, strongly advised to clean up his act. He tried, so he told me, but, y'know, he said it made him grumpy and snappy, so he went back to his old ways. He told me he'd rather die smiling than snarling. Excuse me.'

Suzy Stillrock stands and walks into her kitchen. I hear her pour water into a kettle, hear the click of a cigarette lighter, the deep intake of a welcome drag of smoke. She says from out there, 'Do you want a cup of tea, Mr Heineken? A coffee?'

'No thanks.'

'I won't be a minute.'

'That's fine.' I wait. She does me the courtesy of finishing her fag in the kitchen, then she returns to her seat with a cup of black tea. It has a faintly herbal aroma.

'Go ahead,' she says. 'I know you gotta do this like this, because you don't think he –' She breaks off, puts a weary hand over her eyes.

'There are circumstances about the death that are unusual, yes. In your opinion was he suicidal? Had he ever shown such a tendency in the years you knew him?'

'No. Hey, see, he's … he was … an impulsive kind of guy, and his failures with all those damn screenplays really ate away at him, but, y'know, not Rory, I …'

There's no need for me to push this one further. She can't be sure. Or it's in her interest to not want me to rule out suicide. In the absence of any investigative breakthrough by us, an inconclusive coronial report will suit Stillrock's killer very well.

She takes her hand away from her face, gives me a piercing look.

'Wait a minute, what do you mean "unusual"?'

'I'm not at liberty to discuss details while our investigations are ongoing. Sorry.'

'He's my husband. Surely I have the right to know?'

'In due course. I'm aware that his motorbike accident in Los Angeles may have been a suicide attempt.'

'Yeah, well that was before I met him, and he wouldn't ever let me ask about it. Came at a really bad time for him.'

'Yes, dumped by his studio and the subsequent rape allegation.'

Suzy shakes her head. 'Rory, rape? No way. But I never figured that one out either, it was even a more no-no subject than the bike "deliberate accident" scenario. Y'know, forcing himself on a senior studio executive to try to get his job back? Go figure! But if he did, well surely that showed that my poor man was in a state of greatest mental turmoil.'

'When did you and Rory return to Australia?'

'Oh, you know, when there was no other choice.'

'Okay. So you lived as a married couple in Hollywood for quite a few years. Then you "rescued" him, you say. From what?'

She's sipping her tea, pulls away from it, stares puzzled at me.

'You seem to know weirdly much about Rory in Hollywood.'

'Yes, but I don't believe everything I read.'

'Okie-dokie.' She enunciates it as if I'm a bit simple. 'Rory drank too much, he took too many drugs, he partied too hard, and he fell in with a set of swingers and that did him no good either, 'cause in his disturbed overactive mind he thought fornicating on camera was, y'know, out there and sticking it to the establishment that had stuck it to him after his accident. Bad career move. He just looked silly. So I got him out of all of that, before he got totally washed up, just another loser on an ebbing scum tide.'

'By marrying him.'

'Yup. But by falling in love with him first. I'd always thought he was just great on screen. And you know, underneath it all he was vulnerable. I got in and under there. He appreciated that.'

'Right. Just a few more questions, Suzy. In your opinion, is there anyone who might have wanted to cause harm to him?'

'Emma Lexington,' she replies without hesitation.

'Why?'

'Because she is so poisonous she would do what she could to prevent him coming back to me.'

'Where were you on the evening that he died, Suzy?'

Whether she's seen it coming or not, the question's like a slap in the face. She pales.

'Where *was* I?'

'Yes.'

'Oh my ... was I here? Yes, here, nursing Salvador.'

'What was wrong with him?'

78

'A blue-tongue lizard bit him. The vet shaved a little patch of his fur and I had to apply ointment for two days. *Here kitty kitty!*'

The cat comes back in, onto her lap. She holds up a foreleg. Sure enough, a small shaved area, about the size of a grape.

'You were alone?'

She nods. 'The lizard lives in the neighbour's rockery. They're friends, but Salvie likes to tease it and sometimes he goes too far.'

'Okay, that's fine.' I'm not pushing this one either. But it's not the greatest of alibis.

'Just one more question, Suzy, if you don't mind. How was his relationship with his stepmother Joanna?'

'The best. I mean, she made him, she had such patience with him and she is a woman of wisdom. Jo was good to Rory, almost too good.'

'Meaning?'

'Oh, I guess I put that wrong. He had such a lousy, godawful childhood but out of that she somehow managed to convince him he was special. Some makeover, huh! I suppose what I meant was she could maybe have done the parent thing a bit more, like teaching him to respect others. But hey, you'd have to reckon that would have been asking the impossible of her.'

'Like respecting someone like Robin Meuchasse?'

She shrugs, says, 'Ancient history, aint it?'

I nod, contemplating the oddity of a do-gooder apparently encouraging notoriety. I stand. Leave the stepmother there.

'And what about his relationship with Craig Fine?'

She shrugs. 'Not a relationship as such. Craig looked after his money. Does … did … a good job.'

'That's basically it, then, Suzy. Sorry to have gone on with so many questions, but you'll know why.'

'Sure.' She stands.

I take from my jacket pocket a small plastic sealed evidence bag and show it to Suzy Stillrock, flat out in my palm. In it is the gold Cartier watch we found in the Cadillac, in a ball of car floor fug.

'Do you recognise this, Suzy?'

She shakes her head. Her red hair sways. 'No. Why?'

'No matter. Thanks for your time and I'll be sure to keep you informed.'

We shake hands. Hers is cold, moist.

8

I DRIVE THOUGHTFULLY AWAY FROM SUZY'S COTTAGE, OUT OF Battery Point and along Sandy Bay Road towards the city. I thought she might have volunteered Robin Meuchasse as a confirmed Stillrock enemy. I seriously doubt young Emma Lexington capable of killing him so cold-bloodedly and then mounting such an elaborate hoax. Say he *had* told her he was returning to his wife, Emma's the type who'd be enraged and yelling and out with the nearest kitchen knife, surely?

I've spoken to Craig Fine on the phone. Now to meet him. His financial management company, with glass front door and large single plate glass window frontage, occupies modest offices in Harrington Street. And the man himself is a picture of modesty, which is probably what you want in a good assets shepherd. He's mid-fifties, shiny bald but for the standard monk bit that refuses to fall off. Tailored, lightly pinstriped, dark grey suit, roundish oxblood-rimmed specs. Old-fashioned. Most un-Stillrock-like.

'Detective Inspector, how are you?'

'Good, thanks.' We shake hands and he politely ushers me into a sun-warmed foyer. 'I'm alone today,' he says, waving at an empty reception cubicle. 'Let's go in here, into my office. Coffee? Tea? I was just making a cup.'

'Coffee, thanks, Mr Fine.' Can't refuse twice, eh.

'Take a seat, please.'

I do, opposite his desk, while he fiddles about in a glassed-off kitchenette.

'Instant, I'm afraid,' he says, his voice raised.

I raise mine.

'No problem.'

'Sugar, milk?'

'Yes, no.'

Almost comical, this.

He carefully places a cup and saucer on the edge of his desk near me, sits in his big black ergo chair on wheels, briskly wheels himself along so that he can kill off something on the further of his two computer screens, wheels back until directly opposite me.

'Right,' he says. 'Shocking business. Out of the blue. It's one of those deaths you just can't believe.'

He has intelligent eyes, enlarged by the specs, and manicured hands. All up, shoes included, he's wearing a good few thousand dollars' worth of understated design, and his aftershave is Milan or Paris, somewhere fancy like that. So the modesty of the premises disguises the true nature of his business. That he may be keen to not signal the fact he surfs in money, loads and loads of the stuff belonging to other people. Down to, here Mr Policeman, have an instant coffee. Wouldn't have anything to do with covering up tax minimisation, would it? But I shouldn't form such a spiky opinion so soon.

'Yes, the suddenness of it, the surprise,' I say. 'Until we all find out the reason why.'

He agrees gravely, by way of an impressive method acting jaw thrust. Then he bends forward, sips his coffee, sits upright tapping his specs back into place with a finger. Waiting.

'If I may ask, Mr Fine, how was it that you became Rory Stillrock's financial adviser?'

'I'm more than that, Detective Inspector, but the basic answer is that his stepmother, Joanna Arundel, recommended me to him after he returned from the US. I do pro bono work for her charity company. And as she said to me at the time, Stillrock's made millions and if we don't step in he'll fritter it all away. "We" being me. And that's exactly what I did. I signed him up as a client. He didn't take much persuading once he had Joanna's recommendation. I've purchased property and shares on his behalf over the years. His estate is in a sound position. More's the pity he's no longer able to enjoy it.'

A talker. Good. Run with it. 'Yes,' I agree, 'a pity. Joanna was obviously very important in his life.'

'And how, but then, not now. As he became reclusive I think even she felt the cold shoulder. But the fact is, her importance can't be understated. It's a miracle she managed to turn that damaged young life around. Dedication, for sure. You see the same in her charity work. Also, she's a strong-willed and determined individual and some of that must have rubbed off on Rory, the way he went at his acting.'

'Determined to succeed?'

'My word, yes.'

'How would you describe him?'

'Charming. Gifted. Childlike. Blunt. Hedonistic. Delusions of grandeur.'

'How dull can you get.'

'If Rory was any guide, you need most of those to make your way in Hollywood. But there was this, too. He, uhm, apart from the prodigious sexual appetite, it was as if he never quite grew up and his life was a chaotic cocktail of impulses, and one of them was, he had a reckless honesty and it would get him into trouble, but he didn't seem to care. Like seriously persuading a studio not to use Robin because he, Robin, was a pretend actor, an Australian wannabe. Like acting in a terrible porn film because he liked sex.'

'That's interesting. Tell me, why do you describe yourself as being more than his financial adviser?'

He smiles faintly, nods. 'Rory was in many ways a profoundly irresponsible and unrealistic individual, and no sooner had I taken over management of his financial affairs than he morphed me into his de facto Hollywood agent. Look around!' Craig Fine leans his chair back and sweeps an arm up and down. 'This isn't exactly an outpost of Tinseltown. But I ended up reading his, uhm, turgid screenplays and trying to foist them onto Hollywood studios and producers. I did what I could.'

'Tell me again about the major announcement made by our Arts Minister.'

He raises a frustrated pair of eyebrows above their oxblood rims.

'Mischief on Rory's part. Yes, it's true, we managed to interest a hot-shot young independent LA film-maker in a script. We had a screen hook-up and we talked big names and big money and a turning point in Tasmanian cinema, the perfect film island discovered at last, et cetera. All totally unsubstantiated, but Rory got into the Minister's ear and that was that. As I say, he could be very irresponsible.'

Maybe the Minister applied the carbon monoxide, eh.

'Could the reality of that failure have tipped him over the edge?'

'Possibly. He took it badly. As you say, there's going to be a reason.'

'A question I need to ask you, Mr Fine. Where were you on the night Rory Stillrock died?'

'It was my wife's birthday. We and two other couples, close friends, had dinner at Meadowbank Winery. We all used taxis so no one would have to drive home.'

'How did you find out about his death?'

'Joanna rang. She was in a state. One of yours had just visited her to tell her. I drove out to Richmond to be with her.'

We sip our beverages. He waits patiently, manicured hands placed neatly on his desk.

'Did he discuss divorcing his wife Suzy with you?'

'Yes. He wanted to know if her having left the Tinderbox Road home disqualified her from benefiting from their nuptial agreement.'

'Which is?'

'She takes all in the event of his death. She gets nothing if she is the cause of an irrevocable split.'

'How serious was he about divorce?'

'Hard to tell. Sorry.'

'In your opinion did he have any enemies?'

'Rory Stillrock rubbed many people up the wrong way. Some physically!' He wants to laugh but stifles the impulse by swallowing and swiftly dabbing the tip of his rude finger at his specs.

'Like Robin Meuchasse?'

'They were not best friends, that's for sure. Did you know they were at kinder together and right through school until Rory's expulsion?'

'Small place, Tasmania.'

'Isn't it. And it was Rory, when he was a ghastly little boy, who gave Robin the nickname Snotty, as soon as he knew what the word "mucus" meant and sounded like. In fact he used it at the infamous party last month when Robin threatened to cut his balls off and Rory had to make a drunken getaway in his car.'

'Robin said that, Mr Fine? I'm aware there was an altercation to do with revelations in a recent book. I'm not aware he made an actual threat.'

'Well, it's rhetorical, isn't it? "I'll cut your balls off." Like saying you threw berley to the fish when you mean you had a spew overboard. Well, that's what I thought. I happened to be one of the few who was actually right there when it happened, because I seem to feel I should have some sort of interest in Rory's wellbeing, as you can understand. They were arguing. Rory was being his plain old rude antagonistic self, and suddenly came out with something like, "Oh, get over it, Snotty, go and have a lie down you big wus!" and next thing Robin's chasing him. Robin himself wasn't exactly sober and he tripped and fell, allowing Rory time to get into his car. Then Robin chased the car, slapping at it. But Rory got away and lived to tell the tale.'

'HOW ARE YOU GOING WITH YOUR INTERVIEWS, BOSS?' FAYE'S at her desk with a semi-munched roll of wholemeal mountain bread in which seem to be sprouts and sticks of carrots and capsicums. And she's dipping it into a little deli tub of hummus. Is my junior detective turning into Hedda Andover?

'So far, Faye, this is what I think. His stepmother Joanna rescued him when he was a teenager, his wife Suzy rescued him when he was a comatose film star, and his girlfriend Emma rescued him when he smacked into a brick wall called relevance deprivation syndrome.'

'Deary me, why are blokes so hopeless? Did Rafe speak to you about Robin Meuchasse?'

'No, and …?'

'He found what he calls his F One J One resort. Meuchasse is on Yanuca Island, scheduled to depart Suva and return to Hobart in three days.'

'Good. Let's hope he does exactly that. He had it in for Stillrock, no doubt about that, but that doesn't flick his murderer switch. Where is Rafe, by the way?'

'Video room, looking through those cassettes.'

'Luck to him. Anything else before I uninterrupt your lunch?'

'Something I saw in this morning's *Mercury* boss, I thought a bit strange. In the obit. column, a kind of flaky entry for Stillrock. Sent from Los Angeles.'

The local newspaper's near her and she flicks through it to the relevant page, taps the spot with a forefinger and holds it up for me to read,

> *Stillrock, Rory Jordan —*
> *Oh Rory, taken too young, my sweet friend. I'm keeping our wicked secrets. I know you'd want that. As you fly away, remember me. In hidden love forever,*
> *Viola Vine, Burbank, CA*

'"Secrets", Faye? What's that supposed to mean?'

'Want me to get in touch with her?'

'Yes … no, don't. Get contact details and email them to me. I'll have a think about it.'

Her phone buzzes the short strips of an internal call. She picks up and listens to the earpiece, grins, chuckles, says, 'Geez, okay, I'll tell him, he's here.'

Applying a slow Pufferfish liquorice allsort into my feeding hole, I'm all ageing person agog.

'That was Rafe. The cassettes are, uhm, really pornographic and do we want to go and have a look.'

'All in the line of duty, Faye. Let's do it.'

My desk phone rings. I zip across the corridor. Too late. Too bad. Mobile rings.

'Heineken.'

'Front desk here, sir. There's a Lily Huskisson wants to talk to you.'

'Okay. Put her in an interview room. I'll be down shortly.'

There's nothing flashy about a cop room that shows filmic evidence. In this instance, Rafe has gone massively tech and hooked up a cassette recorder to a plasma screen.

'I've had a quick look at three of them. Brace yourselves, guys.' He slides a cassette into the machine, it clicks and clacks, he hits play.

Even on a quality screen the colour of the video shows its age. And in keeping with a relatively amateur production, if what we're seeing can be graced with such a technical term, there's nothing specifically watchable about it. But plenty to see. Eight or more naked men and women, in a large lounge room, going hammer and tongs at one another. They're talking, grunting, groaning, laughing, urging one another on. Depending on your viewpoint, it's obscene, tasteless, or a not uncommon form of adult socialising. For myself, standing shoulder to shoulder with young Faye, the spectacle is momentarily unsettling. But she and I have peered together at disfigured corpses, up close, so this fleshy heave-ho quickly loses its shock value.

'That's him.' Rafe stabs a hard finger onto the screen.

It takes me a moment to recognise Stillrock. He's half the weight of the dead man in the Cadillac, full head of hair, weird little moustache. He bears a distinct likeness to the Agent Archer of old, the Aussie larrikin made good in Hollywood, but is sadly lacking in the make-up tricks that render a film star so much grander than we mere mortals. He doesn't stand out at all in the orgiastic mob, there's no specific camera attention upon him, even though the film's moving around, zooming in for close-ups, panning back, going back in.

'Idiot,' Faye says. 'No wonder the studios dropped him.'

'Before his crash,' Rafe observes. 'Before the legs got mangled.' He hits the fast forward button. 'Forty-five minutes of this shit.'

'Are the others the same?'

'So far yeah, boss. Two to go.'

'Let's have a look.'

Rafe stops and ejects the cassette, replaces it. Similar stuff, outdoors location, group sex on picnic blankets, on park benches, against cars.

'What's the point of filming it?' Faye asks.

'Jack off later on, mate. Don't forget this is just about pre-Internet days.'

'Right ...'

'Lily Huskisson's downstairs, by the way.'

'You're kidding? What's she want, boss?'

'I don't know, Rafe. None of your business anyway, being off the case.'

'Yeah, yeah.'

He's still touchy about it all. So am I. It wasn't that long ago that Walter tried, unsuccessfully, to have him transferred to the north of the state for pissing in a pot plant in a pub.

Rafe fast forwards the massed outdoor fuck and suck fete, waits a bit, stops and ejects the cassette, replaces it with the last one.

Ah.

This one's different. It is decidedly the product of an amateur. Silent, a fixed, unmoving camera focused on a bed with a yellow wall behind it. On the bed, naked but for long socks, hiding crash scars presumably, smiling lopsidedly at the camera, Rory Stillrock is angled back against the headrest masturbating slowly and with evident pleasure.

Rafe shouts, 'What a wanker!'

We laugh. Faye says, 'My god! How gross!'

Rafe mercifully hits the fast forward button. Stillrock's lazy onanism's suddenly furiously comical meat-beating.

'He was obviously filming himself.'

'I reckon.'

'The yellow wall,' I say. 'There was yellow in the frame of the burnt cassette.'

LILY HUSKISSON STANDS WHEN I ENTER THE INTERVIEW room, and I'm reminded of her slim, petite stature. Noticeably, she's looking far smarter than when I last saw her, on Fink Mountgarrett's can-strewn deck, barefoot then, tiny mini skirt, full of vim and chirpiness cross-legged on a car seat. Today she's wearing what looks like a new black skirt, white collared shirt, both probably Vinnie's, long hair clean and combed, make-up.

'How are you, Lily?' I sit, gesture to her to do same.

'You shouldn't have asked, mate. Look, I'm sick with worry. How long are you going to keep Fink in remand? And he *didn't* steal that bloody necklace!'

'One matter at a time, Lily, please. We have an overloaded court system.'

'Guess what's causing it!'

I ignore the crack. 'His case will be heard soon.'

'Jesus.' She taps agitated fingernails on the tabletop. 'And everyone's saying he's gonna be the first victim of this new mandatory shit, this automatic sentence. How can youse do this to an innocent man?'

'Uh-uh. He whacked one of my detectives. I'll be presenting evidence to the judge, and Fink's lawyer will be doing the same. Assuming he has legal representation.'

'Yeah he's thinking about it. But I'm here to plead with you that he never stole from that New Town place. He's my other half. Fink's my man and he's gone clean, he told me and I trust him. Mate, you *gotta* believe me! Come on!'

She's upset. And I just about believe her. Fink didn't do the job, or if he did, she doesn't know he did.

'Lily, we're investigating this burglary and no one is off limits who we think might help us with our enquiries. But thank you for coming in and giving me your opinion. It's appreciated.'

'Mate. Fink didn't do it. You're gonna make him do time in that god-awful fucking jail 'cause he … *but he didn't steal the necklace!*'

Tears sparkle down her tanned cheeks. She's staring intently at me. Please, can't I lay off him?

Maybe she's being strategic, in here dressed like *she's* his lawyer. Okay he'll do the time for the head-butt, so cut him some slack with the other. But those are hurting tears. I feel sorry for her. Even, in a way, for hot-headed Fink. I was never in the cheer squad for trialling mandatory sentencing, but here it is and Fink's first cab off the rank. Nothing to be done about that. The fact that the Bellyard case has thrown up bugger all is not something I'm about to share with Lily Huskisson, but because we've so little they may get that slack after all. Not that Pufferfish will cut it for them.

'I've got to go, Lily. Unless you have something more you want to say, or tell me.'

She knows I'm a crusty old bugger. She also knows I'm straight as an arrow and a member of the solid old copper school, so she doesn't try and waste my time. She stands, wipes away her tears with the backs of each hand. I open the door, step aside for her.

She stops in the doorway, turns, looks directly and close up at me.

'He really didn't, you know. And I'll tell you this for free, mate, if I hear anything about who done it, even from the man's lips himself, I'm coming straight to ya.'

'Do that, Lily. I would appreciate that very much. In fact, we surely both would.'

9

HERE'S THE THING ABOUT BEING A COP, A DETECTIVE. IT'S TRUE that the business is ninety per cent slog, five per cent luck, five per cent inspiration. But these are not mutually exclusive. Take the extra step, turn the extra page, ask the extra question, and chances are you luck out, stumbling across the one mistake the crook shouldn't have made, but that you wouldn't have stumbled across if you hadn't taken the extra step. So is that luck or perseverance? Bit of both, eh. I feel I may need a fair amount of both, in the matter of Rory Stillrock, unnaturally deceased.

And the thing about Richmond, Tas, postcode 7025, is that this immaculately preserved colonial sandstone town began its life in the 1820s as a hard outlier police district designed to civilise or destroy convicts, bushrangers and Aborigines. Richmond cops were therefore among my earliest predecessors. Funny, that. In Tas from time to time there have been controversies with police commissioners. In Tas not so recently Lieutenant-Governor Sir George Arthur, a selfsame police commissioner, offered a reward for the capture of notorious bearded kangaroo-skin-clothed bushranger Matthew Brady. Brady, famed for never harming women, was outraged and posted his own reward, expressing concern that such a person as Sir George remained at large and offering twenty gallons of rum for his capture.

I'm thinking these thoughts because it's hard to imagine that kind of cruel and unusual past as I drive into scintillatingly neat Richmond. I wonder, for instance, what my predecessors thought of another man of villainous character, Michael Howe, who, near here, cut off a dying mate's head so that the military couldn't take it and claim the cash reward.

Joanna Arundel lives in this town from where she runs a noble charity, TasFoodAid. She's a wealthy individual, owner and occupier of a National Trust-listed homestead on a sizeable acreage along the Coal River. Much of the property is under cultivation, fruit mostly, for her charity. Not that Mrs Arundel gets her hands dirty. She employs a manager and farmhands, in this way also helping the Richmond community. She's a good woman in every way, and her wild and wayward film star stepson, despite his excesses, never did her reputation any harm. In fact, her well known championing of his talents all those years ago, shoehorning him into Hollywood, was seen as an admirable Tasmanian triumph. That is, from Flynn to Stillrock had been a bloody long time between drinks.

A driveway flanked by big hawthorn hedges becomes a garden of dense summer green and mature English trees. The Georgian style house is two storeys of convict whitewashed brick, casement windows, original-looking roof shingles, scalloped white wooden gables framing the steep roof of each wing. It's an impressive old place. Orchards are visible in the distant background, shrouded ghostly white with bird netting.

I use the brass front door knocker. Hear from inside a faint, 'Coming'.

Joanna Arundel is less dowagery than I'd imagined, less blowsy and authoritative than the photos I'd seen of her over the years in social pages and elsewhere. Elegant in a commanding way, her grey hair is neat and shiny up in a substantial bun, her eyes crinkly blue and lively behind specs with drop down chain, pale blue summer dress, upmarket sensible shoes, rings, earrings, necklace. And, I can't but help notice, she's wearing a wristwatch identical to the one in my pocket, only silver, not gold.

'Good afternoon, Mrs Arundel. Detective Inspector Franz Heineken.'

We shake hands, softly.

'Do come in, Detective. You know, I'm surprised we haven't met. What with the charity and so much police involvement in that kind of thing.' High class Australian accent, not a drop of Strine.

'True.'

She precedes me along a green-carpeted front hall and we shade right just before a fine spiral staircase, into what seems to be the drawing room. I feel like I'm in a museum. A smallish, square, functional room. Cast iron mantelpiece, upon which is a cabinet clock, a silvered frame mirror up above, two colonial chairs, a cedar roll-top desk in one corner at which even Arthur might have sat and, I can't but help noticing, a bell-pull hanging from the ceiling near the fireplace. Probably not tugged in a hundred years.

Mrs Arundel gestures to a corner of this room, to a classy old brown leather sofa with two matching chairs. Nice casement views out over the sleepy river. We sit. And she's out with it.

'I have to say I thought you, as a senior officer, would have spoken to me before now,' she says. 'I am Rory's parent, his stepmother. Craig Fine telephoned me today, saying that you had spoken to him. Should I not have come first?'

'I'm sorry. My schedule's unusually busy just at the moment.'

'The fact is,' she says, put out, 'I was originally advised of my stepson's death by a somewhat uncouth young man with a bandage on his lip.'

94

'My colleague Detective Tredway.'

'Yes, and I don't mean to tell you off, but it has been profoundly trying, waiting and waiting. Why will you not release the body? I telephoned the Coroner's office and was simply referred back to you people. And when I called *your* section, a young lady said you were busy on another case! Oh –' She turns away. 'Excuse me.' She takes a deep breath, to compose herself.

'I'm sorry, Detective.'

'And now we both are, so let's call it evens, Mrs Arundel.'

She manages a smile. 'Yes. Poor Rory. His life was such an unpredictable and bumpy journey. But when he was happy, he truly was. He understood joy. And I suppose he's at peace now.'

'Mrs Arundel, to answer your question, we were obliged to do a complex range of toxicology and other tests. They suggested he'd consumed a very considerable amount of alcohol over a long period on that Saturday afternoon and evening. But even so, it's possible he drove somewhere.'

'He didn't just get in the vehicle and, and … start it up?'

'We don't think so. And our opinion is that he wouldn't have been able to drive himself.'

'Did you see any of his Agent Archer films? He never used stuntmen, you know. It was Rory in all of those actions scenes on his motorbikes, and of course in cars. He insisted. He taught himself to become a very skilled rider and driver. But perhaps that young flouncing floozie of his drove him. Emma. Did you ask her?'

'We're speaking to a number of people who knew him. For the record, Mrs Arundel, when did you last see Rory?'

'He came here on the Wednesday before he … He raced up the driveway in such a rush we thought he'd crash into the house! Craig had just told him the movie deal was off, the principal backer had pulled out. Rory as you may imagine was absolutely devastated. Came straight to tell me. Naturally I consoled him, commiserated with him.'

'You said "we"?'

'Two of my charity colleagues were here. We were in the front garden cutting flowers for that evening's meeting. They left us alone, of course.'

'So the news affected him badly?'

'Rory was desperate to resurrect his career, somehow. He'd worked endlessly on those screenplays, and finally it seemed that he'd been welcomed back into the fold, so to speak. Yes, he was utterly devastated. I hate to use this kind of hackneyed phrase, but that deal was the last shot in his locker.'

'Do you think it made him suicidal?'

She frowns at me. 'Detective, my stepson's dead. He killed himself.'

'We're not ruling out foul play.'

'*Foul play?* What a bizarre notion, despite what the stupid newspapers have said. They just want to sell more, of course. So this explains the delay. I think it would have been courteous of you to say so before now.'

My mobile buzzes a message. 'Excuse me.' I stand, a pace or three into the room, read the message from Faye. *Emma Lex Women's Day exclusive sez RS death definitely sus.*

All we need. I drop the mobile back into my pocket, remain standing, as she says,

'Robin Meuchasse? Impossible. Oh, there was no love lost between them, but Robin is a gentleman. Besides, the sight of blood makes him faint. He's just not the type. Why do you think Robin's always played sensitive souls? Because that's what that boy is! And who *on Earth* else is there to have wished Rory harm? And *why*, for goodness' sake? Was anything stolen from the house?'

96

'No evidence of theft, no. Were you aware that he may have been planning to divorce Suzy?'

'This wasn't the first time they had separated. Suzy was very good for him. Whenever I thought it judicious I encouraged Rory to let that silly young floozie Emma wash through him so that he could get back with Suzy. He had, well, impulses, and a young attractive nymphomaniac was ...' She breaks, off, shrugs, no need to elaborate. She looks at her hands in her lap.

'Mrs Arundel, I'm aware that when he had his motorbike accident in Los Angeles there was speculation he'd tried to kill himself. What did he tell you about it?'

She nods.

'That was an awful time for Rory. After all the years of trying so hard, then becoming successful, only to have it all come crashing down because his studio was gobbled up by another one. Yes, he did try to kill himself.'

'He actually told you?'

'Not in so many words. But, Detective, believe me, Rory wanted to end it all that night. I say this because high emotional stress triggered an impulse in him to self harm. I experienced it when he was a teenager, and the medical people at the mental health hospital were aware of it. Not that I was going to abandon Rory to *that* institution.'

'Mrs Arundel, do you recognise this?' I take out the watch in its evidence bag, walk back to her holding it out in my palm.

'My watch! That's my watch! She laughs happily, then stares almost accusingly at me.

'Where did you find it? I lost it *ages* ago!'

'In Rory's car.'

'Goodness me. That's wonderful. Of course, I rode in his car many times with him.'

'When did you lose it?'

She rises smartly.

'I can tell you that exactly.'

She walks to the roll-top desk, opens it up, slides out the writing top. In the recess are box-like compartments, each neatly filled with documents. She pulls one towards her, flicks through its contents, then does the same to another box until she pulls out a tax invoice receipt.

'Last April the fifteenth,' she says, handing me a jeweller's receipt. 'The watch was given to me by my late first husband. I was heartbroken when it disappeared and I was determined to buy another. But I could only get this one.' She holds out her wrist. 'Also a Cartier eighteen carat, but silver, as you can see. Oh, isn't this marvellous. Thank you so much.'

I hand her the watch. There's no justification for me keeping it. She takes it out of the bag, winds it, takes off the silver watch, straps on the gold one, admires it. Hands me back the evidence bag.

'Well, that's about it, Mrs Arundel. Unless there's anything more you might want to tell me, at this stage.'

'We, that is, Suzy and I, and Craig, we want to plan the funeral as soon as possible.'

'Of course. I'm sure the body will be available for release very soon.'

She stands at the casement window, her back to me, looking out.

'What a waste of a life. Do you know, Detective, that in my charity work I see all sorts of poor and suffering individuals. And I sometimes wonder why some of them choose to live. But they do.'

She turns to me. 'And those who make the fateful decision to end their lives are in a way as brave as those who struggle on. Rory was many things, not all of them pleasant, but no one, *no one*, could ever accuse him of not being brave. I'll see you out.'

'Your charity work is admirable,' I say, once we're in the sunshine and I'm at my car door. 'I noticed the bird netting. Stone fruits?'

'Yes, mostly, and table grapes. For some reason we're struggling to find pickers this year. Fewer backpackers.'

'My student daughter's recently returned from Perth. I'll let her know. She likes fruit. And money.'

Joanna Arundel smiles. 'The pay is modest. But your daughter is most welcome to call me, and with a group of friends would be even better. Goodbye, Detective.'

Your average dumb-ass dick would hightail it out of Richmond at this point. Not Pufferfish. I normally buy my liquorice allsorts from a little place in North Hobart, but there is, in Richmond, the finest confectionary emporium in the southern hemisphere and they do top allsorts of the type to keep a busy old crime caper bloke energised and regular and ready for the next step.

10

'SO TELL ME, FATHER OF ONE, HOW DID YOU FIND THE FARE?'

'Different. Unusual.'

'Careful, brother. I used sharp big knives to cook it.'

'Sharp big knives for green lentils?'

'The onions, mastermind, and the green and red capsicums and the carrot and the eggplant, and the dicing thereof. But seriously, how was it?'

'Good.'

Hedda's trendy top-floor Battery Point flat, she, me, various Sunday lunchtime wines, and a lentil bolognaise she cooked and served. Not only was I not aware there's a difference between a green and brown lentil, I'd never yet experienced wholemeal pasta.

'Righty-ho, I've filled you with yummy lentils, so you can fill me with salacious insider goss I'm not supposed to know. Who killed Rory Stillrock and why?'

'If I had a four-sided coin I'd toss it and let you know.'

'Yeah right, come again?'

'Spurned wife, unhinged lover, bitter rival, aghast stepmother. Not necessarily in that order, although I can't see an ageing charity queen with a silver bun and specs on drop-down links murdering the creature she made famous.'

'Think Frankenstein.'

'Think logic, Andover. However he made it, Stillrock had money, lots of it. Always worth killing for, which is why in theory anyway I'm inclining towards the wife. Suzy Stillrock was, is, intimately familiar with his habits, his house. It was their house, the car was their car.'

'Evidence?'

'One long dyed red head hair of hers on his person nearly three months after they last saw each other. And no alibi on the night. A cat with a sore leg is just not good enough, Detective Sergeant.'

'Don't know about that, a dog once ate my homework. But seriously, you're not influenced by this *Women's Day* exclusive are you, Puff?'

'No. But the fact that Emma Lexington and the magazine's lawyers have gone as close as they can to accusing Suzy Stillrock is intriguing. Almost strategic, you would think. At 10.30 tomorrow morning we're interviewing the flouncing floozie.'

'I beg your effing pardon?'

'The stepmother's loving term. The wife refers to her more colourfully. Look, was he murdered? Yes. By whom? Don't know. Unless Robin Meuchasse steps up to the plate, which he can't do just now. The Fiji cyclone has detained him in that Pacific paradise. Besides, he's a party of interest in an unexpected death, not a suspect in a formal murder inquiry.'

'Mhm. Oh, well, to important matters. A horizontal arvo in peace. Like the wines? I chose carefully. What do you think of the merlot?'

'It's … not corked, it's … aluminiumed? But Hedda, why are you people in Drug Branch so quiet these days?'

'Don't laugh, but all the publicity about mandatory sentencing is saying, like, the cops have morphed into lawless fascists so best lie low for a while.'

'So Fink Mountgarrett's stirred the pot.'

'Yep. How's he doing back inside?'

'Easy. Smart of him to plead guilty and avoid a high profile trial. The less spotlight on him the better.'

'Nothing to do with a certain necklace?'

'You said it. Anyway, yes, our man's happily tucked up in Risdon. In fact he'll be getting his first visitors about now. His Lily of the Valley no doubt, tearing strips off him for being a hothead.'

'Mate, surely he pleaded guilty to get the minimum halved. Union not happy.'

'A joke, as the tabloid press is fond of saying.'

'Is it?'

'Take Fink. He kicks back in there, he'll be renewing a bunch of old acquaintances, teach a few young 'uns some tricks, and out in time to plant the winter brassicas down there in his beloved Huon Valley.'

'And then marry his sweetheart. So did he nick the stones?'

'Probably. And maybe in collusion with his best mate Titch Maguire, who I can't get a bead on. A dark horse.'

'He is that. So, frustrations all round. Poor you.'

My mobile rings. Usually means an incident. Hedda pulls a face, looks warily at me. Surely not …

'Yes?'

'Radio Room here, sir. Just to let you know Senior Constables Calder and Sharpe are responding to an assault in a West Hobart house. Victim is a young Indian-born lady. It seems she's been lying there for some time. The medics gave her a shot of pentobarbital. So she's stable, but critical. Head injuries, broken arm.'

'Anything on who did it? Is there a partner?'

'No sir, well, she lives alone. It seems the neighbour saw her cat waiting at the front door last night and again not long ago. So he went across and saw her in her lounge room.'

'Robbery?'

'No particular evidence of that.'

'Okay, thanks. Ask Calder and Sharpe to give me an update at about four o'clock, unless there's good reason to do so before then.'

'Will do.'

I disconnect.

'What's up?' Hedda's rinsing plates.

'An assault on an Indian woman. Better bloody not be an interstate copycat job. She's in an induced coma.'

'Ouch, that's no good.'

I toss my mobile onto a cushion, sit, begin undoing my shoe-laces.

'Come on, Andover, we haven't got all afternoon, leave the frigging dishes alone and get your gear off.'

'Oi, Defective Inspector, I'm booking you for language and misogyny. Punishment, you go in a fierce leg hug.'

'Bring it on, Delectable Sergeant.'

I'VE TAKEN AN IMMEDIATE INTEREST IN THIS ASSAULT. IF THE young woman was bashed because she's Indian, that makes it much more than a domestic or a burglary. In Melbourne and Sydney, where Indians have been targeted, a vacuum generated by nasty extremist talkback has sucked in the police force, the state governments and diplomats in both countries. We don't need that here.

I park outside the West Hobart house of Indira Patel, behind a Forensic Unit station wagon and the marked TPF car of Senior Constables Cody Calder and Kristal Sharpe. Calder's in it, on the radio.

'G'day Cody.'

'Afternoon, boss.' He exits the vehicle quickly. 'Constable Sharpe's having a look at the back garden. The perp came in through the kitchen door round the back and left that way.'

The house is typical of this part of the suburb: red brick, steep roof, probably two bedrooms, smallish front and back gardens with wooden fences and bushes between each neighbour. Easy enough, especially in darkness, to sneak through to the back. Early evening it is, but late afternoon heat lingers, dryly oppressive, the great mountain hanging over us darkly shadowed against a brilliant blue late summer sky.

'What have you got?'

'Not much.' He unlatches the picket gate, steps aside to let me through. 'It seems she's been taken by surprise, because there's minimal sign of a struggle. Plus she's not very big to defend herself. The intruder probably had her left arm pulled up behind her back, that's the nature of the break. And two blows to the head, the blood's pooled in one spot. No sign of what was used to hit her. The neighbours have been talkative but not really helpful. Like, they don't know who her friends are. They do know she works in a tip recycling shop. She wasn't missed there because she doesn't work on Sundays.'

We enter the house. It's got the neat clutter of a young woman's place, with much pre-loved furnishings. What chance from her tip shop, I wonder. The duty forensic in the lounge room's dusting for prints. Apart from one upside-down bentwood chair, and a scatter rug concertina'd against the skirting board, the room is untouched. On the faded old Tas oak floorboards, a plate-shaped black mark, with blood spatters around it, attended by flies.

Senior Constable Kristal Sharpe comes in from the kitchen.

'Afternoon, boss. I haven't found anything in the garden. But one hedge is hard up against the fence. He could have tossed something to the back of it. Be hard to spot.'

I nod. 'So what's odd about this?'

'That the motive's not theft,' Calder says.

'Or sexual,' Sharpe says.

'He's come in, brutalised her, on his way,' Calder says.

'The back door wasn't locked,' Sharpe says. 'Unless she unlocked it and let him in, which you'd think unlikely.'

'Okay, so it's not a b and e, but can we be absolutely sure?'

'Maybe he was after something specific, boss,' Calder says, 'like a valuable item.'

'Wouldn't that mean she knew him?' Sharpe asks. 'She lets him in, he turns nasty.'

I point to the room, its bric-a-brac furnishings. 'All good ideas, but she doesn't on the face of it seem wealthy.'

'Revenge? Maybe she dobbed him in about something.'

'Again, possible.'

'So we're beginning to think they knew each other,' Calder says. 'But if they do, the bloke would know she'd surely tell someone he beat her up. Like, tell *us*.'

'Consider what he did,' I remind them. 'He twisted her arm up behind her back. Why?'

'To get her to tell him something she didn't want to.'

'Yes. But what about something other than the possibility of cash or some such? And can't you hear the threat? "Tell me or I'll break your fucking arm." And she can't scream because it's too painful.'

'Information!' Kristal Sharpe says triumphantly. 'The bastard broke her arm to make her tell him something about another person.'

'And then,' Calder says, 'he smacks her down to give himself getaway time. One to drop her, one to knock her out.'

They look expectantly at me. I'm nodding. But I don't have the answer and we're unlikely to get it from Indira Patel for a while because she's in ICU with a dangerously swollen brain, pressing against the skull, and she'll be kept in her coma until that swelling's down, which I'm advised could be a week or more.

'The information theory has possibilities. Have you got an employer contact for me?'

'Yeah.' Calder whips out his mobile, thumbs it. 'Clara Olivetti is the manager of the tip shop. Her boss.'

'Call her. If she's available I want to meet with her now. Wherever's convenient for her.'

I WOULD IMAGINE IT'S A SICK END TO YOUR SUNDAY TO HAVE TO front up to a cop and be told that one of your employees has been assaulted and may have irreparable brain damage. Clara Olivetti is no exception. She's devastated. But she also bears gold. We're standing in the high-ceilinged, leadlight-coloured hallway of her elegant if tired Victorian house in Lenah Valley. Now that we're face to face I've told her the seriousness of Indira's condition, and she's got her hands over her mouth and nose, her breathing erratic, loud, her eyes glistening. Her long elegant fingers bear rings, she has bracelets, she's wearing an ankle-length cotton print dress, her hair is streaked with grey.

'Oh no! Indira, she's so young. Are you sure?'

'Yes, it's definitely her. There's a reasonable chance she'll pull through. We just have to wait, and hope.'

Clara Olivetti breathes in deeply, composes herself. And she needs no prompting.

'On Saturday afternoon there was an incident at the shop.'

'What was it?'

'None of us actually saw what happened. Indira told Ross and he told me.' She swallows. She's shaking.

106

'Let's go and sit down, Clara. Maybe in your kitchen. I reckon you could do with a cup of tea.'

'Yes, I'd like that.'

She turns. We walk. Whatever she's got, I need it delivered as calmly as the circumstances can make it, and there's nothing like a strong tea. And being engaged while you talk. The kitchen's got a classic old linoleum floor covering, and formica-topped red and white and green and white tables and 'Fifties kitchen chairs with shiny curved aluminium legs on rubbers with shiny studded backs. She fills a kettle, opens a cupboard, two mugs, unscrews a big glass jar, two tea bags. Engaged. Talk, Clara.

'Ross Whiteside, whom I also employ in the shop, said Indira told him a man came in yesterday afternoon and wanted to know about a stereo player she had sold. He wanted to know who she had sold it to. She ... Ross's exact word was she refused to tell the man because he was scary.'

' "Scary"? He threatened her in the shop?'

'No. She refused to tell him who she had sold it to because she thought that might, you know, place the buyer in some danger from this individual.'

'That was good of her. Brave of her.'

'Indira is a young woman of high principles, she ...' Clara breaks off. The kettle starts singing. She pours. I've got an important question for her.

'Did Indira tell Ross who she sold this stereo to?'

'I've no idea. Ross was on the way to the shop in his car, to take over from Indira. He'd phoned her to say he'd be a bit late, and she just mentioned to him that a man had wanted to know about this stereo, that he was quite aggressive. She'd, she told him to go on his way I suppose.'

'Can you call Ross, please? I'd like to talk to him.'

'I'll get my mobile.' She leaves the kitchen. I do the teas. A fat sugar for me. She comes back in, instrument to her ear, talking, hands it to me.

'Ross Whiteside?'

'Yeah. Oh, this is terrible. Poor Indira.'

'I'm Detective Inspector Franz Heineken. It's important that you try to remember everything Indira told you. Straight answers, Ross. Did she describe this man to you who she said was scary?'

'No, mate.'

'No physical characteristic? Like, a big bloke, or beard, long hair, shaved head, tatts, dirty clothes?'

'Definitely no. She was just, she said something like, Hey, Ross, this bloke came in, aggressive and scary, demanding who had I sold the stereo to? And so I said to him even if I knew, I wouldn't tell you, because you're up to no good ...'

'Ross, did Indira tell *you* who she sold this stereo to?'

'No, we had to cut the call, she had a customer, I was in traffic. But that wasn't the point. The point was she stood up to this bloke, whoever he was. I mean, maybe she had no idea who she sold the damn thing to. Tip shoppers are like the biscuits, mate, hundreds and thousands, in and out, browsing, getting the bargain or the thing they've been patiently waiting for.'

'What time did you swap with Indira?'

'Two o'clock. Afternoon shift.'

'What else did Indira say to you in the phone call?'

'Nothing, sorry. It was just, that's what she said. That was it. And when I got in I was straight into it, being late, and she left. Always flat chat on a Satdee arvo.'

'Okay. Thanks Ross. You're working tomorrow?'

'Yeah. Start eight-thirty.'

'One of my detectives will call in and get a formal statement from you. Thanks for your help. I'll hand you back to Clara now.'

She talks briefly to him. Then we sit at a table, with our mugs of tea.

'Clara, this stereo. Can you tell me anything about it?'

'I've been racking my brains. We get stuff dropped off all the time. Sometime on Friday I'm sure I remember seeing an old stereo at the re-usables drop-off shed. With those big boxy old speakers from the Seventies or Eighties, about up to my knee?'

'Did you see anyone drop it off?'

'No, sorry.'

'Where were you when you saw it?'

'Oh, up in the shop, probably just at the entrance, looking down as the vehicles park and the people get out and put the stuff down, take it to where they should, you know, wood with wood, kitchen sinks with kitchen sinks, bikes with bikes.'

'Do you recall about what time you saw it?'

'Again, no, sorry.'

'Surely a stereo goes inside?'

'Oh, sure. One of us will take re-usable stuff inside during the course of the day, and assess it and stick a price on it. Remember, this is a tip shop, our margins are tiny, non-existent. We don't have staff hanging around waiting to cart things up to the shop, and the public are just getting rid of their junk. If they thought they could sell something they'd take it to second-hand shops, not us.'

'What about the staff on the weighbridge?'

'They're not mine. You'd need to go through the Council for that.'

'Okay. I'm sorry about Indira. I'll keep you informed of her progress.'

'Thank you.'

'And here's my card, if you hear or remember anything you think I should know.'

11

MONDAY MORNING AND THE DEEP PLEASURE OF DOING INTIMATE business with famed Chief Superintendent Walter D'Hayt. It's a sheer mystery why seagulls don't crap on his statue. I've steeled myself with a short, tough black and a couple of Richmond Village special liquorice allsorts. Will they be enough? Plus I'm a bit light-headed, a bit off-colour, maybe. Into his office I go. His delightful family members grin at me from their framed photograph on his desk.

'Morning, Franz, take a seat.'

'Hello, Walter.'

'So,' he says, sitting back and steepling his fingers. The calm and authoritative one. 'You're ruling out a racial motive for the bashing?'

'Yes, for the time being. What little we have is that the assailant is presumably the man who verballed her in the tip shop, wanting to know about this mysterious stereo. That he then may have waited until she clocked off, followed her to her home, waited again until dark and then gone in.'

Walter affects a dubious expression. 'Can we be sure about that?'

'Of course not. But I doubt she knew the assailant, and let him in. It was a vicious assault. She has no known association with bad elements. Quite the opposite. She moved in young, happy working class circles.'

'Alright, point taken. What do you know about this stereo?'

'Nothing. At some point during her shift Indira would have gone down to the drop-off shed, carried the stereo up to the shop and assessed it, tried it out with a vinyl LP, put a value on it or stuck it in the back for repair or recycling. Logically, it was in working condition and she put it on sale, unless …'

'Unless what?'

'Just thinking. Speculating.'

'So the point is, what's valuable about an old stereo?'

'Box-like old speakers. Big enough to stash something in one or both of them, around the amplifying discs.'

'Which the person dumping the stereo would be ignorant of.'

'You'd think so, Walter.'

'Stuff in the speakers. That's got possibilities.'

'The problem there is sound distortion. Indira would have put an LP on it and had a listen, before tagging it for sale. If there was distortion she would be unlikely to have put it on sale.'

'Presumably not. The fact is, we *assume* the bashing relates to the stereo. So I need to get two pieces of information to the media. First, and most important, it's unlikely to be racially motivated. Although just at the moment, with that bloody *Women's Day* article about Stillrock, we're being seen as sneaky untruthful bastards.' He scowls, hating it when the public doubt him. 'And second, that it may relate to her being an employee at the tip shop. How do we frame that one?'

'Three lines. Someone might know something about a stereo dropped off at the tip shop towards the end of last week, probably on Friday. Someone might have seen Indira having an animated conversation in the shop on Saturday. Someone might have noticed suspicious behaviour in her street that evening.'

'Sounds good.' He stands briskly and takes his uniform jacket from its coat hanger. 'I'll go and talk to the cameras. And then –' He flashes out his arm to expose his wristwatch – 'at 10.30 we'll do the Emma Lexington interview. She had better bloody well pitch up.'

'She'll be here, alright. Victor La Salle's representing her.'

'Oh, great.'

Out we go, on our briefly separate ways in the cop shop at the bottom of the planet.

TALL, SLIM, SWAGGERING VICTOR LA SALLE'S A HIGH PROFILE defence lawyer. We're worth plenty of money to the smarmy egotistical bastard, with whom I've locked horns on numerous occasions. He rudely flaunts his wealth and success at slipping white collar cowboys off the hook, and is recognisable about miniature Hobart in his flamboyant suits, flamboyant ties, the flamboyant russet thatch with its flamboyant parting. Even the prick's haughty bronze-tanned cheekbones are flam- boyant.

There's nothing fancy about our TPF HQ's interview rooms, with their heavy tables, scrapey chairs, audio and video recording gear, CCTV monitors and high barred windows. So it is that, waiting for us in Number 3, Emma Lexington and Victor La Salle sitting together look out of place, overdressed and just way too well-heeled to be cooling them in here. For starters, his broad mauve tie and her glossy lilac lipstick clash expensively, though maybe that's just me.

He stands, languidly, so therefore does she, her same medium build I saw freaking out on Tinderbox Road. He's on the point of reaching out to shake hands, thinks better of it on this occasion by bringing a hand up to minutely adjust his tie knot.

I do the biz. 'Emma, Mr La Salle, hello. This is Chief Super-intendent Walter D'Hayt, sitting in this morning. Sit down, please.'

La Salle will be well aware that this is big for Walter because of the negative impact the *Women's Day* article is having on the TPF. And slimy, overly after-shaved Victor will be just as well aware that the piece was thoroughly legalled by the magazine's lawyers, so no ammo for us cops there. Thinks Victor.

'Good to see you again,' La Salle says to both of us, sitting comfortably back in his crap plastic tangerine chair and placing one hand on his closed briefcase on the table in front of him.

'Likewise,' Walter says, but I doubt that even one hundred per cent pure CS D'Hayt means that.

'How are you, Emma?' I ask.

'Fine, thank you.'

Her blue-green young eyes regard me coolly. Her thick blonde hair frames the vague chubbiness of her pretty face, its little pout.

'Good. Well, let's get started.' I push the button of the recorder and tell it who's here, date, time, to the sound of Walter clearing his throat and La Salle's manicured fingernails drumming lightly on his briefcase.

'Emma, as you know the purpose of this interview is to ask you some questions about the article that was printed in the latest issue of *Women's Day* magazine, in which you make various statements about the death of the actor Rory Stillrock.'

'Sorry, but are they "statements"?' La Salle says. It's one of those soft, polite, client-protecting opening interjections. Sometimes they work, sometimes they don't. On this occasion, get fucked, Victor.

'Are they?' I pointedly ask Emma, not him.

He says, 'My client made no actual statements of fact in the article. She simply spoke honestly to the journalist.'

Emma's looking at him, nodding, looks at me, nodding now at me.

I stay silent. It takes a while. Walter knows the score. He'll be staring at La Salle, while I concentrate on Emma.

Time ticks by.

'Right,' La Salle says, 'Sorry, you addressed your question to Emma. My apologies.'

'Yes, my question was to Emma,' I say, now looking at him. 'Mr La Salle, I can't be sure if you're representing or impersonating Miss Lexington, but the two of you should have sorted that out before coming in here.'

'Just ask me what you want,' she says.

'The article states that Rory Stillrock was in the passenger seat of his Cadillac. In the sworn statement that you gave us on the day of the discovery of his body, you agreed not to divulge details of the death. You were told that this was because releasing such information might hamper our investigation. Did you tell the journalist that the car was locked and that he was found in the passenger seat, and that this therefore amounts to proof of foul play?'

'Yes. Obviously it was me. Look, you can't keep things like that secret for ever. Everyone's talking about it. Don't blame me!'

'Emma, there's a big difference between the media speculating on vague rumours and you giving a paid interview.'

She's defiant. 'The public has a right to know. And I wasn't prepared to lie to the magazine. I'm not like that.'

'So you also revealed that there was no suicide note?'

She nods, a little caustically.

'Please speak for the record, Emma.'

'Yes, yes I did. For the same reason.'

'Do you realise the seriousness of what you've done?' Walter asks.

She glares at him. 'Rory was murdered! You can't just sit on all that stuff!'

'I'll put that another way,' Walter continues. 'By disobeying the terms of your sworn statement, you're in breach of the Law Enforcement Act. And by potentially jeopardising an investigation into a death you're in breach of the Criminal Activities Act. Either or both of which can result in jail time.'

'Oh, piss off! You're just saying that in your stupid bloody uniform to scare me!'

'My client was acting in the public interest,' La Salle says. 'She made that perfectly clear in her answer. It's not her fault that the media has begun to question your investigation.'

Their strategy seems clear enough. They think I'm going to heavy them for 'allegedly' trying to put pressure on a sensitive police investigation. Well, I *am* going to heavy them. But not only about that.

I say, 'Emma, you repeatedly told me that Rory was murdered. In the article you're actually quoted only as saying that his death was, quote "suspicious". Why did you not state directly in the article that in your opinion he was murdered?'

La Salle wants in eagerly but manages to hold his silver tongue.

Emma shrugs, says, 'Ask the magazine's lawyers, I reckon.'

I look around. Can't see 'em, eh. 'Did you say in the course of your interview with the journalist that in your opinion he was murdered?'

'Look, where's this going?' La Salle demands. 'The published words are there, why are you trying to twist them?'

'Emma, did you say in the course of your interview with the journalist that in your opinion he was murdered?'

'For sure.'

'So the article's not an accurate reflection of what you said?'

'It's … Look, we spoke for ages and they have to, you know, fit it into five hundred words or whatever.'

'Would you please tell me whether the article is an accurate reflection of what you told the journalist about the death of Rory Stillrock?'

'You don't have to answer that,' La Salle advises her, 'because the question is irrelevant.'

She clams up.

'Why is it irrelevant, Mr La Salle?'

'Detective Inspector Heineken, my client has no say in journalistic editing procedure.'

I wait a bit. Then say, 'Emma, a few minutes ago you said that the public has a right to know, and that you weren't prepared to lie to the magazine. You said, "I'm not like that." How much money were you paid for the article?'

Silver bites his tongue.

'Twenty-five thousand.'

'Were you happy to accept it?'

'They wanted to know about him. He was a famous Australian. I found him dead. They asked me for an interview. I gave it. Getting paid is what happens.'

'Are you disappointed that the magazine inaccurately reported what you said?'

'I object!' La Salle waves a flamboyantly angry hand. 'You keep trying to insinuate that my client should have some control over what is standard journalistic reportage.'

'Emma, every time your lawyer heads me off at the pass, the longer the pass becomes. I ask you again, are you disappointed that the magazine inaccurately reported what you said?'

'They wrote what they wrote.'

'For the record, I take that to be an evasive answer.'

'It's not!'

'Alright, then, in that case I can only conclude that you are happy with the article, otherwise you might have tried to publicly correct it. So to us, you say he was murdered, to the public you don't. And you phoned Suzy Stillrock and accused her of murdering him. But in the article you're quoted only as saying that Stillrock told you that he had decided to divorce Suzy. You don't say in the article that in your opinion she murdered him.'

'No. Because there has to be proof, obviously.'

'And who's paid to look for that proof?'

She gets it. Ah, the cops. You, Mr ugly old relentlessly unpleasant dick sitting opposite me.

'Please answer the question, Emma.'

'Well, you guys, obviously. But –'

'I take you back to the beginning of this interview, Emma. Chief Superintendent D'Hayt advised you of the seriousness of your going public, of potentially jeopardising this investigation. Is that worth twenty-five thousand dollars?'

She shakes her head, confusion setting in. You're with the grown-ups now, Emma. Crying murder's tough stuff.

'Please answer the question, Emma. Did you decide to do the interview and take the money for it, knowing that you might make the investigation more difficult?'

'No, Jesus!'

'You see, Emma, we *are* talking about murder, right? You've been in my ear that Suzy murdered her husband Rory. You've gone as close as the magazine's lawyers permitted to saying to the public that she did it. You have seen to it that murder rings loudly in the summer air, Emma, and part of the fallout is that the public thinks we cops are making a stupid mess of it all. Well, yes, we are looking at murder. But not necessarily at Suzy as the murderer. Where were you, and what did you do, on the night that Rory Stillrock died?'

'*Me?*'

'Yes, you, Emma Lexington. If I'm investigating a murder, and you have very much encouraged the view that he was murdered, why should you be off limits as a potential suspect?'

'I *loved* him! I *found* him!'

'Suzy Stillrock also claims she loved him. And she has sixteen years more than you to prove that. And she didn't leave fingerprints all over the death car. But answer my question, please. Where were you, and what did you do, on the night that Rory Stillrock died?'

'I was … I was, I mean, I meant, I …'

She clams up again. I shouldn't say this but I do.

'Mr La Salle, can you possibly interpret that? I, I, dot dot dot, I mean, I meant?'

He stands, all six foot flamboyant something of him. 'I would like to adjourn with my client.'

'Your client's going nowhere, Victor. But you know where the door is if you need one of your Cuban cigars. Where were you that night, Emma?'

'At, at my flat.'

'Alone?'

'Yes, yes I think so.'

'I thought you lived with Rory?'

'Yes of course I did. Just not all the time.'

'Why not?'

'He, we, were quite happy with it that way. Sometimes he just liked to be alone. Writing.'

'So on that night had he asked you to stay away?'

'Uhm, I can't remember. Probably.'

118

'"Probably"? You already can't remember what happened between you and he so soon before he died?'

'He, uh, yes, I was there in the day then he asked me could I stay in my flat ...'

'So he could write? Having just had a breakthrough deal fall over? Writing would be the last thing he'd want to do, surely?'

She's looking pleadingly at me. Can't I just stop? Sorry, Emma. It's called work.

'Why did he not want you there that night, Emma?'

'I ... I thought, I think he may have ...'

'Someone else?'

La Salle interjects 'Leading question! You can't!'

Too late, Victor. Done.

Eyes shut, no longer hearing her lawyer, Emma nods her bowed head. Tears darken her silk top.

'Speak for the record, Emma.'

'Yes. I thought maybe he was going to have someone else there.'

'Who?'

'I don't know.'

'Sure? Absolutely sure?'

'Yes.'

'How did you feel about it?'

She shrugs.

'Emma, the recorder doesn't pick up shrugs. Did you feel jealous? Hurt?'

She begins to cry. 'Yes ...'

'So, let me summarise for you, Emma. On the one hand you stayed away, at his request, and you thought it was because he might be seeing someone else. You don't have anyone to verify that you were not there that night. On Monday morning, you rang the police saying you had driven there from Hobart and found him dead in his car and that Suzy had done it, murdered him. You've now more or less confirmed that in print, across the country. It's called jury influencing. "I read it in the paper so it must be true." Your fingerprints are all over the place at the death scene. You have no alibi. What's to stop me concluding you're stitching up Suzy because you know very well we're treating it as murder, and she has a motive, his estate, whereas you apparently don't? Until now. Jealousy.'

'I didn't kill him. *I didn't kill my Rory!*' She screams and leaps up at me. The table, Walter and La Salle get in her way. The uniform monitoring the interview from the CCTV room rushes in. I wave him away. La Salle's soothing Emma, his arm around her. She's heaving, sobbing, moaning.

'I didn't kill him, I didn't, I didn't. The person there did it, the person there!'

'They ate a takeaway at his house on the night he was killed, Emma. You can't cook, can you?'

'Objection!' La Salle's mightily pissed off, and I don't blame him. But I do ignore him.

'Why didn't you say anything about jealousy in your sworn statement, Emma?'

She sits up straight, deep breath, stares at me, her eyes shiny.

'I thought it was Suzy he was seeing again. It made me feel sick. But I pretended to him I, I didn't suspect that, I went with the pretence he just wanted to be alone. And so, when I drove there that morning and, and found him, I knew it was her. Murdered him. My Rory. But I couldn't, I didn't want to say that he, he, had asked me to stay away …'

It makes a kind of sense. The pain of rejection. Hatred of Suzy, and a blind conviction that Suzy was the mystery visitor, ergo, Suzy did it. But not too blind to have nutted out the danger to herself of appearing jilted, because that would look like a

120

motive. If I can't have my Rory, nor can you. A motive, which, until a few minutes ago, she did not have.

'Just one more question, Emma. Why didn't you get the spare keys and open the car instead of smashing at the windows?'

The question surprises her. 'I didn't think about a key. I was, I just wanted to get him out of the car.'

'Okay. Emma, do you have any plans to travel out of Tasmania in the next little while?'

'No.'

'So if I need to contact you again, you'll be in Hobart?'

'Yes.'

'Good. Interview terminated.'

I'M BUGGERED. NOTHING A COFFEE WON'T FIX. ON THE WAY UP, Walter and I have digested the turn of events. Now, watching me fill the perc with powder, he says, 'Good work, Franz. She wasn't game to spill that. La Salle was shocked.'

'And she's made him look stupid. Well done, Emma Lexington.'

'Think she did it?'

'Not impossible, but not likely. I'll put my money on the visitor.'

'Suzy.'

'Or Robin Meuchasse.'

Walter thinks about it all, nods to himself. 'Right. Keep me informed.'

I sit at my desk, lean back, sore neck. Really need a swim at the shack. A day or two unwinding. Some chance. Faye at the door.

'How'd you go, boss?'

'Emma's managed to put herself in the frame. She was possibly being moved sideways by Rory.'

'Really? Boss, I wouldn't pick her for a killer. Ripping Suzy's eyes out, yeah! But that, you know, middle of the night creepy exhaust fumes?' Faye looks doubtful. I nod, It's a fair point. But sexy young Emma's no angel, not if she managed a relationship with fractious, cranky, deviant Rory for the better part of a year.

'By the way I got a contact for that Viola Vine in Los Angeles, boss, who wrote the strange obit. lines.'

'Thanks. Send it to me.'

She stands in the doorway. 'You okay, boss?'

'Yes. Just a little stiff.'

'Right.' She gives me a parting glance, disappears. A minute later and my machine pings a new email. And the percolator sings. I need that coffee.

Seated again, an allsort, no two, need the sugar, and a sip of the hot stuff. That's a bit better. I'll make that call. Eighteen hours ahead of California. Hope she's not the type to take an afternoon nap. Too bad. I dial.

'Hello, this is Viola speaking.' An LA drawl, throaty. Cigarettes maybe, or a singer, both.

'Viola Vine? My name is Detective Inspector Franz Heineken. I'm calling from Tasmania, Australia.'

'Why, hel-lo! And what can I do for you, sir?'

'It's in connection with the actor, Rory Stillrock.'

'Oh, poor, poor man. He was a honey. I miss him so.' She sighs down the line. I have an image of the voice, of her in a satin dressing gown on a balcony overlooking the Pacific Ocean. Though she's probably in a dull room in a dull suburb.

'Yes, his death came as a shock. Viola, I'm the detective in charge of looking at the circumstances of the death, and although it has been reported as suicide there are some unusual factors I'm looking into.'

'Oh? Such as …?'

'In particular I'm keen to talk to someone who may have been with him shortly before he died. The purpose of my call to you is to ask how well you knew him, and do you know if he had any enemies?'

'Gosh sakes, is that one helluva question or what, did he have enemies? Well, you know, Rory was famous for being a straight up and down Aussie. He said what was on his mind. He annoyed the hell out of plenty of folks over here. But, sir, that doesn't mean that all these years on someone's gonna have gotten on an aeroplane and gone down there to your Tasmania and *killed* him!'

'I didn't quite mean it that way, Viola. More a general question. You see, in your obituary notice that you put in our newspaper you wrote about you and he having had secrets. So I wondered, what kind of secrets? I was thinking, if he had secrets about others, they might not want him to reveal them?'

'I get you now. Yeah, well, he and I had a, you know, we were very loving with each other sexually and spiritually. But I didn't let on to his wife, Suzy. Maybe he did, I wouldn't know. But heck, we're looking at what happened a long time ago, sir. And he was well known for his sexual appetites. He even went in some videos.'

'Yes, we're aware of that.'

'I think it is right to say goodbye to those you loved. I just like to pen some words when my friends die. And Rory was special to me.'

'That's good of you.'

'I wish I could be more helpful, but it was a long time ago.'

'No worries, Viola.'

'Oh I'm not worried, sir, just a little sad is all. But tell you what, if I think of anything I'll be sure to let you know.'

'Okay. I'll email you my details.'

'You have my email address?'

'I do. We're very sophisticated, we Tasmanians.'

She laughs. 'And I knew from Rory that you're also charming.'

'Thanks for your time, Viola.'

'A sad pleasure, sir. Have a nice day, now, won't you?'

12

BY MIDWEEK I'M PREPARED TO ADMIT IT. SOMETHING'S CAUGHT up with me. Woozy head, grating cough, mucus waterfall in the throat, and a half-closed eye. Rafe sums it up when he sees me standing at the door of their room.

'Mate, stay away, you've got flippin' pink eye.'

Boots on the desk, he's got the *Mercury* in his lap, which he holds up at me in mock defence. On the rumpled back page, a former bricklayer from Ulverstone celebrates a five-for against the Black Caps. On the front page, wedge-tailed eagles and white-bellied sea eagles castigated as 'worthless' but costing the state millions by having flight paths in the way of proposed wind farm turbines.

'I knew there was something, boss.' Faye shows concern. 'You don't look too flash.'

'No, not great.'

'And you sound like Deep Throat,' Rafe says. 'Take yourself off! Seriously. We're good. We can run the show.'

'I might, I might.' I'm halted at their doorway. Not going any further in. But we need to catch up.

'Rafe, where are we with the Indira Patel bashing?'

'They're planning to bring her out of the coma on Friday night. Her condition's stable, so they're optimistic. But, who knows, maybe residual brain damage.'

'Public response?'

He shakes his head. 'Same as yesterday, not much. Twelve calls but they're just chatter, none with anything about a stereo. There are three with vague possibilities, so I'm onto them today. Going to see an old couple at Gagebrook, a builder at Howrah, and a currently unemployed of Fern Tree. Boss, maybe she *was* done over by a racist. Maybe I should go looking there.'

'No. Not while we're being publicly pasted on Stillrock. One spot fire is enough. Faye, where are you with your overload?'

It's a gentle ongoing crack at Rafe for being pulled from the Bellyard case.

'Well,' she says, 'we're looking at a dead end on the necklace. I talked to Mr Bellyard again, I had another go at trying to locate Cawler in Europe, wherever he is. As of now, it's cold. Whoever broke into that safe has well and truly got away with it.'

'Okay. And Stillrock? I take it you listened to the transcript of my interview with Emma Lexington yesterday.'

'I did. Great interview, boss, you wormed it out of her and she's a silly girl, but like I say I'm not sure she's capable of doing the deed. What else I have for you is that Robin Meuchasse is due back here on Sunday. He's booked a flight out from Fiji, first class to Sydney, connector to Hobart. So we can do a meet and greet on the apron, if you like.'

'Do that. And can you both interview Suzy Stillrock, please. We need her reaction to the *Women's Day* article. Make sure you read my notes from my first meeting with her.'

'Sure, boss.'

'Mate, you're stuffed. Go to the doctor. Go home.'

VIRAL CONJUNCTIVITIS, SOME OTHER INFECTION. THEY ALL ADD up. And breaking young Emma Lexington took a little out of me. I'm struck low. Hardly ever happens. Pufferfish needs to paddle his scavenger fins and tail into a dark, quiet place.

There's this shack I have on Bruny Island, south of Adventure Bay, my isolated forested place once a contested spot, a spark of anger between its first owners and white fellas. Now, driving there, nearing Kettering, one-eyed and loaded with a prescription antihistamine, much of everything seems to amount to nothing. I'm weeping pus and phlegm, sick and sorry and going to hide alone.

Rinse the body in the warmish salty sea. Open the bung eye wide underwater, swim painfully out to the sacred rock, hang off it in the swell a while. Then allow waves to propel and float me back to the tiny fine sandy beach, upon which I graze my tummy. Stand, with effort. Beating down late summer sun. Young gang of warbling magpies, hop-strutting on the fringes of the sand, unafraid and wondering who I am at their place.

Later, dark blackly moonless outside, with some wines in me that shouldn't be there, and part way through Hedda's lurid paperback, the tiny lounge room still aromatic with the two pies and large plastic tub of coleslaw I bought at Margate. Phlegm's gone. Head's hot, spinning scenes. Stillrock. Mountgarrett. Indira, Joanna, Lily of the Valley, Craig, Emma, Clara Olivetti and her faded hippieness, Viola, and who's mystery Robin and where is he ...?

THE MOBILE DRAGS ME FROM PROFOUND SLEEP. BRIGHT OUTSIDE light. Jeez, after nine, I slept as if dead. Nora.

'Hi Dad, how're things?'

'I'm crook, flu. Sleeping it off.'

127

'Shit, sorry, I woke you.'

'It's okay, I need to be up. So what's with you? Found any work?'

'Nah. There was something at a restaurant, but it fell through.'

'Pity.'

'Anyway, Dad, I was wondering if I could take a couple of friends to your shack.'

'When?'

'Like, today? For a few nights?'

'I'm here, Nora. At the shack. Lying low.'

'… Oh. Oh, look, sorry, I mean. Gee, you don't sound good.'

'Just a cold.'

'So, maybe we can go down, I dunno, at the weekend? I've told them all about it and they're just so, wow! Envious.'

Nora's sensible. She'd never do anything dumb at a precious place like my shack, wouldn't bring flaky idiots here, to a senior cop's hidey-hole. But she knows me. I don't always give, just because I'm asked.

'Your mates haven't got work?'

'No, why do you ask? Youth allowance is the pits, but at least we're alive.'

'I'll let you use the shack, on one condition.'

'Sure, what's that?'

'Heard of TasFoodAid?'

'Uh, yeah? … No? …'

'I was talking the other day to the lady who runs it, out in Richmond. They grow fruit and give it to charities, so it's good work. But she's struggling to find pickers this year. Phone her, her name's Joanna Arundel. Mention me. The pay's not much, but it's money. And as much free fruit as you can take away. To the shack. Do two days' picking with your mates and I'll give you two nights at the shack.'

128

'I mean … Well I'll have to ask them. They might not want to.'

'Don't ask them, Nora, tell them. Good fun, good cause, pocket money for cask wine and round steak for two days in paradise on a South Bruny private beach, crays and abs just offshore.'

'You're weird, Dad. Okay. I'll ask, I'll … what's the name again?'

'TasFoodAid. Richmond. Mrs Joanna Arundel. If you're lucky you may even get tea and jam "skoans" in her National Trust house on the Coal River bank.'

'Yeah, right. When are you coming back to Hobart?'

'Friday.'

'Sorry you're crook.'

'Nothing that'll kill me.'

'See you, then.'

'*Vaarwel, dochter*.'

She'll be thinking, grumpy old bastard. I'm thinking, grumpy old bastard.

13

'HEDDA. HOW ARE YOU?'

'More to the point, Franz, how are *you*?'

I'm on the Bruny-to-Kettering ferry, in my car in hot early morning sunshine.

'Betterish. On my way back. I'll be in the office in forty. Where are you?'

'Stanley.'

'What's happening up there?'

'Fishing boat. Bales of five-star Tasmarijuana destined for Melbourne. Well, we're following up on a tip-off but so far all we've found are fresh fish, snap-frozen fish, fishing long-lines, fish cleaning gear, and fish-finding sonar.'

'Some tip-off. Your people are being used in a turf war, Andover. Wise up.'

'Yeah, yeah. Mate, two reasons for the call. One, how are you, established that, sounds like you've been wagging, two, want a feed Sunday evening? Your place.'

'Why mine?'

'To try out your new oven.'

'Say again?'

'Your new oven we're going to buy this weekend to replace the cheap little number you should never have bought in the first place.'

130

'It came with the house. Well, okay. It's kind of you to buy me a new oven, Hedda. And you can be the first to cook in it.'

'I will. You're buying a Glem Bi-Energy wall oven, it'll cost less than three grand, and you're paying. What's that noise?'

'Ferry's docking. Let's talk when I'm in. I happen to be fond of the oven I've got.'

'Bulldust, mate, come on, I know what I'm doing. So it's a deal, hey? Nine sharp Sunday morning we're in Hardly Normal, all eager, I talk to and bargain with the salesman, you stand in the background like a miserable put-upon husband, waiting to extract your credit card. With me, oh prickly one? Come on, Puff. It's not going to hurt a bit. You may even like the feeling.'

'I'll think about it. See you.'

I drive thoughtfully off the ferry. What's she up to?

INDIRA PATEL'S DEEP-SLEEP EXPRESSION, HER BARBITURATE coma, makes her look serene, lying on her back in her ICU bed. The cast on her broken arm tells a different story, as does her shaved head, two lines of sutures, eight stitches in one, twelve in the other. I know, from a photograph, that before her attack she had shoulder-length hair, dark and glossy, and a toothy grin. Clara and Ross, and others who Rafe's spoken to during the week, all described her as very friendly, with a bubbly personality, that kind of thing. For this reason alone I'm strong on the theory that she didn't know the person who bashed her.

It's late Friday morning, hot and motionless outside, a bad northerly due sometime tomorrow, off the mainland, from the Red Centre across the Mallee, over Bass Strait losing little of its dry heat and a million blowflies. But now is now and Rafe and I are listening to Dr Irinya Krneta, longtime neurosurgeon at the Royal Hobart Hospital. Behind her, the room's window has a strange split view, half brittle-dry Mount Wellington forest, half advertising billboard of a grey-bearded old bloke on a donkey on a jetty, spruiking the world's best premium beer, brewed in Launceston. The room's smell? The usual. Distinctive drug chemicals, softer warmish humanity. Indira Patel has, after all, been lying here exuding both for a week.

Dr Krneta says, 'The patient's responded reasonably well to the reduced cerebral blood flow, and intracranial pressure is now normal, as we predicted. But there are minor brainstem lesions, from the force of the blow on the skull, which pushed the brain down, with a force about equivalent to falling off a bicycle, say, onto a hard surface, without a helmet. I suppose you want to know when you can talk to her?'

'Yes.'

Krneta consults the patient chart. 'She's been on withdrawal for twenty-two hours. She'll wake sometime during the night or tomorrow morning. But of course, only then will we know if there's residual damage.'

'Of course.'

'And I will decide when you can actually talk to her. You know why.'

'Yes, shock, regression. We've every concern for her well-being.'

'Good, Mr Heineken. Is there anything else?'

'Could one of your staff let me know when you've made the decision?'

'I'll call you personally.'

She means she brooks no shit with detectives, in the matter of damaged individuals in her care. As if that's new.

But then she says, 'Do you think it was racial?'

Can't help herself, eh. Everyone in Tasmania, and not a few beyond, keen to know. Who bashed the Hobart Indian?

'Ms Patel will hopefully answer that, Dr Krneta.'

LATE FRIDAY. JUST ABOUT THROUGH THIS DRAGGING HOT DAY, head well on the mend. I'll be asleep early, though, probably won't even be dark.

Rafe at my office door, keen. Lip all but normal.

'Boss, there's a bloke downstairs with his son. He says they've got something to tell us about a stereo.'

A Mr Tasker and his five-year-old son, Damien, clutching a large scrapbook. We go into in an interview room, the silent lad staring up at me with large unblinking eyes.

'So what can we do for you, Mr Tasker?'

'Well, I dropped off a load of stuff at the tip a week ago, last Friday. Damien was with me. Then I saw your appeal on TV, about a stereo, and it meant nothing to me. I mean, I saw no stereo at the tip. But Damien did. And the reason we're only coming to you now is because, well, do you want to tell the Inspector, Damey, mate?'

The little boy nods, staring up at me as he has been, says to me, 'Why aren't you wearing blue clothes?'

Three men grin.

'That's a very good question, Damien. It's because I don't work so much on the street. I have an office up in this big building.'

I hand him one of my cards. 'You can have this.'

He studies it closely. The embossed badge seems to convince him, yes, he's a policeman.

'Mummy and I were cutting out old newspapers today.'

His big sentence, his big eyes on me. Buttressed by his carefully watchful dad.

'That's nice, Damien. What for?'

'My scrapbook for kinder.' He opens it out on the table. Glued on a page is the photo Walter had placed in the *Mercury* last week. A 1970s common Bang & Olufsen stereo, best we could come up with as a hopeful approximation.

Damien says, 'And I saw this picture and asked Mummy what it was. And she said that when she was little it played music with black plastic plates. But they don't make them any more. And I asked Mummy, is that why the lady took hers to the tip? Because it had become rubbish?'

'That's interesting, Damien. What was the lady doing with it?'

'I watched her while daddy was busy. She was at the shed. She was trying hard to get it out of the front seat, because it was big. Then she put it on a table in the shed and went away.'

'A stereo like this one? With big dark boxes?'

He nods enthusiastically.

'Do you know what kind of car she had, Damien?'

'A Straylian Holden ute.'

'Do you remember the colour?'

'It was white, but with dust all over it so it looked brown.'

'And what about the lady?'

'Uhm …' He looks doubtful. 'I think she was shorter than Mummy.'

'I can help you there,' his father says.

'You're doing very well, Damien. Do you remember what kind of clothes she had on?'

He shakes his head.

'Maybe you remember her hair?'

He screws up his face. 'Maybe quite long? I'm not sure.'

'That's okay, Damien. I bet you were looking at that funny old music thing, hey?'

He nods importantly.

'Did she have stuff in the back of the ute, Damien?'

'Yes.' He takes a deep breath. 'A chair a lamp, a guitar, a football and big black garbage bags and stuff.'

'Good, that's very good, Damien. Mr Tasker, would you be able to give me an approximate time you were there?'

'Oh yeah, I can do better than that. I wanted my stuff offloaded and back in the car by five past four, because I like to listen to the Phillip Adams repeats on Radio National. And my wife's one hundred and sixty-five centimetres.'

'Good. Well, thank you very much, Damien. You're a very smart young man.' I shake his hot little hand, then his old man's again, as does Rafe, and we usher them out into the heat.

'We'll take it, boss, a dirty white ute, a shortish female, an accurate time. Say the ute went in and onto the weighbridge at four. She'd be driving out at say, ten past. Pays the fee. Bloke in the weighbridge has punched in her postcode, Bob's your carbuncle.'

'And in this case, Damien's our sleuth.'

MINE'S AN OKAY OVEN. IT WOULD BE A CHAMPION IN A REMOTE Congo village. Yes, the narrow rubber seal is already lifting, and yes, the grill component is disproportionately large, making the oven part too small. And the brand name, *Kopria*, sounds like Greek for bullshit to me. But I chose this place with all fittings, and being single I wasn't charged up about the whitegoods, they looked fine. Shiny, new. Sucked in old cop. Yes, no, maybe, but the fact is I was more interested in the proximity of the house to town, to the Southern Outlet and Bruny, its view of the mountain, even its view of the tip. I liked its profound anonymity, and the steep down-sloping drive, the profusion either side of the drive, on the narrow slopes, of man-size scotch

135

thistles among half-buried ankle-twisting dolerite rocks. And the auto-gate, the thick white faux Spanish walls and heavy door. If some villain finds out where Pufferfish lives and wants to come and do him harm, he'll have his work cut out.

Two boiled eggs and a packet of instant pasta for supper, washed down with no-name orange juice. Still muggy-headed. That crowned garlic and rosemary-spiked roast lamb for one in the *Kopria* – its last supper – will just have to wait, eh. Maybe for an eternity, if Hedda's real about her new-oven-for-Puff movement. Whatever that means.

I'll be asleep before dark. Brushing my teeth, I ponder again our business, how it works. The public have no idea how useful they are, in the matter of providing information. Take young Damien Tasker. Thanks to his kinder scrapbook, we've now linked the stereo and potentially Indira's assailant to a female ute owner living in a narrow band of southern Tasmanian postcodes.

SATURDAY MORNING. INDIRA PATEL IS PROPPED UP IN HER BED, multiple white cushions behind her like Sydney Opera House shells. Her brown skin's waxy, old Easter egg grey from poor internal maintenance, and her large red-veined eyes struggle to focus on anything, let alone me. She's not a well person, and Dr Krneta, in the room with me, Rafe, and a colleague of hers charged with legal responsibility to monitor 'invasive patient contact', namely cops on a case, is agitated. This should not be happening. But the thing is, Indira, upon being surfaced into true wakefulness earlier this morning, called for us. Called for the TPF, the Tasmanian Police Force. And the urgency of her call regressed her, so they gave her a mild shot, but she persisted, and so here we are, it's not yet nine in the morning, and I'm about to do a duet with a re-drugged post-coma victim of scummy human behaviour, a man beating a young woman almost to death.

'Indira,' Dr Krneta says, 'this is Detective Inspector Heineken. He will help you.'

Krneta motions me forward. Indira takes my hand. She feels it and holds it, and, like a strange human rush, I feel in its feeble grip that she has been wrestling something in her coma state. She grips more tightly. Strength.

'What happened, Indira?'

'You must help Johann.' It's a bare whisper.

'Who is Johann?'

Tears on her cheeks, the colour of honey.

'Who is he, Indira?'

'I rang him.'

'You rang Johann? About the stereo?'

A feeble nod.

'He came and collected it from you, Indira?'

Her head lolls, eyes sink back.

Krneta stands in the way.

Rafe says, 'Johann Dellacroix, the bloke with the stall at Salamanca Market. Be him for sure, boss. There's only one Johann in this town who does up old musical stuff.'

HOBART'S CBD IS SO SMALL THAT WITHIN MINUTES RAFE AND I are zigzagging through traffic down Campbell, into Davey and pulling to a sharp cop halt on the pavement at the top of Salamanca Place, the broad avenue sloping to the row of famous old sandstone warehouses built for a licentious, thriving port, its river a bloodied whale slaughterhouse. This Saturday morning, stalls are erected as far as the eye can see, all the way to the distant old grain silos long since converted to swanky apartments. Early morning it is, but faithful browsers, and curious tourists, congest the paving and this friendly tent city of unique island commerce.

Down we go through the slowly moving throng, trying not to be rude about it. Along past displays of Tasmanian timber breadboards, chopping boards, neat jars of leatherwood honey, pre-loved clothes, books, hundreds of them, another time I'd be buying a few, jewellery, scented candles, soaps, bath stuff, fruit leathers, toys, bric-a-brac, thylacine and Tasmanian devil tea towels, Salamanca Market's distinctive aroma of barbecued bratwurst and onions, and rhythmic Peruvian pan flutes, framed artworks, woollen beanies, blankets, and an empty space where Johann Dellacroix, Saturday after Saturday, in all weather, sells 33, 45 and 78 rpm records.

I show my ID to the neighbouring stallholder. He's sitting in a deckchair, reading *The Age*, no one interested in his wind chimes just for the moment. He stands.

'Would you expect Johann here today?'

'Oh, yeah. Something wrong?'

'When did you last speak to him?'

'This time last week, mate. Just to say hello, then goodbye. Nice bloke but he's a quiet sort.'

The stallholder on the other side has nothing to say either. Rafe's phoned the Council person who administers the market. No word from Johann about him not being here today.

HQ calls me with his home address. Up in the hills behind Mount Wellington, in the backblocks of Collinsvale. It won't take us long to get there, but even so I want some uniforms. Anything could be going on up there. It's a Glenorchy patch, so I call through to Main Road. They'll have a car there before we arrive. I advise a cautious approach.

In the car we speed up Davey, the blue and reds flashing, into Harrington and back down Macquarie to the Brooker Highway. Rafe keeps to a relatively sane speed.

'What do you reckon, boss? We could have done with this information a week ago.'

'That's the worry.'

I make a call.

'Clara here.'

'Clara, hello, Franz Heineken.'

'Hello …'

'Indira is out of her coma. We're hopeful she'll make a good recovery.'

'Oh thank God for that.'

'She's spoken. But it's still early days. I just wanted to let you know.'

'Can I visit her? She doesn't have any relatives in Australia.'

'You'll need to ask the hospital that. One question, Clara, you people know Johann Dellacroix?'

'Yes, of course. Dear Johann, he restores old … the stereo!'

'It seems Indira phoned to tell him about the one that was dropped off at the tip shop. You do this kind of thing?'

'Yes, there are clients like him who ask us to let them know about certain items. Johann has a huge record collection, at his place up near Collinsvale, and he's got a workshop there. He restores stereos and gramophones, electric typewriters, that sort of thing, and sells them to the second-hand shops. It's how he makes a living.'

'And his Salamanca Market stall.'

'Yes. Is he, is he okay?'

'I can't answer that, Clara, so please keep this to yourself for the time being.'

Rafe's ducked off the highway near Moorilla, testing the engine and brakes as we climb and turn and avoid traffic.

Faye comes alive on the car radio. 'A Glenorchy car's on the way to the property, boss. What I can tell you about Johann Dellacroix is he's sixty-two, single, lived at the house you're going to for twenty-seven years, and he makes his living restoring musical equip –'

'Old news, mate.'

'Rack off, Rafe. And a few years ago he got in a blue with another fellow about a stereo, as it happens. About who had seen it first at the tip. They had to be separated by staff, and it went to court. So, not sure if it's related.'

'Could be. Do a background on the other party.'

'About to, boss. Cheerio.'

Along Glenlusk Road now, climbing, fewer properties, bigger blocks, very rural, amazing views over the lower Derwent Valley, the narrow river broadening, suburbs, open ocean, distant peninsulas, islands. Cows and goats hang around in paddocks. They advertise properties here as paradise twelve kilometres from the Glenorchy CBD. I can see why.

A dirt road leads to Dellacroix's place, set well in behind trees, though the house itself is in a large cleared area, but for a mature wattle tree, tall and spread and bright green in the oppressive heat. The marked TPF car's out front, empty. A scared, skinny bitzer dog's outside, barking at the open front door. An old Kombi van occupies a solid wooden lean-to. The cleared area's typical, stuff lying around, free ranging chooks, a pile of ancient tree stumps off to one side, a large unkempt vegie patch with startlingly tall silverbeets and a profusion of staked tomato bushes, heavy with deep red fruits big and small, unpicked. Pumpkin vines trail out of the patch across dead yellow grass, fat pumpkins here and there like grey boulders.

The house is a beauty, a classic old forest dwelling, myrtle and blackwood on raised foundations with a wraparound pole bluestone verandah.

A uniform appears at the front door, cap off and held to his face, covering his nose.

'Bugger,' Rafe says.

He parks, we get out, walk. The dog turns to us, half ready to attack but scared witless.

A second uniform comes out and they stand together on the verandah, gulping sweet rural air.

'Got a body in there, sir, decomposing rapidly. Jeez, it's not good.' The sergeant takes a hurried step forward and spews mightily over the edge of the verandah onto the papery-dry grass.

We step up. The vomiter's deathly pale, his constable partner, all nineteen or twenty years of him, sweating profusely, his face unnaturally shiny with it, his eyes big with the disbelief that assails you when you step across the boundary from the casual to the horrific. It gets me every time, even after all these years.

'Thanks, guys, appreciate it. Wait out here, if you don't mind.'

The interior is, for the most, a bachelor's, that is, not very clean, the chairs and rugs in the hallway and lounge room have probably been there for as long as he's lived in the place. Last winter's ashes still in the magnificent stone fireplace you could just about stand in. Open-style kitchen with a great view, but the stove looks like a Fifties model and the filth-spattered oven's not a patch on my *Kopria*. Pity there isn't a garlic-studded roast lamb in *it*, anything to cover the stench of rotting flesh.

The astounding feature of this large, rustic old lounge room is that its walls have floor-to-ceiling shelves, purpose built, and they're jammed neatly full of sleeved LPs.

'Bloody oath!' Rafe mutters. 'He must have every vinyl ever made.'

On we go. Following the smell, basically. Through into a dim passageway, off which rooms lead, doors open, a couple of bedrooms, a junk room, another with a reasonably sophisticated home brew beer facility. The end of this passageway is where we need to go. Rafe's behind me. The door ahead's wide open. I imagine the young constables where we are. Downright spooky in the windowless gloom it must have been. Their Glocks out and held high, for sure.

It's Johann Dellacroix's workroom, dividing left and right off the doorway. Like an extra large rumpus room at the end of a family house, the width of the place. It has big windows for him to see well while working. There are two long tables in the middle of the room and work benches along the walls. They're all laden with an amazing clutter of musical instruments and players, in every conceivable state of repair, disrepair, many seem abandoned long ago, or more likely kept for the day a part comes in handy. Tools line another wall, hanging on up-angled six-inch nails hammered solidly into the thick horizontal wood planks.

The table on the left is where, it seems, he was most recently working. A portion of it is cleared, screwdrivers and a small metal bandsaw, as if in use, single screws scattered about, a length of electrical wiring, a rectangle of some kind of board with screwholes in it. Like a backing board, about the size of one of the decent breadboards we saw at the market a short while ago. Old chipboard, though, daggy.

Opposite us is a pair of closed double doors, mostly glass. They open onto the back verandah. Johann Dellacroix is lying in a classic foetal, defensive position on his bluestone floor. It's Johann? Well, bits of visible grey hair suggest early to mid sixties. He's wearing a long brown leatherwork apron, which is moving sinuously from the maggots underneath. Many more of the puffy white worms, and an intense cloud of densely black flies, are about the unrecognisable face. The heat of the past week has speeded putrefaction, with an odd result. The body is still bloated with gas, but the face, probably because it's been entirely exposed, has collapsed and already looks more skeletal than a human face, a skull, albeit dripping flesh.

Rafe opens the rear double doors, steps outside. I bend forward for a closer look. The head is black, where I can make it out, black with what looks like thick road tar, blood. So he would have been struck a number of times, judging by the amount of blood and in particular a slanty, crush-like depression in the matted tarry mess. That's one mighty blow, with something like a heavy spanner.

Flashback to Stillrock's garage. Spanner there, starred Caddy windows. Phew, head's spinning, light. What's that in the exposed death claw hand? I'll just bend down to prise it out. Oh no! Woozy, don't faint-fall onto this. Unlike me but it's the conjunctivitis hangover, and I back away, walk out, stumble out. There's Rafe down on the tatty typically Tasmanian summer lemon lawn, just appreciating not being back in there with stinky mister decomposed.

I suck in a great lungful of hot fresh air, then another, through mouth and nose. See life at its simplest, pecking order. Chooks out front, ducks this side, five or six, large ducks with those angry-looking red fleshy knobs on their beaks. Muscovies, that's what they are, Muscovy ducks. Poor things, who's going to look after them now, and the dog? Sun's warming up, high in the eastern sky already, making the river far below shine like a glistening yellow super-highway threading through our gentle valley.

'Oh, that's a bad one, boss. Poor bastard took what I saw to be two smacks to the head at least, and by surprise you'd say, the work apron on. Front door unlocked, these back glass ones as well, too easy.'

'Rafe, we need this place roped off, and a forensic van up here. Go around and tell the young blokes to get that done, and can you talk to Walter?'

'Sure, boss.' He gives me a bit of a look. 'You right, mate?'

'Just got to go back up in there, and get something.'

'Rather you than me, mate. I'll go tell the little ones.'

Stepping back into my job, is what it is, once the emotions have had their say, which they now have. Johann Dellacroix, music repairer, stinks to high heaven. But I have to go back up in there and in any case it's soon to be a carefree space of Forensic Unit personnel, photos, dusting, scooping up gunk. The skinny bitzer's paw prints will be everywhere and it probably licked its master over most of the seven days he lay there, licked him as a dog will do to wake the master, then maybe to taste him as well, not that I saw bite marks. And further sad proof that Tasmanian devils are gone from this part of the State, no longer build their dens under solid old Tassie houses like this one, or they would have been up in there feasting and cleaned him to the bone.

Back into the death zone. I'm careful not to touch, to contaminate potential evidence, clues. Big black flies swarm up. His fluids are rim-marking the bluestone. I hadn't seen that, should have, sharp back of twelve-inch ruler on knuckles, could and should do better. Notice things, Franz. Anything.

It's in the claw. To the massed dismal music of flying raisins I prise apart the nauseatingly stiff-soft thumb and forefinger, take what I want that was in them. Back away, sweet crooked elbow to face, out again.

I wait in the sprawling backyard. Looking across the dead yellow grass at what is an impressively large duck pond, a back hoe job decades ago, judging by the mature old bulrushes. Waiting

144

for Rafe. He comes back. To find me staring at the crumpled thing in my hand. So he stares at me.

'What the hell's the matter, boss?'

Yucky though it is, I can read, quite clearly, alongside the stern grey Catholic profile, the words *Narodowy Bank Polski*. Johann Dellacroix died not with a felafel but a zloty in his hand.

Gruesome or not, I laugh at the sheer bloody paradox of it. And say, 'Looks like you're back on the Bellyard case, Rafe.'

WE WALK AROUND TO THE FRONT, DIGESTING THE POSSIBILITY, the probability, that the murder of Johann Dellacroix – the bashing of Indira Patel, for the sake of a stereo – is linked to the theft of the diamond necklace from Mr Gavin Bellyard's New Town home. His wad of zloty banknotes was stolen with the necklace and here surely is one of them. A dying man's grasp at his assailant?

The Glenorchy boys have taken refuge under the grateful shade of the wattle tree. In the glaring sunshine scrawny bantams peck enthusiastically at the sergeant's vomit.

'Could one of you bring me an evidence bag, please.'

The constable hops it to their car, brings me a bag, holds it open while I drop the zloty in, seals it. Rafe takes it. I stand there with my fingers in need of a rinse. I'm thinking of the duck pond. But not just for my fingers. You might conclude that the smarter the villain, the quicker he'll get rid of incriminating evidence. True. But as we know from long experience, this carries some risk with it. Speed before calculation. And, yes, even for the smart villains, a body of water's just about irresistible. And in my breathing sweet air round the back, concentrating on the pond, rather than the image of Dellacroix, I saw something on its brown surface, out in the middle, no larger than, say, what you might buy in a tacky Cairo tourist shop. A little pyramid. For that is what is poking out of the middle of the pond's surface. It could be nothing. On the other hand, it could be something. And my fingers need a rinse.

'Round the back, please,' I say to Rafe and the constable, and to the sergeant, now emerged from the wattle, 'You stay here, and make sure nobody comes in. But call me when forensics arrive.'

'Sure thing, boss.'

Back around we go. The pond's some way off from the house, across the papery grass crackling under our shoes.

'What's that?' Rafe says. He's seen the thing in the water.

'We should find out.'

At the edge of the pond I kneel, rinse my fingers in the warm, turmeric-hued water. A little way along, speckled Muscovy ducks emerge from their elevated wooden house at the pond's edge, eye us warily.

'Weird,' Rafe says. 'It's not a pump or anything. I reckon it's been exposed with the sun drawing water off at such a rate.'

'Constable,' I say, 'would you be okay wearing a dead man's wellies?'

'Yeah, no problems, sir.'

'Though I'm sure Rafe's happy to do it.'

Rafe's not happy to do it. Doesn't say so, just a look.

'Alright then, if you don't mind, I saw a pair of his wellies up on the deck. Go and get them. Better drop your dacks, the water's bound to be deeper than the boots.'

Self, Rafe and the Muscovies watch the constable enter the water, his trousers, jacket, shirt and tie and cap off, red underdaks, pale skin, olive-green wellies to just below his knees. Water soon slurps over the rims of the wellies.

'The bottom's really soft,' he says, making his way cautiously towards the pyramid object. 'Muddy.'

146

'Be duckshit,' Rafe says.

'Careful when you get close to it,' I say. 'Don't step on anything. And feel down with your hands.'

The constable does just that. He stops when he's about a metre away from it, the water over his knees. He puts his arms into the water, feels gingerly about.

'Some kind of box … And there's another.' His words bounce off the shiny surface.

'Okay, take hold of the one that's exposed and lift it slowly, see what happens.'

He takes another step forward, bends right over it, arms submerged to his armpits, then he stands slowly upright, a box trailing wires in his arms.

'*Whoo-ee*, that's Bang!' Rafe shouts, 'Olufsen better be there.'

'It's a stereo speaker,' the constable says across the water. 'It must be attached to the rest of the thing.'

'Do you want Rafe to come and give you a hand?'

'Should be okay.' He bends again, feels about, more relaxed and confident now, knows what it is, and it's just water, no Tassie crocs in here. He's fiddling underwater, carefully but with firmness, and we soon see why. He lifts, exerting himself because of the pull and weight of the water, the entire stereo up, its two speakers on top of it. Water drains loudly from it, back down into the pond, down his body.

Then he turns, nearly overbalances. It's a close thing.

'Fuck it,' he says, 'the wellies are stuck in the mud. I can't move.'

'Okay. Hang onto it. Rafe, looks like you get your wish after all. A dip on a hot summer's day.'

He's quick, because the young constable's clearly feeling the weight of the thing. Rafe strips to his underpants, bare feet because he doesn't need to get stuck and there are no other wellies.

He takes the big boxy bundle from the constable, and together they make their way out of the duck pond. Rafe puts it down on the papery grass. The arm of the turntable's skewed, both speakers minus their backing. A dolerite boulder the size of a shot put sits in a speaker. To weight it down, didn't quite do the intended job, did it, in fact rolled the speaker upright, into view.

And wedged into the other speaker, against the amplifying disk, is a shallow rectangular box Rafe and I recognise straight away, the clincher to this extraordinary morning, the ornate walnut box that once upon a time housed the Bellyard necklace.

14

I'M NAMED AFTER A SLUGGISH, ROTUND, DECIDEDLY UNPRETTY and deadly species of fish. And so it is with almost a sense of kinship that at long last I clap eyes upon Robin Meuchasse, the somewhat famous St Helens-born stage, television and cinema actor who still chooses to call Tasmania home, though his website now says he was born and raised in 'the world famous Bay of Fires'. Fair enough, perhaps he attended home school on an orange lichen boulder crashed by waves, but I doubt it, not least because he went to kinder and then school in Hobart with one Rory Stillrock. What attracts me to him is his fancy rainbow gear, the canary-yellow scarf, green cotton shirt, satin indigo waistcoat, their combined colouring making him resemble a poisonous South American tree frog.

He's taller than on TV, with a decent spread of wealthy middle-aged plumpness, tanned, piercing brown eyes under prominent eyebrow ridges, full head of caramel hair, parted in the middle. His face looks younger than the rest of him. Deep actor's voice, firm, positive handshake. No wedding band, expensive wristwatch.

Murder fresh on my mind. Mr Meuchasse is seated opposite Rafe and me in an interview room, his clobber seriously at odds with our collar and tie drabness. His ongoing expression? Mildly amused.

'Thank you for coming along, Mr Meuchasse, so soon after your return from Fiji.'

'A pleasure.' He smiles at me. 'Anything to oblige.'

'As you've been advised, this is a formal interview in the matter of the death of Rory Stillrock. We have, as you may already know, interviewed others –'

'Good! So we'll all hang together!' He laughs generously.

'– Others who were close to him or in contact with him shortly before he died. So, yes in that sense you're not alone. You know he was murdered, then?'

'Oh come on, I was making a joke!'

I look at Rafe, who looks at me, and we look at Meuchasse.

'Sorry,' he says, reddening under the tan. Just ...' He shrugs. Best let it go.

'I'll start here. Is this your voice, Mr Meuchasse, on this recording?' I push the play button. We listen.

'"It's me. You aren't answering your mobile. When and where do you want this drink?"'

Robin Meuchasse clears his throat. Those melodious words came from nowhere else. He holds up an arm and, frowning, waves an explanatory finger, says, 'Yes, yes he'd called me and left a message saying sorry, and could we make up.'

'For what?'

'You don't seem to know much about us.'

'If you could answer the question, please.'

'Well for starters, we knew each other from a young age. We, uhm, as boys our friendship was also physical, constantly physical ... But then as we suddenly were older and professional competitors we distinctly lost the urge to spill one another's seed. So ... Well, anyway, we came into contact at a party, this was, oh, three weeks ago? And a shitty little book had just come out, a book about Hollywood, a gossipy book and supposedly Rory

150

had intervened with a production company to prevent me from being signed up for a movie role. So I confronted him. He was his usual drunk, belligerent, laughing, sneering self, a sad parody of himself, actually.'

Meuchasse stops and looks down.

'Rory loved getting under my skin.'

And stops again.

Pause.

We wait.

'So where is this going? Oh, please, look, you've got your job to do, but I didn't kill him, guys. Push that barrow as far as you can, but I did not kill Rory Stillrock.'

'What was his answer to your phone message?'

'He rang back saying sorry, sorry for being a dickhead at the party and could I get over it, and he offered to buy me a drink to apologise face to face.'

'You agreed?'

'Oh, yes. Rare indeed for Rory to say sorry. But for me there was more than that. I really wanted him to, to be humble in front of me. Not grovel, just be humble. Be aware of the consequences of his actions. And, you know, there's this thing, schadenfreude, pleasure at another's pain. A big deal he'd done with a studio for one of his scripts had just fallen through. I wanted to see his hurt close up. You probably don't know much about that deal.'

'We do. So you met at his house?'

'Yes. Late on the Saturday afternoon before I flew out early the next morning. Rory had wanted to meet in town, in a restaurant or high profile bar. No chance, I said.'

'Why did he want to do that?'

'So that people could see us, word get out we were pals again. Conclusion, Robin has forgiven Rory.' He shakes his head. 'I was never going to give him the satisfaction of that. Not after what he tried to do to my career.'

'Right. You were prepared to forgive him privately, not publicly.'

'Yes.'

'What happened at his place? What did you do?'

'He grabbed a couple of bottles of Portuguese rosé, gave me the flutes, and we wandered down to his gaze-about. Sorry, he called it that, his gazebo near the cliff. Rory always had a way with words, though not necessarily a good way. Witness his appalling scripts. I read one. A tasteless potage of clunky dialogue and overcooked description.'

'He gave you one to read?'

'No. A furtive email attachment via a friend's friend. Alas for him, Rory's clever tongue never translated to print.'

'How long were you in the gazebo together?'

'Oh, the time it takes to drink two bottles? We did relax after a bit, laugh at some of the old stuff.'

'So no hard feelings? I understood he was notoriously direct, that he was rude to the point of being proud about it.'

'Oh yes, rude Rory, no doubts there. I just happened to catch him alone when he was genuinely down. Hit hard. By the reality, I think, that it was just about all over with his career. Saying sorry to Snotty was almost an afterthought, he was so fucking glum. And probably the Suzy decision didn't help.'

'What do you mean by that?'

'You saw him dead, right. Was there a small round bandage on his face?'

'Over his left cheekbone, yes.'

'Earlier that day she'd gone to his place to confront him, he said, about the Lexington girl, and so he said to Suzy he'd decided to divorce her. He, uhm, kind of jumbled how he explained it

152

all, but apparently she lost it. Hell hath no fury, you know, as he explained it, and she gave him what he called the mother of all backhands. Those exact words I do remember, because I remember thinking, paradox in there somewhere, the way his women used to have to mother the poor bastard all the time. Her ring sliced his cheek.'

I'm nodding, listening, nodding, Rafe too, toy dog coppers. This is news. Suzy Stillrock told me the last time she saw Rory Stillrock was many weeks before his death, the pair of them on one of his motorbikes shouting happily at each other in high speed wind.

'Did he say what happened after that?'

'Only that it bled like hell, you know, like a shaving nick. So, that had him pretty down as well.'

'Did he say anything to you about Emma Lexington?'

'Not really. I barely know her.'

'Did he say why he had decided after so many years to divorce Suzy?'

'No. Ask her that, not me. I mean, sorry, he didn't go into detail. He only told me because I asked him why the bandage, I was half hoping, what do you know, the ageing brat's got a zit, but he told me straight up, Suzy. Could have fibbed, didn't. Not our Rory.'

'What time did you leave his Tinderbox home?'

'About six? Hard to tell when the sun's still high, and the sweet pinky wine's mellowed your attitude. It was the first time I'd felt sorry for Rory Stillrock. So my "Shat on Freud" moment, as we used to call it in drama school, turned out just a bit sour in the end. I'd rather not have had it, poor dead bastard.'

15

YOU COULD CALL IT FALLING IN FOR THE FALLOUT. HUNT'S
OFFICE, its three-sixty degree views of estuary, mountain, city,
sky, and across down through the big green summer trees
of St Davids Park to Salamanca Place, now all but deserted
of what so recently was its vibrant tent city market, minus
Johann Dellacroix. Rafe and Faye are with me, Hunt and
Walter out of uniform, recalled from their weekend. Hunt's
wearing a pale green cotton collared shirt with a sailing club
slogan emblazoned on the breast, ditto-coloured trackies, tan
deck shoes. Ergo, the man has been sailing, which he does of
a weekend. Walter looks fit and energetic and just out of his
bicycle lycra. Hunt's PA Priscilla's present, she's a closed book,
hers open now to take notes. She's a faultless person in her role.
Hunt's dumped a six pack of frosty-cold Cascade Premium
lagers on the King Billy table, and Priscilla has placed a tray of
nibbles on it, a large tray shaped like a shiny footy oval. Tomato
sauce dip bowl, sausage rolls, party pies, sushi rolls.

We tuck in.

'So where are we with this one, Franz? It's taken a strange and
dangerous turn. The young Indian's lucky to be alive, as it is.'

'There are complexities, which I'll work through one by one.
First a recap of the chronology of events. I'll then summarise

154

the suspects. I'll then bring to your attention the problems we face in this investigation. I'll then look at what we have in our favour. That's four. And lastly, arising out of those, I have some suggestions.'

'Sounds good. Go for it.'

'First, the theft from Gavin Bellyard's New Town home. A professional safe-breaking job, netting a diamond necklace valued at two hundred thousand Australian dollars, and a wad of Polish zloty banknotes valued at approximately one thousand Australian dollars. There was very little forensic or other evidence at the scene for us to go on, there was minimal subsequent public feedback and our network of street and undercover sources came up with nothing. It meant a thoroughly professional job.

'The bashing of Indira Patel became the first real link to the theft, once it became clear why her assailant was after a stereo dropped off at her workplace, the city tip shop. She, under physical duress, told the assailant that Johann Dellacroix had bought the stereo from her. The assailant murdered Dellacroix, approximately eight days ago, and took the stolen necklace from its box that had been hidden in one of the stereo speakers. The assailant threw the stereo and speakers into Dellacroix's duck pond. That's the chronology.'

Hunt nods. He's the sushi man. I continue.

'What about suspects? Fink Mountgarrett was our first, logical suspect. As a career criminal he's been found guilty once of safe cracking and the likelihood is he's been responsible for a number of unsolved cases dating back many years. Furthermore, his second cousin Deon Cawler worked in the Bellyard home last year and Cawler's fingerprints were on the painting hiding the safe. Cawler had legitimate business in the house as an employee of a firm that fixes rising damp. As such it could be argued that he merely removed the painting in the course of his work –'

155

'Which is exactly what a defence lawyer will do,' Walter says.

I nod. Yes, Walter, we're slowly working that one out.

'– But for us there's a greater likelihood Cawler told Mountgarrett about the safe. Unfortunately Cawler's somewhere in Europe and untraceable. Even if Interpol locates him, or he returns to Tasmania, he's hardly likely to tell us that he told Mountgarrett about the safe. All we do know is Cawler wasn't in Australia when the theft took place, eliminating him as a suspect.

'So what are the problems? The necklace was stolen, made its way into a stereo speaker, for which Johann Dellacroix was murdered. You'd have to say the first problem is that our logical suspect in the theft, Fink Mountgarrett, has a reasonably good alibi when it comes to Dellacroix.'

'Yes,' Hunt agrees, to laughter. 'Sitting in our prison.'

'Theoretically, therefore, Mountgarrett could arguably be cleared of any involvement in the theft. Our second problem is we're relying on the word of a five-year-old boy for crucial information, namely, that a short woman in a dirty white ute left the stereo at the tip recycling depot a week ago last Friday.'

I take a slug of beer, bite of proletarian sausage roll.

'The good thing about the kid,' Rafe says, 'is he wasn't prompted. And he had no doubts about it being a white Holden ute.'

'Our next problem,' I continue, 'is Indira's assailant. She described the man who confronted her in the tip shop as having longish dark hair, wearing a dark green beanie, and with a four or five day growth. And he was wearing sunglasses. The best she could say about his size was medium build, slightly stocky. So he's a generic, really, a bloke not particularly distinctive. There are no fingerprints in her house, which tells us he wore gloves. He smacked her from behind, then held her head to the floor,

156

twisted up her arm, got the information he needed then hit her again, to enable his getaway unsighted, and to take on Dellacroix before she could warn him.'

I finish the sausage roll, wash it down.

'I'd add these, as problems,' Walter says, 'the mess with Mountgarret's mandatory, and the media obsession that we're withholding information on Rory Stillrock's death. We're not looking good just at the moment and we're going to have to probe very carefully with the Dellacroix murder. This is tricky turf. But go on, Franz.'

'Some positives, potentials. Thanks to Mr Tasker and his son we have an almost exact time when the ute dropped off the stereo at the tip. The woman used the weighbridge to discard stuff at the tip face. Residential postcodes of vehicles using the tip at that time are, as you might expect, mostly the Hobart area, with a few exceptions. There are hundreds of registered utes in this catch zone. In the ten-minute period when the Taskers were at the tip, one tip user gave a Huonville region postcode. Just one.'

I pause. They watch me intently.

'Fink Mountgarrett owns a 1995 white Holden ute. It's battered, he uses it to collect and cut wood that he sells off the roadside. It's generally dirty, certainly was when we visited him the day of the altercation. Faye drove past his place yesterday. Faye?'

'It's had a good wash.'

Hunt says, 'You're suggesting it was washed as a result of our media statement about a dirty white ute?'

'Could be, sir.' She looks at me. On I go. Tension's up.

'Mountgarrett's de facto is Lily Huskisson. She's petite, with long dark hair. Damien Tasker said the ute driver was a small woman. He wasn't sure about her hair, but he did say it might have been long. Indira said the man who bashed her was of medium, slightly stocky build, longish hair and unshaven. Titch Maguire, Fink's close friend, fits that general description. Except he's got a rough buzz cut, not long hair.'

Hunt nods, says, 'And I suppose if we go and look at him we'll find he's had a shave? Franz, aren't you drawing a long bow? Apart from the elephant in the room?'

'This is a bits and pieces investigation, Grif. And yes, I'm speculating that Mountgarrett stole the necklace and hid it in an old stereo that was in Lily's house, knowing that we'd be likely to get a warrant to search his place. But not her place, she was never a suspect. And it's inconceivable that Lily would then get rid of the stereo. Unless, of course, she didn't know what was hidden in it.'

Out you go, elephant.

'They're partners, for goodness' sake!' Walter says.

'Partners in love, not crime. The word has been around for a long time now that Fink Mountgarrett's retired from his life of crime, largely because of pressure from Lily. She's reputed to have said she'll give him the flick if he doesn't give the game away, just as she gave away her trade as a sex worker. It was a deal between them. And he's said to have done just that, gone clean. Hence, no word from our sources about him and the theft of the necklace, or any other recent job, come to that. Lily pleaded with me to believe her about this, last week, that he's clean. And I didn't think she was having one over me, not at all.'

'I reckon he did this as one last job,' Rafe says. 'Like, same as sorting out his super.'

'Okay,' Walter says, 'so Mountgarrett hides the necklace in her stereo without her knowing. And she suddenly decides to get rid of it while he's inside?'

'It's quite possible she was cleaning out her place, like any of us do from time to time. In her case, preparing for her man to marry her, once he's out. Mountgarrett himself told me they're planning to join their two houses together, that he's going to bash in each end wall and turn their place into a flash ranch overlooking the river. That suggests preparatory work, such as getting rid of junk. And remember, it was an ancient, broken stereo. Faye?'

She says, 'I can confirm that Lily had what looked like a heap of junk in her house. I glanced in the windows when we were there the first time, when I was calling for a paddy wagon.'

'Alright,' Hunt says, 'bearing in mind this is a theory, is speculative. I can understand Mountgarrett's ears pricking up when he hears the cops want to speak to someone about a stereo left at the tip. So you could usefully enquire at Risdon if he's been agitated lately. But even so, there must be plenty of old stereos out there.'

'Exactly. It's something we have to work on. Just as it's possible that Titch Maguire is the assailant. He's the right size, unshaven, and the fact is, whoever bashed Indira Patel disguised himself by wearing a woollen winter beanie on a hot summer day. Why not a cap with a low peak, or a hoodie? A beanie's snug, head-fitting, it keeps a wig on.'

'Where would you want to take this, then, Franz? With so little to go on, you might find hauling Maguire in for an interview is counterproductive.'

'I agree. If he's our man, he's had a week to work up a story, alibis. I want to stalk him, not flush him. I want the element of surprise, mainly because it's virtually all I've got, so my suggestion is to put him and possibly Lily Huskisson under surveillance. And to keep under wraps the fact that the Bellyard theft, the Indira Patel bashing and the Dellacroix murder are linked. The killer mustn't know we've found the stereo, less still that we know what was in it.'

159

'Franz,' Walter says, 'don't you think we've played enough games with the public?'

'Whoever killed Dellacroix needs to believe he's getting away with it. He'll be feeling more secure with each day that passes. I want to turn that to my advantage.'

Hunt finishes his beer. 'I'd like to hear about your surveillance plan, before signing off on this.'

'If the theft and murder have nothing to do with Mountgarrett,' Walter says, 'then we'd be crazy not to make public the link between the necklace and the murder. We need every piece of information we can get, and going public's surely the way to do it. Maybe the stereo went to the tip deliberately, to be collected, but the Indian girl got Dellacroix there first.'

'Could be,' I say, 'but as a theory it's got no more weight than the other. If we go public all we can do is sit back and wait and hope. At least I've put forward a strategy, based on evidence.'

'Highly circumstantial evidence.'

'Evidence all the same. And the minute the killer knows we're onto the stereo, he's out of here. If he hasn't already gone. Let me put a tail on Titch Maguire for a few days. Nothing happens, fine, then we do an interview. Give me three days to watch him. And her.'

'Alright, alright,' Hunt says.

Decision time.

'Let's have a good look at them, Franz. Let's put Lily and Titch under the microscope.'

'HEY, PUFF, CHECK THIS OUT.'

Hedda, swinging a hula hoop around her agile hips, then up over her head around a raised arm, back down again, languid and rhythmic, to her singing, 'All the leaves are brown

160

and the sky is grey, I've been for a walk on a winter's day, I'd be safe and warm if I was in LA, California dreamin' on such a winter's day'.

Nice.

By any measure nice, bringing back a Sixties social fashion that was also healthy, mix in the Mamas and the Papas of that vintage. But today a few million obese Aussies would struggle to fit into a hula hoop.

Sunday evening. Oven's in. Hedda split a fingernail installing it, so had to instruct me in how to make 'her' roast chook stuffing. I now know how to finely chop pine nuts, celery, capers and dates and work them with fresh sage and thyme into breadcrumbs, diced onions and milk. In the new oven, it all smells good. I'm starving, tired, need a big sleep to fix me for tomorrow. Still the residue of that flu bug. The Meuchasse interview threw a spanner in Suzy's work. And how the development in the Bellyard necklace case will play out is anyone's guess. If it plays out.

Hedda's not regressing, she's got a car boot full of hula hoops for a police charity health gig she's coordinating next weekend, so she's been practising. Quite good too, sashaying around my kitchen, into the lounge room, singing.

Back in the kitchen she stops suddenly. The hula hoop clatters to the shiny new floorboards. She has a sip of her riesling, sits on a breakfast counter stool, watching me slice an array of salad ingredients onto a bed of cos lettuce in a large glass salad bowl, one shallot, a cucumber, cherry tomatoes, a red capsicum.

'So, mate, question without notice, how the hell did that necklace box end up in a Collinsvale duck pond? By the way, as a Dutch foreigner, I bet you didn't know that Collinsvale used to be called Bismarck, but they thought it might be a good idea to change the name during World War One.'

'There's a possibility the stereo was dropped off at the tip by pre-arrangement. Say for a tip-face employee to pick it up, or a member of the public, and we're looking at that, but that will take time and in the meanwhile I'm gunning for Fink Mountgarrett and his scurvy mates. They're all I've got.'

'You don't sound too optimistic.'

'With good reason. Another warrant down at their Huon nest's out of the question, and there's not been a word on the street that Fink did the job, he's an old pro, no fool, he kept quiet, so we'll just have to watch his missus and his best mate and hope they leave a trail of sparklers through the dark woods.'

'Yeah, right, you are seeming to want to pin this butterfly down. Our Fink definitely nicked the shiny neck knick-knacks?'

'Who else?' I slide the salad bowl to one side, open the fridge door, take from a rack in the white cavity a bottle of Paul Newman's salad dressing.

Hedda gives it a disapproving stare. 'My oath, no, too much sugar, too much spice. I'll tell you how to make one.'

My turn to be myself in my own home, a bit put out.

'You're joking? Salad dressing is salad dressing. But at least this is Paul Newman. I could have bought two bottles of Home Brand for the same price.'

'Jeez, misery guts, take it easy, we're here for you. Got any garlic cloves?'

'No.'

'Balsamic vinegar?'

'No. I don't buy that sort of thing.'

'At least you have a quality Tassie extra virgin olive oil, hey? – 'cause I bought it for you, hey?' She cackles, then sighs. 'Franz, you've got SMS, mate.'

'That being?'

'Single man syndrome.'

'And I have news for you.'

'What?'

'I think you'll find that Paul Newman's isn't so bad. And as it happens I've a new bottle of Michael Caine's Limey Pickle for the chook.'

'Ho ho. He's not a bad actor either. *The French Connection?* No, that was Gene Hackperson.'

'From memory, yes. And segues neatly into what I've been waiting to ask you. What's Tassie got to do with this drug-linked Arabian connection, so called?'

'Too soon to know.'

'You're being cryptic.'

'No, mate, realistic. A rumour about a Bahraini sheikh wanting to buy up property here, big time. A mysterious fella who wants to put Tassie on the international celebrity polo circuit, but who apparently makes his squillions through the Afghan opium trade.'

'My troubles pale by comparison.'

'Gotta watch this space. Hey, how're you travelling with the late great Rory Stillrock?'

'Don't ask.'

16

THE LAST TIME I COMMUNICATED WITH SUZY STILLROCK SHE was in her svelte Battery Point cottage, in which the tall woman in her non-widow's white frock told of her life with the deceased film star. Now, in a TPF HQ interview room, seated opposite Faye and me, she's changed. Markedly. Gone is the long swishing red-dyed hair, against that white. A neat bob-cut, I suppose it goes with the smart grey-skirted suit. She might as well be a different person. Not so easy to spot by readers of *Women's Day*, perhaps.

I can smell the last cigarette on her breath, across the table.

The interview is set up.

From her eyes, she's wary.

'What is it you want with me?' she asks.

On the basis that you never answer a question with a question, I say, 'Suzy, just the truth'.

She looks at me, then at Faye.

'No comprendo, amigo,' her husky US twangy voice says.

'I'll get straight to the point. When last I spoke to you in your home at Battery Point, you said that the morning of New Year's Eve, when you and Rory rode on his Dominator motorbike, was the last time you were with him.'

I wait.

'Yes.'

'Did you see Rory on the day of his death?'

'How could I?'

'Suzy, I have reason to believe you confronted him that day.'

Faye says, 'Did you slap his face?'

The shock of it coming from my junior works in ways that none of us in this room could have anticipated. Suzy Stillrock turns full on to Faye. They stare at each other. For once, I'm completely forgotten.

Suzy's eyes flare and she inhales deeply, as if to unleash a fearful denunciation. How dare this little girl say such a thing. But instead she smiles, enigmatically.

'Yes. I did slap him. Hard. Just once. It's always worked before, and I had no reason to believe it wouldn't this time, with my Rory. Sorry I lied, but, work it out guys, the stupid bitch made me. Go ask her why. She's *framing* me. Earn your goddamn salaries!'

Suzy Stillrock pulls her lips tight, bangs her arms folded together, thrusts herself back in her chair so she can glare at both of us.

'Why did you slap him? '

'Oh …' She uncreases her angry mouth and chin, takes a deep breath. 'Rory rang me and said he wanted to discuss things with me. So I went there. I was about to turn into his driveway when I saw the bitch's car coming out. That so pissed me off !'

'What did you do?'

'I drove on, then went back.'

'She saw you?'

'Nope. It wasn't her I wanted to confront. Goddam Rory! I said hello to him by getting out the car and slapping him as hard as I could, and I gave him an ultimatum there and then. Me or her, he had one minute to decide. I told him to get real and work out she was screwing him for his money, not his looks or fame

165

because he didn't have either of those anymore. What else would she want with someone more than twice her age? That hurt. He said he had to think about it. But he did text her right there in front of me and tell her to stay away a couple of days. Then he asked me to stay the night. But I know how to control Rory, I said, no way Jose, I'm too damn angry and besides, I'm caring for another man tonight, Salvador. That put Rory in his place. The great immortal Stillrock less important than a lizard bite.'

'What time of day was this?'

'Early in the afternoon, I guess.'

'Suzy, you admit to deliberately lying. We've had to prise it out of you. And because we now know that you were with your husband on the afternoon of the day he died, and because you furnished no alibi for the night he died, I'm beginning to believe you were the person with him that night, because he most certainly was not alone. Were you with him that night?'

'No!'

'When exactly did you leave his property?'

'How the hell should I remember? Jesus, call it three, call it two thirty, we had our moment and I got out of there.'

'That's three, two thirty in the afternoon or the early morning?'

She gives me a hate-filled look. But she holds herself together.

'The afternoon, Detective.'

'Why was your cat more important than him that night? It makes no sense to me.'

'Because a good dose of hurt, physical and psychological, made him wake up to himself, brought him back into line. Look, Detective, and your teenage partner, Rory had major female issues. He loved us all and we, y'know, *served* him, his pleasure, but we also, when the moment came, had to dominate him. I

166

doubt the slut-fuck ever worked that out, the cruddy pouty stupid little Tasmanian bitch.'

'Glad you're not referring to me,' Faye, says. 'Or am I swept up in that?'

'Get on!' Suzy Stillrock laughs crudely. 'Hey, girl, don't take offence.'

Cops never do, eh, soulless, heartless, lungless, kidneyless creatures that we are.

'So you had the altercation with him,' I say, 'that included you slapping him with force enough to make his face bleed.'

'His left cheek. He's had my backhand before. This ring here nicked on the point of his cheekbone. He went into the bathroom to fix it. He came out with a homey little round skin-toned bandage over the cut. We both cried. We so loved and were for each other. And he was always coming back to me. Rory was always coming back to me. I saved him. And you want me to answer your real question? If I had been there that night I goddamn *would* have saved him!'

We wait. Tight-lipped, flint-eyed, she has the call. By an effort of will she calms herself. She says,

'I knew him intimately and so I can tell you this. The angry child never left the man. Telling the truth was Rory's ultimate act of self-preservation. He hurt people through it? Sure he did. It was his way of saying, now you know how I felt. After I left he must have contacted her again and told her it was over between them, I can hear him saying it to her, all you wanted was my money, so fuck off ghastly little Emma. And that's why she killed him. And now I got nothing more to say to either of you.'

'Alright Suzy, you're free to go but I advise you to acquaint yourself with legal assistance, because I'm not satisfied with your explanations relating to your whereabouts on the night your husband died.'

She stands. 'Mr Heineken, I'm about to go and fetch the best lawyer money can buy. And when we come back, you'll feel the sting.'

'If he was murdered, Suzy, it's the culprit who needs to feel the sting, not me.'

'SO WHAT DO YOU RECKON, FAYE?'

She and I are in my office, she with a mug with a tea bag in water, self waiting for the percolator to murmur, liquorice allsort being worked out of little brown bag.

'We're stuffed on good evidence, boss.'

'Or stuffed too full of it. We need to consider and apply, Faye. I think we need to look again at it all, the evidence, and apply each piece to each potential suspect. Remembering that we really only have two, Suzy Stillrock and Emma Lexington.'

'Robin Meuchasse?'

'Forty to one, though stranger races have been run.'

'What about his stepmother, Mrs Arundel, and the investment bloke, Craig Fine?'

'He's got a solid alibi, remember, and why would she? We need to start nearest the heat source, and that's Suzy and Emma. They ignited the firestorm and they, one of them, for me, must have done the deed. The logic of the evidence we have points that way. And Faye, I don't think a man, read Robin, killed him.'

'Oh, so it's a female crime? Why?'

'Lack of force.'

'Well, okay. Got to persuade him into the car, into the passenger seat, on a pretext of going somewhere. He'd trust someone intimately for that, boss.'

'Oh, yes.'

I pour my coffee. Faye takes her tea bag out of the mug, holds it pinched between fingertips over the mug, walks around behind my desk and drops the tea bag into my wastepaper basket. Not so long ago, this wouldn't have occurred, her crossing my sacrosanct space. It just goes to show the power of a burning five-cent tea bag.

A parcel for me, brought in by a mailroom worker. No need for my envelopener. The parcel, a FedEx, has been scanned, opened and searched.

Faye and I peruse it. *Personal* written in big spidery letters above my name and the TPF address. I shake its contents gently onto my desk. Well, well. Artefacts.

A script of one of Rory Stillrock's Agent Archer movies, heavily annotated in handwriting and awash with margin doodles, this script surely used to learn his lines.

A framed photo of the actor in his prime, arm casually draped around the shoulders of a beaming grey-haired, square-jawed man. Simple scrawled caption, *With Heff, his place.*

'So who's Heff?' Faye says.

'Hugh Heffner, I reckon.'

Faye picks up a folded T-shirt, with signatures on it around an image of Stillrock posing on a motorbike.

A Betamax cassette.

And a note in a spidery scrawl.

Dear Detective –

Thank you for taking time from your busy schedule to contact me about Rory Stillrock. That got me to thinking and I searched for this bunch of stuff of his I knew I had somewhere in my condo. I don't want it, and I sure as hell wouldn't put it on e-bay! Nor could I find an address for his widow Suzy, but that may be just as well, for

*she will be grieving right now, so maybe best you pass
it all on in time. I don't know what's on the video — old
technology!*

Yours in love and friendship,
Viola Vine

'Where's Rafe?'

'By now probably back up at the Dellacroix property, boss,
after showing Mr Bellyard the necklace box, for his stat dec that
that's the box that was in the safe.'

'In that case you and I had better deputise for the said Rafe as
official Stillrock video watcher.' I pick up the black video. 'Let's
wander down and see what Ms Vine may have inadvertently
sent us.'

WE VANDEMONIANS ARE A RUM LOT. OUR GENERALLY GENTLE
natures belie an unpredictably insular island mentality. Consider
this. We occupy paradise. We are stubbornly never no more than
half a million souls in this large, temperate and verdant, ocean-
rich island that could comfortably settle, clothe, house, employ
and make happy many more. It's as if no one else actually wants
to live here, in this heart-shaped place geographically laughed at
as a pudenda forest. Not to mention near-genocide and the once-
shameful convict stain. And the two-head incest jokes, the bad
teeth, the eternal greenie wars, poor education retention rates.

There can't be anything in all of this, surely?

According to Viola Vine's video, there is.

And it's shocking.

Me and Faye are in a small light-muted video room, the
principal one being in use for a seminar. The tape is silent. This one
features the same king-size bed, yellow background wall and fixed

spy camera position that had us watching Stillrock masturbate. Now, he's just as naked, with the weird little moustache, but not alone. Doggy style he's energetically screwing his equally naked stepmother and, by his grinning gestures at the camera, she clearly doesn't know they're being filmed. Her hair was still dark back then, many years ago, and well below her shoulders, which it surely still is. She's talking, looks like she's urging him on, her breasts swaying vigorously. Stillrock takes her hair in his hands, rides her like she's a horse, her hair his reins. It's not violent or even painful-looking, but enough to bring her head up and, by her open-mouthed calling, a thing she much enjoys.

'Christ,' Faye says softly. 'His mum …'

'Stepmum.'

On and on they go, until Stillrock takes himself out of Joanna, brings her head around and works it down onto him, and once she's got her face buried energetically in his crotch, he relaxes back against the bedstead, winks at the camera, gives it a thumbs up then puts his hands behind his head, smiles and closes his eyes.

'You bastard,' Faye says.

'Motive, Faye. The cassette burnt in the fireplace on the night he died.'

'Another of these? Him and her?'

'I think we're entitled to draw that conclusion for the time being, don't you?'

17

CCTV FOOTAGE OF NON-CONTACT VISITS AT THE PRISON IS stored for a few weeks, then the tapes are wiped and re-used. That's fortunate for me. Driving along the East Derwent Highway, which cuts busily and noisily through sleepy suburbs, I'm intrigued. The stereo was dropped at the tip on a Friday afternoon. The next morning Fink had two visitors, Lily and Titch. That afternoon Indira was quizzed in the tip shop about the stereo. She was assaulted that night, forced to reveal that Johann Dellacroix had taken the stereo. He was murdered that weekend. Let's say sometime during that Saturday night.

Intrigued because there's a compelling logic to this sequence of events. They're riveted together, and in this business we rely on cause and effect in working out crimes. Bad behaviour's seldom spontaneous, even when it appears to be. There's almost always an understandable cause. Jealousy. Money. Revenge. Money. Drugs. Money. Fear. Money. Silencing ... Joanna Arundel, now who would have thought that? Theirs must be a complex backstory. Did she silence her stepson?

Fine rain tipples the windscreen, slanting from on high across the river. A great horseshoe rainbow sticks up out of the zinc works, high over the bridge and harbour, down into the casino. I consider deviating shorewards to the Lindisfarne shopping centre, to the second-hand bookshop there with its goodly pre-loved array of novels. Another time. Felonious Town beckons.

The line of fast-growing eucalypts planted to soften the landscape by hiding the island's prison still have a way to go. An original complex of buildings and phalanx of squat newer pale grey blocks and high outer fences, it's built on a hillside along the perimeter of the suburb that bears its name. As ever, small groups of muscular brown native hens browse on pastures near the creek running a hidden course along the prison boundary. Flightless they are, but nature, having taken that away from them, imbued them with a healthy instinct to flee on long powerful legs. Turbo chooks, we pointyheads call them. Unusually, dominant single females run male harems. Probably not a bad life. Probably pretty safe living on no man's land between a highway and a huge razor-wire fence.

I'm taken straight through to the monitoring unit, park myself in front of a flatbed screen with a keyboard which I can use to call up footage of a particular date, time, a particular part of the prison complex. I can zoom in, out, fast forward, freeze, copy, print colour frames for use in court. Drugs, weapons and mobile phones are the three areas of concern. CCTV footage of visits goes some way to keeping the inflow in check, though the good old-fashioned technique of hurling things over the outer security perimeter fences still works well, hence construction of new ones, bigger, higher, better. But even non-contact visits need to be monitored electronically. This system needs to work for me. And now is as good a time as any to show why.

So. The visitor register shows that on Saturday morning, at eleven am, inmate Mr Adrian 'Fink' Mountgarrett received two visitors, Ms Lily Huskisson and Mr Titch Maguire. In the control room I therefore call up this footage. The screen blips open, to a wide view of the non-contact space, being numerous booths, inmate separated from visitor by a glass screen with chat hole. It's otherwise a friendly space. Kids can play on washable carpet squares with rounded plastic toys. Guards are unobtrusive. I zoom in on a booth.

'Cup of tea, Mr Heineken?'

It's a surveillance duty officer. A long time ago his old man, then a cop at Tasmania's most isolated single-man station, Liawenee, was gunned down by a lake shack owner whose wife had been cheating on him, with the cop, sadly.

'Ta, white, one sugar thanks Jason. Who's that next to Fink?'

'Brody Quarry. Came in last week, Vic boy, Broadmeadows, that knifing at Claremont?'

I zoom in, watch. No audio, not legal to listen in on legal conversations. Fink looks healthy, relaxed, the pale ginger goatee beard nice and trim, bit of larrikin length to the wisps behind the head. Fink knows his jail culture, its nooks and crannies, or as they say, its crooks and nannies. Lily and Titch, the other side of the glass, they're all at peace, yacking away, Fink is in and will soon be out, it's a career hazard. His kind of going to jail is no worse than shedding shares on an unpredictable bear market, or copping four weeks for 'accidental' front-on high contact playing footy. And they do look happy, Lily in particular animated, loving her man through a glass lightly, so to speak.

But then she says something, gaily. As if it's nothing, but Fink, and I'm not close enough to the intimate action of the three of them to be certain, kind of looks down and around as if to source a sharply unwelcome smell. Then he erupts, arms flying. Lily looks shocked, Titch stunned. Fink just as quickly subsides, aware of drawing attention to himself. He locks his hands together, as if praying. No help from above. Lily's talking animatedly, worried. Titch is frowning, perplexed. Fink puts his hands out, talking all the while. Then he laughs, or seems to be trying to get her

174

over his outburst and Lily sits back and shakes her head. Normal conversation resumes, but sitting back with her arms folded she's lost her earlier sparkle.

Fink and Titch share a blokes' laugh. A joke, maybe. Fink leans forward and blows Lily a kiss. She relents. Then puts a hand to the side of her head and circles her forefinger at her temple. Fink nods, grins – yeah, I'm crazy, alright. The three of them laugh. Fink points behind him and appears to be telling a story, what goes on in there makes a man a little crazy. Lily and Titch listening, nodding. Then she gets up and walks off camera.

I pause the frame, activate another monitor to follow her. Toilet. I return to Fink and Titch, frozen, Fink watching Lily walk away. I roll the footage. Fink, his expression grim, leans urgently into the chat hole, talking rapidly. The words draw Titch forward. He listens intently. After a short while he nods. Lily enters the frame. Titch sits back. Fink smiles at her. Normal conversation resumes.

It's all I need, though I watch out the rest of the visit. She didn't know he nicked the sparklers. And I don't think Titch knew either. Cunning Mr Mountgarrett. A bit too cunning, seeing as what's happened.

The visitor register also shows that the following Monday Titch, alone, visited Fink. I find the footage, watch them confer briefly, Titch doing most of the talking.

I've been stalking villains for over thirty years and, stake my Bruny Island shack on it, what Titch said to Fink was that he did the job. Got the necklace. Did he also say he needed to commit murder to do so? I reckon. They're hard boys, grew up close, faced the system together. That Fink almost certainly hadn't in the first place told Titch he'd done the Bellyard job is in keeping with his trademark of leaving a minimal footprint. He knew he could do the New Town Bellyard job on his own, so why tell even his best mate? The old pro doing one last job. Did he need help? Ah, go away! Always done it meself, do this one meself, and out of there. Soft footprint.

That's what I think. Following the logic of the crook. *Someone*, not Father Christmas, not a Sudanese refugee welcomed to Tasmania, cleverly stole an expensive diamond necklace from an almost entirely unprotected Hobart home. Easy picking. Who? Safe cracking has complications. Deon Cawler, second cousin of Fink and somewhere in Europe, found the safe.

That a person cracked.

Eventuating in the murder of a long-time Salamanca Market stallholder.

Time, for sure, to put hidden cop eyes on free Lily and Titch. Because we still have nothing by way of admissable evidence against them. No point therefore even pulling them in for a chat. They are, so to speak, 'safe'. For now.

18

'IN THIS DAY AND AGE, IF HE WAS A CELEBRITY AT ANY RATE, he'd be pitying himself as a sex addict and checking into a clinic. Back then, no such thing. And the record's clear, that even when he was growing up in Hobart he was a precocious little fucker, if you'll pardon the pun.'

I'm in Walter's office. He nods, contemplating it all. The video evidence Rory Stillrock has presented to us, in the investigation into his death, isn't in itself damning of Joanna Arundel. What they got up to was their business. Indeed, they evidently were enjoying themselves, much to Walter's discomfort when we viewed the video together a short while ago. It's the circumstantial case she's going to have to navigate, with great care, namely, whether she was instrumental in the burning of a similar video in Rory's fireplace, around about the time of his death.

'He was expelled from a school for so-called sexual misconduct, wasn't he?'

'He was,' I say. 'He was caught with a young female teacher. So, by whatever warped means the relationship between him and Joanna became physical, it's vaguely explicable –'

'And when,' Walter says, 'I mean to say, this is hard to bloody comprehend. She's a highly respected individual!'

'Was.'

'We must be dead careful, here, Franz. You're going to have to build this further before we can make a case.'

'I know that. It's obvious though that his taking such footage, apparently without her knowledge or consent, sets up a potential motive.'

'Arguably yes, but here's what I can't understand, and what any defence counsel would use to hammer us. Why would she become murderous over something that took place maybe twenty years ago? Something that's obviously never come to light, either, or people would surely have spoken about it.'

'Point taken. So, let's say we have a fifty per cent motive.'

'Remind me, how did she react when you first spoke to her after his death?'

'Sorrowful, resigned. Controlled and calm. None of the wariness that tends to expose guilt. Which is why I never remotely considered her. But I don't like that video. Its cruelty alarms me.'

Walter reflects upon it. 'You're going to have a hell of a job associating her with the video burnt in his fireplace, aren't you?'

'Forensically, yes. That's impossible.'

'Well, I say again, Franz, why would that make her want to kill him *now*?'

'Perhaps he'd just told her about it, shown it to her for the first time. He did have his pornographic cassettes under lock and key. And she made him destroy it. No more evidence of their shameful relationship. Whereas for Suzy there's been an increasingly powerful motive. Every day that went past was a day he and Suzy drifted apart, with Emma Lexington doing her best to make that permanent.'

My turn to pause, to ponder the tantalising, frustrating bits and pieces.

'This is going nowhere fast,' he says. 'What's your next move?'

'Another chat to Craig Fine. I think I can prise more out of him than last time we spoke.'

'Good. But remember what I said about Joanna Arundel. What she got up to, what we saw on that video, was their business. And it doesn't translate to murder. We're in enough of a bloody mess with this so-called suicide without fingering a pillar of the community.'

'Believe me, Walter, I've no intention of doing that to her.'

19

TITCH MAGUIRE'S PLACE IS A REASONABLE DISTANCE UP THE hillside near Franklin. Its view of the dark, broadening Huon River and down along to the D'Entrecasteaux Channel and beyond must be fairly agreeable. Also from his place he'd clearly be able to see across the broad tranquil river and along to the two weatherboard homes of Fink and Lily. So he's their neighbour, in the crow flying sense. By road, however, another matter. Any time Titch wanted to visit them he'd have to drive north to Huonville, crossing the river on the bridge, then back along the other side. But he did say he had a boat.

It's day two of the watch on him and thus far, nothing. I arranged an upstairs room in a Franklin building for our purposes, with a good visual of the road leading up to Titch's house, a dilapidated weatherboard with peeling tin roof on a leveled, overgrown block.

Rafe's home, for three days and nights, is about as basic as you can get, but far, far better than twelve hour stretches in a surveillance car. Rafe's allowed to be off watch, sleeping, from ten at night to five in the morning. Three days, and if nothing happens, that's it. Yesterday, day one, Titch went out once. Rafe had time to slip out into his car and follow Titch's 4WD Toyota into Huonville, where Fink's mate bought himself a takeaway, a slab of Vic Bitter, bottles of brandy and a big white parcel of meat from a butcher. Rafe's got a video-cam and a telescope mounted on a tripod, which he's also been using at the riverside window, through which he's got a decent view of Lily's house. She's been out and about a couple of times, in her Daihatsu, Fink's clean battered ute conspicuously out of sight behind his place.

Faye's with me in my office going through our notes preparatory to having another shot later today at Craig Fine, Stillrock's erstwhile financial adviser and press-ganged agent. It's just after eleven and I'm beginning to feel the midday hunger pangs come on.

'Want a coffee, Faye?'

'No thanks, boss. Make it for you?'

I shake my head, rising. A short black and an allsort will stun the pang a while. All in the line of duty, eh.

'– And so what I reckon,' Faye says, 'is that Craig and Joanna aren't that close socially, because even though he does the pro bono for her charity, I've found no evidence of the Fines and Joanna ever –'

Phone.

'What's up, Rafe?'

'Titch has got company, boss, two flashy blokes in a black Merc coupe, it's a Hertz hire. They've shaken hands, businesslike, gone straight inside his place.'

'Flashy as in?'

'Shiny boots, smart jeans, collar shirts untucked, shades, accessories, lightweight coat on the one. One's about forty, other early to mid thirties. Minted crooks, boss, take my word. Not from here.'

'Reckon Titch knows them?'

'By the body language, no. But, y'know, no admiring of the scenery on their part, no introductory chat out the front. This is definitely straight inside to business.'

'Okay, we'll ID them through the rego. Got some pics?'

'Yeah.'

'Email them through. When did they turn up?'

'Now. Well, five minutes ago.'

'When they leave, follow them. I'll come down straight away and keep watch on Maguire, if he doesn't go with them. Here's Faye.'

ONCE OUT OF THE CITY I USE THE LIGHTS OF MY UNMARKED Commodore to speed along the Southern Outlet and onto the Huon Highway. Faye will have advised the traffic people. The climb to Vinces Saddle, the summit at Lower Longley, is fun, the long and winding descent into the Huon Valley less so, all that sharp brake dancing.

Faye calls in as I'm approaching the Mountain River and Crabtree turnoff.

'Boss, they hired the vehicle at the airport at ten this morning. They being Niko Nikolides and Paul Palace. They're Melburnians. Nikolides owns properties in Footscray and Yarraville, one a nightclub with a fairly seedy reputation. Palace is a bouncer at that club. Neither has a record, though Nikolides has attracted the attention of both the ATO and ASIC in the past on suspicion of hefty tax minimisation through offshore holdings.'

'That's interesting.'

'Yep. And Palace has been a person of interest in more than one fracas involving clubbers and serious injuries. They're booked to return to Melbourne on today's three o'clock flight. And that's all I've got just at the moment.'

'Push the Vics for what you can. A Fink link would be nice though I won't be holding my breath.'

'Will do, boss.'

Slowly through Huonville, across the bridge over the dark water.

Franklin's a charming little place spread thinly along the western bank of the Huon River. Pub, cafés, antique shop, Victorian theatre building, boatbuilding school, rowing club, footy oval right on the river bank. Assorted watercraft sit on the sparkling, motionless water. Behind, the hillsides slope up, largely cleared but with forested patches increasing further back. Altogether, Franklin's about as charming a rural hamlet as you could wish for.

Plump and wide in the Huon River, the grey-green grassy expanses of the North and South Egg Islands stretch a long way, middling the waterway and so appearing to reshape one broad river into two narrow ones. The visual effect is confusing, then intriguing. A ferryman, so it is said, once made his wage taking Cygnet-side folk through the narrow Egg Island Canal to Franklin to watch the talking pictures in the theatre, then back again in pitch darkness.

I park near Rafe's unmarked Ford Falcon. Along the side of the building, in through an exit door, up the flights of steps. Rafe unlocks and opens the door.

'They're still up there, boss. Long meeting.'

I walk to the rear window. The black Merc and Titch's Toyota are clearly visible in front of the house on its flat quarter acre cut into the hill, no attempt at growing anything. If not for the vehicles the place might be unoccupied, so dead looking is it. The front door's closed.

I use the telescope. Sunshine glare prevents me seeing through the front windows of the place.

'Hopefully they'll bump him off,' Rafe says, 'then we can arrest them at the airport with the stones and get this shit done with.' He laughs.

183

'Well, unless the Vics give Faye more on them we're just going to have to watch and wait.'

'Jesus, boss! An unemployed non-entity like Titch Maguire gets a visit from two Melbourne crooks who've flown here just for it, and we do *nothing*?'

I carry the telescope to the front window, begin seeking out the Mountgarrett-Huskisson estate across the water.

'What's your suggestion, Detective?'

'You musn't let Walter heavy you, mate. I mean, what else are those scumbags doing up there?'

Found their weatherboards. The Daihatsu's out the front of hers. Shame her earnest nest-building had to come to a sudden halt.

'Their business, Rafe.'

'Yeah, right, all good. "Their business." Same logic as fucking your stepmum's their business?' Rafe makes a throaty, infuriated sound. In his mind's eye he became a cop, a plainclothes crime detective, to do the right thing by society. And that includes the holy grail of busting in on a gang of heavies doing dirty deeds, Glock in hands, catching them red-handed, bravery medal to follow down the track. From time to time spectacular raids happen, but they're rare. And dangerous. Rafe could go up and in there and stop a bullet for his trouble. And, not that I want to remind him, he played a not insignificant role in the jailing of Fink and the public hassles that's generated.

Faye calls. 'Nothing more on Nikolides and Palace, boss, but the Vics seem happy to do some digging on Nikolides in particular, using his suss visit here as the trigger. He's obviously pissed them off somewhere along the line.'

'Good. I'll get Walter to send them a surveillance request.'

We wait in silence, looking up at the house, the two vehicles. A long meeting indeed.

'Coffee, boss?'

'No thanks. But a steak sandwich smeared in garlic mayo and country cut French fries would hit the spot.'

'Yeah, so why've I been eating dry Mi goreng noodles and baked beans? Hey, let me go and find something, I've been smelling some pretty good tucker out there.'

'– No.'

Out they come, the three of them, and the blue heeler. Rafe gets behind the video-cam, begins to shoot. I use the telescope. Hard to read what's happened. They're not smiling, nor is there a dead-rat-in-the-place look on their faces. No one carrying a package. But the speed with which the two interstaters get in their Merc maybe does say something. Titch watches the vehicle do its three point, head off, and back inside his house he stomps, leaving the door open.

'See ya later.' Rafe's into his holster and leather jacket and out the door.

There's telescopic vision a fair way into Titch's house. Passage, mess, slice of an ugly lounge room. The sun's heightened angle enables me to watch him cut through a front room, he bends, picks something up, disappears. I keep watching. Nothing. I hear, faintly, Rafe's car engage. The likelihood is he'll tail them fruitlessly to the airport. They don't have much time for another appointment, put it that way. No matter. We're onto them, and our Vic colleagues will hopefully get something from their surveillance.

Mi goring, eh? There must be bread or fruit or something in the kitchenette ... No, hold even that, here's Titch Maguire, getting into his Toyota, abrupt take-off. Out I go, locking the door, down the stairs, out through the exit door, which locks itself, to my car, engage, ready to go. I have a clear line of sight to where Titch's road engages with the public road. He turns my way. Going to Huonville? To Hobart? Neither. Near me, he swings onto the dirt strip alongside the footy oval, and I watch as he parks next to the riverbank, gets out, dog bounds after him, and they walk a few metres to an aluminium runabout tethered to a stake. The dog leaps nimbly in, barely rocking it. Titch follows, sits, flicks the rope off the stake, one tug on the engine cord and they're off. It's that quick, and so am I, though not in a hurry, in case any of the good folk of Franklin are watching.

Back up in Rafe's surveillance eyrie I watch keenly as the runabout enters the Egg Island Canal, the ancient cutting narrow, sides thick with vegetation, making it look even narrower. Kind of fascinating, this, seeing him so engaged, like some old Huon Valley cockie who knows the short cuts, except that this Titch has just been rubbing shoulders with, as Rafe would say, bad guys from elsewhere.

I use the telescope, bring him up close. His faded black and red check-shirted back's to me. I watch him drag on a smoke. The dog stands up at the prow, turns happily to its master, then back facing front. I can almost smell the tobacco, the diesel, lingering in the narrow cutting.

The boat turns sharply once out the far side of the canal and increases speed. Soon, he angles it in towards the far riverbank and I can see why. Lily's Daihatsu is bumping along a dirt track towards the river. The car halts underneath a tree, out she gets, a carry bag in her hand, and she stands watching his runabout come towards her. Its ponytail whitewater wake disappears as he cuts the engine, drifts the boat to the bank. Titch grabs something to steady the boat, uses his other hand to help her in, then he re-engages the engine, spins the boat in a practised arc.

Angling back at the canal. Lily's sitting facing him, her back to the dog in the prow. Titch steers them into the canal, slows.

186

It's not a body of water for speeding in, could be submerged branches, and the overhangs.

Then I spy, with my big eye, something remarkable. Their knees are almost touching. Lily leans forward, so does he, and they kiss. I grab the video-cam, begin filming, fearful they're too far away. The boat putters on, Titch holding the tiller as they kiss, perhaps he's watching over her shoulder. They break apart just as the runabout leaves the canal, Titch laughing, can't see her face, then she turns to watch the bank on my side approach and she looks as happy as the dog.

Titch drops the tie rope on its stake, they're in his 4WD and away, just like that, for the short journey back to his place, up its road, park. I've got the video-cam rolling again. Lily grabs her carry bag, pushes shut the front passenger door. Titch, arm around her and a brandy bottle hanging from one paw, boots his front door open and they enter his house, and the door, maybe he backheeled it, shuts fast.

20

YESTERDAY'S BUSINESS AT FRANKLIN PREVENTED ME FROM keeping my appointment with Craig Fine. Faye had therefore invited him to present himself at HQ at eight o'clock this morning. He's prompt, waiting, as we make our way to the foyer. Same modest, near apologetic look, expensive dull suit, white shirt, grey tie, thin monk halo of brown hair, oxblood spectacles enlarging his intelligent eyes. He stands mutely watching us, briefcase in hand, a perfect nobody curiously aligned to a deeply flawed somebody.

'Good morning, Mr Fine. Thank you for coming along. This is Detective Constable Faye Addision.'

'How do you do,' he says to her.

'G'day, how are ya,' Faye replies brightly. Her handshake's a handshake, his offering a lifeless arm.

As soon as we're seated in an interview room, around which he's gazed in vague apprehension, I activate the recorder. If Craig Fine wasn't expecting a formal interview, he's not saying.

'Thanks for your time, Mr Fine. I'd like to begin by asking if you've had any representations from Suzy Stillrock or Emma Lexington since you and I last spoke.'

'They've both contacted me, yes, with the same question. Who gets his estate? And I have said to both of them that I'm seeking legal opinions, which is as it should be.'

'Can you explain why, please?'

'Suzy had been away from the marital home for almost a year, after which relevant family legislation would override her claim to inherit his estate, provided it could be proved that he was living in a de facto relationship with Emma. And she plans to provide that, on the apparent basis of Stillrock having told her that he wanted her to live permanently with him.'

'So the twelve-month period is important?'

'Oh yes, for Suzy. After that she would have had no claim at all, if they were still separated. And it would obviously be in Emma's interest to keep them apart until the year was up.'

'Does Emma have proof of what she says?'

'Well, Stillrock indicated quite strongly to me that she was giving him a new lease of life. Indeed, in the depths of his despair over the film script debacle he said that her youth and vitality and optimism meant much to him. But you must understand, detectives, it's not that simple. I could see through Rory. Emma was pleasurable for him, not bedrock. To use one of his crudities, he once said to me that Suzy was built for comfort, Emma for speed. And Suzy has ample proof that she and Stillrock periodically separated, in order to refresh their marriage. And she most forcefully argues that this was the case on this occasion. Just that Emma wormed her way into Stillrock's affections, and deliberately worked to turn him away from Suzy. And, as I say, apart from anything else this expanded the time in which they were apart. That is, Emma actively worked to prevent him asking her back, or her forcing her way back.'

'Do you believe that?'

'Whether I do or not, Suzy has a fair case, in my opinion. As you know, the law struggles to be clear cut in the area of family relationships. And if partners have an informal arrangement that involves mutually agreed separations, how can legislation simply overrule that? Which is why I'm obtaining legal opinion on behalf of the estate of my client Rory Stillrock.'

'So he was, like, a *victim* of two women?' Faye asks.

'Well ...' Craig Fine winces. 'Rory a victim? I don't know about that. It could be that he and Suzy were in a longstanding game, that he was using Emma as some kind of psycho-sexual bait to tease Suzy.'

I don't answer, nor does Faye. We think about that. Then I say, 'Okay, Mr Fine. Just as a matter of personal interest, do you think he was the victim of foul play?'

'Yes.'

'Why?'

'You people would have ruled it out otherwise.'

'Fair comment. Faye, do you have any further questions about Suzy or Emma?'

'I do,' she says. 'You must know Suzy well?'

'Reasonably, but we're not close. My wife and I hardly ever socialised with them. We were not their type.'

'So, would you not be able to say to what extent she loved him? Or didn't love him?'

'Mhm, that's hard. But, if this will help, he knew how much he owed Suzy. Actually, for keeping him alive, in a way, jarring though that sounds.'

'Yes, it makes sense,' Faye says.

My turn. 'And what might you have heard about Robin Meuchasse since his return from Fiji?'

'That he regards it all as a bit of a sad joke. He seems to think Stillrock was born to kill himself. That's what he told me, anyway, at the funeral.'

'Didn't that strike you as callous?'

'Rory was a shit to just about everyone, some more so than others. Robin he took particular aim at, because they were professional competitors.'

'Despite their long friendship?'

He shrugs. 'Stillrock was complex and conflicted. What more do you want me to say?'

'Clearly he was. Look, I know I've already asked you about that script of his that at the last moment didn't get up. If you could just remind us, please, how much that failure hurt him. That script has been described to me as the last shot in his locker. Perhaps it did tip him over the edge.'

Craig Fine frowns, then reflexively dabs a rude finger at the bridge of his spectacles. 'No, Detective Inspector, no. And funny you should use that phrase. That script wasn't the last shot in his locker. Even in the depth of his despair and humiliation at having had that deal snatched away, he told me, and he used the phrase only then, that he had one more shot in the locker.'

'And that was?'

'He said he'd decided to start straight away on his auto-biography. His own story, that no one could, excuse me, fuck up on his behalf, were his words, or tell him how to write it or what to leave in or out. He said he had lived a unique life, and that his tell-all autobiography, with no holds barred, would shock the world, sell in the millions, et cetera. He even told me its working title.'

'Yes?'

'"Agent Stillrock: The Revenge." Inside his pain he was very angry. Not suicidal. Angry.'

'You're saying he had something to live for?'

'Much to live for. His whole life, refreshed in print. So, personally, I happen to believe that he was murdered.'

'By who?'

191

Fine sucks in a deep breath. 'I think Emma Lexington did it. I think she was beside herself with rage because she believed he'd secretly decided to return to Suzy. Using Emma, as I say, as bait for his jealous wife. And I've yet to meet a woman who likes being used that way.'

'Why didn't you tell me this at our first meeting, Mr Fine?'

'This is my opinion. I've no proof one way or another, or you would have had it from me. And in the absence of proof you won't find me speculating aloud. Except in here.' He smiles thinly.

'Talking of speculation, I don't suppose there would have been anything about you in this book of his that you wouldn't have wanted made public?'

He sits back, flummoxed, then grins. 'No! I'm so dull my wife calls me Forty-Five. You know, like a dim light bulb.'

Faye and I can't help ourselves, we laugh, and Fine does too.

'What about Joanna? Anything his stepmother wouldn't have wanted made public?'

'Joanna? You can't possibly think ...' He tails off, big frown, nervous rude finger.

'Same question as I asked you, Mr Fine.'

'Of course, yes, sorry. You have to.'

'We do. We have to keep asking questions, meaningless though they seem to be, right down to that last shot in the locker. So, nothing on Joanna?'

'Well, no, of course not.'

'Good. Alright, well thanks you for your time Mr Fine, it's appreciated.'

For some reason Faye and I escort Craig Fine right out onto the street. Probably because we're so pleased with him. Rush hour traffic's sounds and smells don't amount to much, absorbed as they are between HQ and the big green of St Davids Park.

Pleased because he's handed us the real motive on a plate. Stillrock was killed not because of what he'd done but what he intended to do.

We watch him stride with briefcase swinging towards the traffic lights that will take him to his Harrington Street premises.

'Boss, would it be Joanna who said that? About the last shot in the locker?'

'She did. And if he told Fine about his proposed book, he surely told her.'

Faye doesn't answer. The traffic glugs to a halt. Car people look up at us looking down at them.

Then she says, 'But he wouldn't write that about them, surely, his own stepmum and him? After all that she did for him?'

'It's an intriguing question, Faye, and I'd like to put it to her. Our problem is, good motive, no evidence.'

The mobile. Rafe.

'Jesus Christ, boss! I've been watching the place, Toyota's there, but the fucking runabout's gone!'

21

RACING TO FRANKLIN TWICE IN TWO DAYS, THIS TIME WITH Faye and in a different car, I'm puzzled. If Titch has become aware of our surveillance, how? Or are he and Lily still in his house? Rafe in his eyrie said her car's still under the tree where she parked it when Titch picked her up in the runabout yesterday. So theoretically they're still together, wherever they are, and whatever that means. The problem, such as it is, confounds me. Unless a third party has gone off in the runabout, Titch, and presumably Lily, must have walked from his place to the river under cover of darkness during the night or early this morning before Rafe woke and resumed his watch. The fact he didn't make a point of checking on the runabout is understandable. You wake up, look out the window up the hill, Toyota's parked where it was when you went to sleep, owners still home.

We're flying, blue and reds silently flashing, the highway, as ever, mostly free of traffic.

Faye says, 'Maybe he just went to get the paper. And she's fast asleep. Didn't want to wake her firing up the 4WD.'

'Is he that nice? Can he read?'

'Slipped its mooring?'

'He might share the thing.'

'Yeah, there's that.'

'But my feeling is they've pissed off, associated with the Melbourne visitors. Cause and effect, Faye, the abc of criminality. Pays our wages.'

'But why not just use his vehicle?'

'Have a guess.'

'He knows he's being watched.'

'He does indeed. Or one or both of them are still fast asleep and the sound of gentle and polite copper door knocking will soon find that out.'

'SHIT, GUYS, I'M REALLY SORRY,' RAFE SAYS, LETTING US IN, 'I MEAN I just didn't even think of looking out for the bloody tinnie, did I? I mean who *would*?'

'Possibly me,' Faye says.

'Get stuffed, junior. It was only when it registered with me, where's the dog? It's usually outside in the sun in the morning. So what's the plan, boss?'

I'm looking through the telescope at the house. Just as he said, the Toyota out front, nothing moving in the house windows. Could he have looked down at Rafe through binoculars? Not impossible but I doubt it. Unless we have a rat in our TPF ranks. Unlikely. Or the Vics. Possibly. Or a casual mistake by Rafe, or even me, after all, we're burned into Titch and Lily's retinas.

'Two plans. Plan A if they've shot through, Plan B if not.'

They wait, watching the house, watching me.

'Plan B, we arrest them.'

'*What*? You've been saying they're untouchable.'

'Walter's been saying that. Changed circumstances.'

'Onya, boss! Plan A? If they're gone?'

195

'Franklin's first b and e by serving members of the Tasmanian Police Force. Let's go.'

UP CLOSE THE PLACE LOOKS EVEN MORE RUN DOWN. CREEPERS creep across the low wooden deck of rotting boards. Rusty bits and pieces lie scattered in the grip of grassy mounds, a side wall's stained ugly from a long-leaking drainpipe.

I knock loudly on the front door. Silence. Rafe and Faye go up for a close look through each window.

'Mess in there,' he says.

'Don't bother trying to sell.' Faye cups a hand, peers through filthy plate glass. 'Bong on a table, boss.'

'There's our arrest. He's already done time for drugs. Come with me, Faye.'

We walk around to the back. It's the same, unkempt, a chook pen abandoned so long ago it's sagged to the ground, pulled down by a sprawling blackberry patch, near a large rusty water tank with no top and a ladder against it, nearby hosepipe a sleeping serpent. I try the ancient back door. Locked, wobbly. I see there's a gap between the door and the foot-worn step. I get down on one ageing Pufferfish knee, close one eye, peer into the lock. Key's in.

'Faye, could you bring me a charge sheet, please?'

'… Yeah, righty-ho.'

She's back with the piece of paper in a flash. I've taken out my Tasmanian Air Force knife, selected its pop-out five-centimetre stiletto. It's a clever little tool with an eye at the inner end, to thread line and make a fine needle for tent mending, stitch gaping wounds, that kind of everyday thing. I slide the sheet under the gap between the door and step, insert the stiletto into the keyhole, wriggle it. Manoeuvre, jiggle. Soon enough, and with

196

care, I'm pushing the key head, then it falls, and we hear the soft plunk of metal on floorboard. I carefully pull back the charge sheet. The key fits through the gap.

'Jeez, boss, you're in the wrong profession.'

I unlock the door.

'One other thing, Faye. The raw material for the bong. Hop up the water tank ladder.'

She does. My fast-learning junior up a ladder peering down.

'Eight big plants, boss. Almost to the top. What made you think –?'

'Another old trick, Detective Constable. Suntrap. Silly boy shouldn't have left the ladder up. Let's go inside.'

THE PLACE PUTS ME IN MIND OF AN ANIMAL'S UNDERGROUND burrow. Perfect for the creature but not to everyone's taste. There's clutter everywhere, the air's stale, unmade bed, blokey things where you wouldn't expect them, such as a rusty motorbike wheel rim on top of the noisy, battered fridge festooned with joke porno magnets, and a hole bashed casually through a wall to take an extension cord. But I can see Lily in here, envisage them drinking and smoking dope, laughing, rutting, eating charred snags and steaks done on the filthy barbecue burner out the back.

In each of the two front rooms I look out and down. Could he have seen Rafe in his room looking up here? No chance. Rafe's window, from here, is tiny. Titch would have needed a powerful pair of glasses, and there's no sign of such.

I've a call to make.

'Walter? Franz. Titch Maguire's gone, alright. No question he's done a runner in his runabout.'

'We can be absolutely sure of that?'

'Well, I'm standing in his empty house, his Toyota's out the front and there isn't a note on the kitchen table saying, "gone fishing", so yes, we can be reasonably bloody sure of that.'

'How did you get in?'

'The back door was unlocked.'

Not that I'm going to tell him how.

Keeping watch at the front, Rafe, I see, is ferreting, fossicking in the Toyota.

Walter says, 'So what do you suggest, Franz, as you see it on the ground?'

'Every available uniform within cooee to search upriver and downriver until we find him, or his boat at least. Something spooked him. He's taken Fink's missus with him and that little tinnie with its lawnmower motor can't have gone far. And I doubt I'll find the necklace in this festering tip he calls home, or probably used to call home.'

Walter pauses then clears his upper echelon public service throat down my earhole. Bastard. Rafe's got something in one big paw, goes around the back to come in that way. I wonder what.

'Okay. I'll do a call-out. Tell me where you want to brief them and give me an ETA to point them at.'

'– Hang on, Walter.'

Rafe barges in.

'Check these out, boss, they were in the glove compartment. Never thought I'd find gloves in such a place!'

He's holding up a pair of tough work gloves, newish, but with dark dry stains on both. Puts them in my face.

'Blood, mate, pure and simple, blood. Smell it. The Indian girl's or Dellacroix's, both, I reckon.'

198

HERE'S HOW THINGS WORK. METAPHORICAL HORDES OF TPF officers are eagerly making their way towards my designated forward command post, a dusty highway pulloff just outside Franklin near the Swamp Road turnoff, where I'll brief them, assign them stretches of river. A small TPF water vessel is making its way from Hobart. It'll scour the waterways not visible or inaccessible from the waterside roads, both banks of the river. This process takes time. And only so many officers will be gifted to me. It's not as if Titch and Lily have transmogrified overnight into VDL's Bonnie and Clyde. And off-duty personnel get narky quick when pulled in for a shit job like this. Looking in awkward, wet places. And keep looking until Pufferfish says you can stop. It pisses them off and I can understand why because it used to piss me off too. Only now I call the shots.

Here's how things really work. I'm patiently waiting at the forward command post. In dribs and drabs TPF personnel arrive, unenthusiastically. A call from TPF HQ.

'G'day sir, call from a fisherman at Port Huon, he's just come back in and says his car's gone.'

'What kind?'

'Prado LandCruiser.'

'Where was it?'

'The car park.'

'Ta. *Rafe!*'

Across the dusty space he comes jogging at an irritated clip.

'The fuck's up, mate?'

'Fill your car with people and go to Port Huon. A Prado LandCruiser stolen from the car park. Bound to be them.'

'Right, boss … But can you not just yell at me like that? As if I'm your thick offsider?'

'You are my thick offsider. So listen hard. Given the time between when you missed them and now, they could have parked that runabout anywhere, Forbes Bay, Surges Bay, Police Point, Shipwrights Point, somewhere in and around Hospital Point. But start at the Port Huon car park. Go find, Rafe.'

'Yeah, I will. Boss, just don't treat me like shit on a shoe.'

Faye and a male uniform have stayed back at Titch's place, instructed by me to work carefully through the rooms for evidence that might further implicate him. Not that I'm going there, now. I've got a growing posse of restless troops to keep on hold.

RAFE CALLS.

'Boss, found the tinnie. They tucked her in under a stand of boobialla scrub, pushed her in good and deep. We're talking not one hundred metres from the car park.'

'Thank you, Rafe. What did you find in the boat?'

'Cigarette butts. And half a loaf of white bread in its plastic, big packet of barbecue chips, Tim Tams. You wouldn't want to eat them, though. Crushed underfoot.'

'That's interesting.'

'Going somewhere.'

'Maybe. Probably.'

'Chase is on, then.'

'It is.'

'Boss, if I'm the shit on your shoe, who cleans it off?'

'Rafe, I'm not a hard man. But having said that, I'm reminded that it's high time I caught up with Fink.'

22

EVEN WHITE-HOT MURDER BLOKES LIKE ME HAVE TO REST FROM time to time. Which is why I find myself at home in the middle of this day, wanting a quick nap before going on to the jail to chinwag with Fink Mountgarrett about this and that. Surely I've shaken off that flu bug? The head's heavy, the legs reluctant. I need more time at the shack, the solitude of the place, floating in her little bay between sacred rock and striplet of fine white beach sand, weary body defying gravity.

I'm at the kitchen bar, picking at last night's unfinished pan omelette, half a glass of apple and guava juice. The alarm's already set, on the lounge room floor alongside the couch. Hope the mobile doesn't ring. It doesn't. But the front doorbell does. Great. Better not be Jehovahs or they'll witness some earthy language.

Sing-song voice outside.

'Hi, Dad!'

I open the door. Nora's with a friend. She's carrying a wicker basket.

'Hello, hello, and to what do I owe the privilege?'

She pecks me on the cheek. 'Dad, you remember Jaye?'

'Of course.' We shake hands. 'Come in. What's with the basket of goodies?'

'Guess, mate!' Nora dumps the basket on the kitchen counter, takes out four glass jars.

'The fruit picking we did at Mrs Arundel's place?'

'Yes …?'

'She said take as much home as you want, so we did! Just heaps! Apricots, peaches, greengage plums, strawberries, and we spent the *whole* of yesterday making jams and chutneys. So these are for you, these two are spicy chutneys, they're a bit hot actually, and this is strawberry and this is peach jam.'

Nora grins happily at their handiwork and then at me.

I nod, a grateful old father. Even though I'm thinking, pity I know what I know.

'So,' I say, 'it wasn't so bad after all.'

'Thanks, Mr Heineken,' Jaye says. 'It was good fun, really was. The pay's alright. And this stuff. And, you know, thanks so much for letting me stay at your Bruny place, it's totally awesome.'

Nora takes some other things from the basket, a magazine, a shiny pamphlet, some cards, drops them on the table. She picks up a card. 'And Mrs Arundel sort of said, these are what they use for raising charity, you fill in the card with a pledge of donating however many dollars. So … Not sure if you're interested? Or maybe you can just leave them in the canteen at work?'

'I might do that. Apart from slaving away in your kitchen, how's uni?'

'Oh, y'know.'

'I do?'

'Mate.' She winces at me. 'All good, except there's this one lecturer. Early Australian history. We can't stand each other. Probably 'cause she's only about five years older than me. The other day she failed me for an essay, like forty per cent? So

I'm, why Claire? And she goes, "It's off topic", and I'm like what do you mean off topic? History isn't one dimensional. And she goes, Nora, we work according to set marking criteria and blahdy blahdy yabbada yabbada. I mean, Jesus!'

'Everyone thinks she's a real dick,' Jaye says. 'Basically, she covers up her own insecurities with this mantle of *I am so clever*.'

'That's a shame. Just remember, though, she calls the shots, and you want the marks. Cup of tea?'

'No, we're off to movies. Just thought, well you probably wouldn't have been here and I was going to leave the basket at the front door, like in a fairy tale. How come you're here anyway?'

'Lunch. And a lie down. Getting old, fragile, handle with care.'

They laugh, Nora grabs my arm, prods a bicep. 'Got a way to go yet, Dad.'

I see them out.

Think of them at the shack. Consider their happiness. You're only young once and you're bound to make the best of that, if you can, while you're still in the outer orbit of childhood's innocence. Something like that.

AS FOR JOANNA ARUNDEL AND HER CHARITY NO LONGER QUITE so noble and good. I pick up a card, look at it, let it flutter back to the counter. Do I want to support her? Some chance. The magazine is the new TasFoodAid annual report and it has the same sense of noble deed-doing as the fundraising cards, with its glossy colourful three-fruits logo superimposed over a pea-green map shape of Tasmania. Even as a not-for-profit entity there's still a nice little personal profit to be made by the owner. Take this good-looking report. Scatter it around the right boardrooms and it talks. Be interesting to find out from Mr Craig Fine if

Joanna makes a quiet buck from this enterprise, that otherwise she might, say, donate to charity.

I flip through it. Got to admire her, though. Hard yakka. Can't switch off with her status. I wonder when she last had sex with her stepson. Did she kill him? The pressure's on me to call this investigation one way or another, soon. As of now, how easy it would be to advise the Coroner of the inconclusive nature of the police investigation, and to recommend that this inconclusivity is reflected in his report. Maybe I'm just overtired. Rory Stillrock was murdered but the evidence required to prove that beyond reasonable doubt and then secure a conviction is missing.

So we live. Win some, lose some. Was going to nap? The mobile. Rafe.

'Boss, you at the jail yet?'

'No, why?'

'Been thinking. Is it a good idea for Fink to know we're looking for Titch?'

'No. And I told Walter, deflect public queries about cops scouring Huon waterways. But trying to keep it quiet, Rafe? We might as well stick our thumbs in a bursting dam wall.'

'Yeah, just thought I'd mention it.'

Flipping through the TasFoodAid report, glossy, charitable. What's Rafe really saying?

'Good on you, Tredway, keep up those thoughts, and remember, you're only my thick offsider because Faye's my thin insider, know what I mean?'

'Boss …' He laughs in my ear, and I'm thinking, he really needs to lock down the Bellyard necklace case, because in his mind he mucked it up, but he didn't, in fact the opposite occurred.

I'm looking at a photograph of Joanna Arundel with her secretary, at some warm outdoor function raising Christmas funds.

'– Boss?'

'Rafe, yes, what were you saying?'

He tells me, but will have to repeat himself because, blow me down, in full colour, Joanna Arundel at this warm outdoor sunshine-winking function is waving like a queen, her smile beatific, her wristwatch not silver but gold, the one she supposedly lost long before the photograph was taken.

23

ADRIAN 'FINK' MOUNTGARRETT LOOKS AT DETECTIVE INSPECTOR Franz 'Pufferfish' Heineken and I look at the Finkster, across a scarred table. We're at 'his' place. Just the two of us. Tape's running. Fink didn't know he was about to be interviewed. But it's happening. Something in me still almost admires the cut of his jib, which is his tapered goatee, tiny unshaved tuft in the chin dimple, bogan goat-tail. I can't see Fink and self getting along socially, but he has as much right as me to his seven score years and ten. The difference being he's locked up and I locked him up. And so we talk.

'Well, Fink, you're aware something's going on down in the valley today?'

'I heard, yep. Heard youse lot begun infesting the waterways, mate.'

'Be a reason, surely? Your patch, Fink.'

'Dream on.'

'Try harder.'

'Mate, am I the king of Huonville? No.'

'No, agreed, but you are, or maybe until recently you were, uncontested prince regent of the hoon valley.'

'What the fuck is a "prints regent", mate, and whatever your question was, the answer's get stuffed.'

'If only it was all so easy. I've four matters to lay on you, Fink.'

I'm taking a punt with the first, because for all I know it's part of an arrangement. My man's sitting back now, arms folded, classic posture of calm, facial expression may contain traces of amusement.

I dip solemnly into my briefcase. Take from it and spread upon the table, facing Fink, four enlarged glossy colour photographs of Lily and Titch together.

Kissing in the canal. Canoodling in his car. Giving each other the glad eye out the front of his place, she on tippy-toes. And a rear view of them disappearing into his fetid castle, arms around one another, brandy bottle swinging from a Titch paw. By the foreground blurring in each it's clear they're clandestinely taken images, furtive underhand material, normally the stuff of private investigators. Fink, you'd reckon, knows just how much more serious this is than the work of a fat, greasy-haired p. i. documenting some middle class nookie for a few grand. But we'll see.

No arrangement.

Fink stares down at the photos, jaw stiffly working. Almost hear the teeth grind. Do hear him swallow, inhale sharply through pinched nostrils.

He didn't know. It's betrayal.

My man's face glows red. He's about to blow, flicks narrowed eyes to mine.

'The fuck you doin' to me, cunt …?'

'As you can see, we've been watching him, Fink. And now Lily's got herself caught up in the mess.'

Eyes whipping about, the photos, me, elsewhere, he's calculating fast.

'They're just takin' advantage of me bein' in here.'

'Could be. But also more than that, Fink, much more. Here's the second matter. Titch recently murdered someone. It was in the media. Awful bashing death, maggots. Johann Dellacroix. You know why he did it?'

His eyes again fixated on the images and he's seeing them in a different light, now that we cops know.

'Titch murdered him? No, mate, surely. Why'd he want to do that?'

'Easy. Guess.'

Fink shrugs. 'Dunno. You just saying he did.'

'I am indeed. And so we arrive at the third matter. Titch did it to retrieve a diamond necklace from the poor bastard.'

Fink shakes his head, like he's taken a sharp smack.

I wait. Then say, 'In summary, Fink, you're inside, Titch is outside, and he's got your diamonds and your girl.'

'Bull fucking *shit*!' Fink smashes a backhand across the images and they fly, up he jumps, enraged and violent. The guard rushes him and even though he subsides straight away the guard grabs and twists his arm, heavies him back into his seat. He'll lose privileges for it.

'Leave me,' he says panting. 'Won't do it again, won't, just …
Aahh! …'

A roar of rage and he shakes his head again, bashes the flat of his hand against his temple, a harsh and painful smacking sound, over and over.

I wait.

'The fourth matter is this, Fink. They've done a runner. Something spooked him. It's pure luck the tip worker's alive. You know about the tip worker?'

'Nah.'

'Also in the media. Bashed to within an inch of her life for no apparent reason. By Titch.'

'Yeah?'

'Oh yes. He's gone over the edge, and I'm very, very worried. For instance, he might take a hostage. Though he might reckon he's already got one.'

'Lily?'

I nod. Wait. Allow him to consider it all.

'I could do with a smoke,' he says.

'In a minute. I want you to help me. I don't normally do deals, but think about this. Titch Maguire has blood on his hands, his gloves actually. He's wanted for murder and a further charge of attempted murder. And because he's in possession of the diamond necklace we've been seeking we have more than enough evidence to convict him of its theft. So, even if someone else actually stole it, I can make that irrelevant to a court. And I want Lily Huskisson out of his hands. So you see, Fink, I need to know where he might've gone to ground. Somewhere safe to lie low while he finds a buyer for the stones to get him out of here, away from the likes of me. You should know where the bloke is. After all, he is your best mate.'

'Was, fuckin' was,' he mumbles. But he's calculating again. An out for him. Lily back. In return for telling a cop where to find a fugitive. Ratting on your own's about as low as you can get. Unless Titch just went lower. But he did retrieve the stones on Fink's request.

I wait.

Fink Mountgarrett's cunning face morphs into a skin-creased expression of pure agony, hurt and beaten, intensely conflicted, wondering what's the least bad of two very dodgy-looking options. He, my exhausted man, exhales noisily, clears a croaky throat.

'Lily and I will sort it out. She belongs with me. So yeah, mate, I'll tell you where I reckon he may have gone. But on one condition.'

'And that is?'

'Like you said, he's got the necklace. So he did the job.'

'That's right, Fink. He did the job.'

'You a man of your word, mate? Fuckin' cop?'

'Last time I looked, yes, Fink. Done deal?'

I lean forward, extend my right arm across the table, hand out to shake. Fink shakes it. His fingers are dry and cracked. They must have him on painting maintenance duty or something.

'Done deal,' he says.

'I'll say this, Fink, your lady and your best mate, they are two people you would never have expected to get down and dirty together.'

And I'm thinking of others too, unconnected to Mr Mountgarrett.

'Shits me, mate. You don't fuckin' expect it.'

'No, you don't. Believe me, I sympathise with you Fink. And to think that it all started with an innocent headbutt.'

24

THE BREAKTHROUGH I'VE BEEN LOOKING FOR, WAITING FOR, AFTER the slog, the perseverance, the luck, the extra step, stuns Hunt and Walter, but they're also relieved.

'She has a case to answer,' Franz, Walter says. 'She lied to you about her watch, and that's now the key piece of evidence.'

'No question she wouldn't be physically capable of doing it,' Hunt says. 'And her motive's right up there.'

'Shocking,' Walter, says, 'I mean, I'm ... how's the public going to react to this one?'

Hunt surprises us both.

'You know,' he says reflectively, 'it's funny. The Christmas before last Sybil, among the socks and chocs, gave me the autobiography of the famous Hollywood actor George Hamilton. He'll be getting on, now, Mr perpetual suntan. Played a lawyer in one of the *Godfather* movies. And in his book he cheerfully admitted to having a sexual relationship with his stepmother when he was twelve, and then they continued it when he was a man. And in fact as I recall George Hamilton had a cameo role in *Crocodile Dundee in Los Angeles*. So there you go gents. It's an unpredictable world.'

'OH DAD, THAT IS JUST SO PUERILE! HEDDA WON'T MIND! WE'LL be pitching one small tent in the she-oak grove. She won't even know we're there!'

'Yes she will, Nora. Look, weekends are precious to working people like us, and Hedda needs time alone, okay? So, no, this weekend, no shack, sorry.'

Pause. I look at my office wall clock. Nearly time.

'I kind of told Jaye and his friend we'll be going there. They probably broke other plans.'

'Then they'll have to unbreak them.'

'How's Hedda going to *mind*, actually? She's so laid back.'

'That she may be and even if she didn't, I would. But I will tell you, she's been involved in some difficult work. It's been in the news. The mother injecting her babies at night to keep them quiet?'

'– Oh, right. Jeez …'

'I have to go. Call me this evening and we'll arrange another time.'

'Sure, thanks Dad. Uhm, tell her I'm really, really sorry.'

'It's the job we do, Nora. *Vaarwel.*'

Dutch sign off, phone down, time for a fast hot little black? No. Interviewing on a full bladder pisses me off so to speak, though the technique of mysteriously suspending an interview for a toilet call can have its merits.

Naturally enough, those interview techniques vary according to circumstance. The interviewee can be drip-fed facts, and fact-like insinuations, like quarry eventually exhausted by a predator in pursuit. Or be harried into a sudden dead end by verbal entrapment. Or there is the stealth predator technique, in which a big hit first up on the prey renders it bleeding and helpless.

I've settled on which one I will be employing for Joanna Arundel.

FAYE AND A UNIFORM DROVE TO RICHMOND AND INVITED JOANNA Arundel to accompany them to HQ for a formal interview, the reason given to her that new information required she be formally interviewed, and would she like a lawyer present? Her answer was, no, she would be pleased to swear under oath any information that might assist in finally ending the controversy surrounding her stepson's death.

So be it.

Otherwise, Faye would have arrested her.

Now Joanna Arundel's seated in an interview room, waiting. For me. And I wonder what she makes of my deadpan self, not so long ago passing the summer time of day with her yaffling about white netting protecting her fruit trees.

'Well, hello, Detective,' she says, upon seeing me. 'I almost feel like a *criminal* in this ghastly room.'

Hair in its big grey weightless-looking bun, tailored light cream linen suit, plain court shoes, and in possession of an item, a smart handbag. Me? Instant coffee-brown suit, seriously pre-loved white shirt, new Les Lees tie from a sale rack that was virtually on the Liverpool Street pavement.

'Hello, Mrs Arundel.' I sit, smiling faintly, as is she.

'So what is this further information you have? To bring this all to a close, I trust. It's been too distressing.'

'We do expect closure soon. Which is why you have been asked here.'

'Well, can we get it done with, please. I've a substantial schedule today.'

I nod, equably.

Predator, prey, choice of.

The thing about a predator is that over its lifetime it must expend minimal energy in order to maximise its chances of survival. Hence, the importance of the decision as to how to attack.

Behind her drop-down specs she wants me to get on with whatever it is I want to ask her. So I do.

'I'll get straight to the point, Mrs Arundel. When I first spoke to you at your Richmond home, I handed you your gold watch –'

Pause. Just enough to take in her reaction.

Her eyes flick to Faye then back to me.

'– And you said you had lost it almost a year ago, and you showed me a receipt for the replacement silver watch. Yes?'

'Oh yes indeed. And thank you again.' She smiles graciously. Her arms are crossed demurely on the table. The gold watch glints. She touches it fondly.

'And you remarked how much you continually missed the gold watch, given its sentimental value. So how can it be –'

I reach down to the green recycling bag on the floor alongside my seat, nice young environmentally aware touch, Faye, and bring up the TasFoodAid annual report, open it at the photograph of her indulging in her queen wave, lay it on the table before her.

'– How can it be that you were wearing it less than three months ago?'

She blushes, a hand floats to a shining pink cheek as she stares down at herself, the deadly question demanding an answer. How can it be?

'My age, it must be my *age*!' she says, through a high-pitched, wobbly laugh. 'I'm getting old and forget, and oh the silly watch, the clasp thingy, loose, should have had a watchmaker mend it ages ago –'

We wait.

'– I mean, well obviously I lost it after that picture was taken. And just forgot, as you do, Detective, as you would know.'

Stalking's over. The horrified herbivore has bolted. Let's go, cub Faye.

'No, Mrs Arundel. Here is what I believe happened. You did lose your gold watch a year ago. And you did buy a silver replacement. But then you found the gold watch, somewhere in your Richmond home perhaps, and began wearing it again. Until it came off your wrist when you were helping drunk Rory Stillrock into the passenger seat of his Cadillac, on the night he died. Or do you have another explanation?'

She's flushing with an angry, rash-like scowl.

'Oh what rubbish, nonsense! No! *What?*' An impulsive hand fumbles for a non-existent glass of water, sticky dry mouth.

But she's been around for a long time, Joanna Arundel. She takes a deep, deep breath, reasserting herself. Spine up, defiant sparkle in the Delft-blue eyes, jutting bosom pack.

'Are you both *imbeciles?* Are you truly and honestly deluding yourselves that I, that I, I'm sorry, Detective, but why *in Heaven's name* would I wish to harm my own stepson?'

I nod. She has a fair point. Reach back down into my crafty bag of tricks, bring up Viola Vine's video cassette. Wag it lightly at her.

'One of these cassettes was burnt in his fireplace, Joanna, shortly before he died. You and Rory Stillrock in sexual congress.'

She doesn't reply.

'The things he would have written about you both, Joanna, in his book. He wouldn't have held back, because it truly was the last shot in his locker. And he was determined that everyone should know the truth about Rory.'

She's staring at me. I'm justice, dehumanising before her eyes. I've seen it many times before, the panicky, fearful look, generated by excessive excretion of stomach bile, which does something else too, as the air's blighted with a razor-sharp tang of diarrhoea.

215

She holds stiff fingers over her lips. Eyes darting between me, Faye, me. Decision time. Bluff? How can we know so much? But we do.

Her eyes come back to me, and we spend some time regarding one other. A shared wisdom passes between us, like electricity between two points. We're equals, but not for much longer. Make your play, Joanna, because I'm not blinking first.

I sense a deep shudder move through Joanna Arundel. And she is ready to talk.

But still, she waits. That it should have come to this, when it shouldn't have, but it has, and the man with the dead eyes has brought the cold news, has worked his way through dark, slimy cracks to get to her, to get her.

'Detective Heineken, Rory should never have even *considered* writing a book about himself. Even if it was accurate, it would have been so wrong, because it was only *me* who truly knew him. And therefore only I knew when the time had come to put him to sleep. Does that make sense?'

'It does, if you are telling me that you were alone with him on the night he died and helped him go to sleep in his Cadillac.'

'Yes. I did. I did what a good mother must. My Rory had suffered enough. If you like, I euthanised him. Time anyway for that law, don't you think? Well?'

'Joanna Arundel, I advise you that you are under arrest for the murder of Rory Stillrock. You do not have to say anything, but what you do may be used in evidence.'

She laughs. '"Do not have to say anything!" Oh, you are a pitiful lot. *Pitiful!*'

We wait. She makes a heaving sound, looks wide-eyed at Faye, shakes her head, pats an instinctive hand on her bun. Large tears slide down her cheeks. And now Joanna Arundel pushes her arms forward along the table, drops her head into them and moans loudly, deeply, repeatedly, as if giving birth, dying.

My thoughts are for young Faye. She'll be feeling pretty crook at this display of anguish, but won't be showing it. We went in for the kill because that's what we're paid to do.

When Joanna lifts her head, her dangling specs are broken, eyeliner and eye shadow smudged all over her wrinkled face, penciled eyebrows broken up.

'Do you know,' she says softly, 'how much that boy suffered? He had such a terrible childhood.'

She sniffs loudly.

'One day, and I remember it so well, he came home after school completely tormented. He was just … The older boys had bullied and mocked him for not having real parents. The head teacher had caned him for being naughty. He said he wanted to kill himself. I took him in my arms. He was shivering, like a little animal. And I soothed him in my lap, just talking softly and stroking his hair, as you do. The temptation to comfort him with my body was overwhelming. And he slowly stopped the shivering, grew calmer, and then, and then, he was near my breast, and seemed to want, so I, gave. And he was, even then, I could or should have stopped us, but he, yes, he *thanked* me, in his way even though he was, oh, fourteen, we actually knew what we should do and he loved me. It *was* love, you see, was …'

She halts, unable to go on.

Faye says, 'Would you like some water, Mrs Arundel?'

'Yes thank you, dear, if you wouldn't mind.'

The guard brings in a plastic cup. She drinks noisily, water splashing her chin and top. Long dank grey tendrils of escaped hair drape her arms and the table's edge.

Joanna Arundel's telling us a story that has been waiting a long time to come out.

'That half hour instantly became his thrilling secret, my dreadful mistake. But, you see, my unconditional love gave him strength and resilience, and he had a child's implicit trust that it was right and necessary to end his torment. I can tell you, well, I must tell you, that for me it became a shameful pleasure, a secretive, seductively physical power. I lied to myself that I was doing this only for Rory.'

She stops. Her face is glistening with bright sweat. I can smell her acrid underarms. She swallows, shakes her head, the damp heavy hair, and on she goes.

'I lived with a most terrifying dread that he would blurt it out to someone, in his impulsive shouty way, but he never did. So you see, that was my gift to him, to uplift him, make him famous, my job then done. At great moral cost to me, but done.'

'A moral cost to him?'

She sighs deeply, raggedly. By way of answer says, 'You must understand. I will try to be accurate, because I know it means a lot to you people. He, my darling Rory, is –'

She stops.

We wait.

'... Was. Was, oh dear me ... That skinny child had to put up all sorts of self-protective barriers to shield himself from a world of taunting and hurting. Those barriers were ...'

Joanna Arundel sits back, heaves deep breaths into her, closes her broken-up eyes. When, after some time, she opens them, we're no longer there, and her expression's dreamlike.

'– But oh how I used to *laugh* at the brilliant wit and sarcasm, stunning in one so young, like a boy Oscar Wilde, yet the child also had the survival ferocity of a litter runt to snatch and devour. It was then I realised, saw with my own eyes, that there were two Rories, and how he moved in and out of character effortlessly. Far from being disturbed, schizophrenic, whatever they tried to say it was, and of course the fools had *no idea* what it was, I realised what a fabulously natural actor he must be. For me, it was like stepping through a waterfall to the hidden dry spot behind. I was elated at the realisation, and decided there and then to push and push him into the world of make-believe, to turn my little Rory into a famous actor. I had the money to give it a damn good go, a powerful urge to succeed and not a few connections. And so we set out on our remarkable journey. And we did succeed. We did it.'

She refocuses on us. She's exhausted. Her eyes well up with tears.

'Go on, Mrs Arundel.'

'You must remember I was barely thirty. I had only one focus, and that was to help the tormented boy. He had been thrown at me by a man I should never have married. But I did all that I could. He was the most beautiful, saddest child I had ever seen. He was so afraid of his temporality that he talked like a jackhammer, as if deranged. But he wasn't, and he had become mine, my responsibility, and I began to realise that I had it in my power to help him. That was the best way I could make sense of what was happening. That our wrong love was right, somehow. And he seemed also to understand that although I was his new parent I was also his oldest best friend.'

'Did you ever try to stop the relationship?'

'Oh, what an ignorant question. No. Such utter merging doesn't "stop", Detective. It lasts forever and ever, an indelible stain. Surely you understand that. I have been living with it all this time, a grotesque flowering plant inside my body. For Rory, I helped him to find paradise, but then, as I always thought, he finally rose up, confused angry and afraid. The child had never left him. And finally I was to blame.'

'For what?'

'When it all went wrong in Hollywood. I rushed to be with him, took the first available flight after the accident. He was under sedation in hospital. When I was allowed to see him he, he … *accused* me … He wanted people to know about him and me. It was his defence against being called a rapist. I begged and begged him to say nothing, to keep our secret. He reluctantly agreed. But after that our relationship changed. He then had less respect for me.'

She slaps a hand across her eyes. We listen. She cries.

'Accused you of what, Mrs Arundel?'

'When he was pleading with her he said she became me and he thought he must kiss her to make it right and she didn't like it, but he couldn't stop, he said, so it was my fault, all those years ago, it was too awful, my fault, my fault …'

'The studio executive's rape allegation?'

She nods, her head slack, as if we've been punching her.

We wait. Then she says, 'Rory invited me to his house that evening without saying why. A rare, surprise invitation. He had become reclusive, you see. I was thrilled. He was drunk when I arrived, nothing new, but I had bought a lavish Indian takeaway with all the trimmings and I thought we were in for a wonderful evening. Then he told me he had decided to write his autobiography. Do you know, when I said he would destroy me if he wrote about us, about our relationship that way, he became irritated. He said, words to this effect, Jo, you're not my real mum. You loved me. You were the only person in the world prepared to save me, even if it meant you doing that. Are you now saying you didn't love me, Jo?'

She stops. We wait. She seems utterly spent.

'What did you say to that, Joanna?'

'What did I say? I remember pleading with him, but he laughed. He was so drunk, high as a kite, a ruined man, a very

220

angry, hurt, dreadfully compromised individual. I could no longer give him what he wanted, by agreeing that he should write about us. He said the book would be worthless to him if he didn't tell the truth. And he said, well then, 'let's look at the truth, and he went upstairs, came down with a cassette and put it on in the theatre. Just him and me in those big plush velvet seats. I was terribly upset when he showed me that video. Wouldn't you be? And he knew that even though he'd secretly filmed it years and years ago, in the fog of those Hollywood years, he had done wrong, he had betrayed me. Even though he assured me he had never shown … That it was all for his amusement only. So I made him burn it. But he laughed, dropping it onto the fire. He laughed, because he said we were both equally sick. That is when I saw how damaged Rory Stillrock really was. Beyond repair. Everything bad in his life seemed to have curdled in him. And as if writing it down would help! I did so plead with him. He said he would think about it. Detective, I could not take that risk.'

'How did you get him into the Cadillac?'

'Oh, easily, how do you think? I suggested we drive into the city and get a newly released movie. I pretended I was no longer upset. He agreed. On the way, we stopped at Kingston and I bought him some chocolates from a machine. To stuff him to the greedy gills, help put him to sleep. He was snoring and bubbling away before we even got to the Proctors Road turnoff, so I drove over the bridge and back. Did you know he was ready for death? Rory was but a heartbeat away from leaving us on his own terms. I thought it a powerful symbol, that his heart had gone bad.'

'And when you returned you left the engine running, locked him asleep in the vehicle with the spare set of keys and asphyxiated him with its exhaust fumes.'

'Yes. It did occur to me that if the vehicle was locked, logic would have said he did it. I did not want you to catch me. But now you have'.

'Is there anything more you wish to say at this point, Mrs Arundel?'

'Yes. I completed my lovely stepson's life cycle, as it was meant to be. I thought it so wrong that he should damage himself any more by his beautiful recklessness. You see, I made him what he was, and so it was only right that I closed his eyes at the end. He was never destined to grow old and weary. Rory may no longer be here, Detective, but he's very conscious of us. When they know the right thing has been done by them, the dead watch over us.'

Joanna tries to finish her water, drops the cup, water splashes. She holds her face, hides it in her hands. Into them, she mumbles, 'I did not make the decision to kill him, it came to me. Rory sent it to me, as he sat there drinking whisky and smoking his cigars, a dying shadow of what I had made him. I had to destroy my own monster. *Oh, oh, oh! I am so afraid!* Who might forgive me?'

I see again the accusing crimson stare, demanding of me that I do something.

25

ANOTHER DAY, ANOTHER JOB.

West of Dover, the unsealed Esperance River Road winds towards Hastings Forest and the mighty Hartz Mountains National Park. Our convoy's four, being a Jeep 4WD in which are five troggies, that is, Tactical Response Operations Group boys, some gung, some ho, all keen to put into practice endless training. Rafe and self in a Pajero 4WD, followed by a marked TPF vehicle with three Kingston uniforms, this isolated part of Tasmania being their patch, and a paddy wagon in which to hopefully bung the miscreant, Titch Maguire. Yes, this is a manhunt, but not dragnet style. A ratio of twelve to one's plenty in the bush, and even if Lily's his hostage that's still plenty of us versus one of him.

Warm, low, rain-dark clouds obscure Adamsons Peak and the lofty green dolerite giants marching away towards the southwest coast. We're looking for a long-abandoned fruit pickers' hut, in a valley cut off by an old growth forest coupe cable-logged a quarter of a century ago and left to regrow. Fink described a track off a logging road, and a hut with provisions in it, cans, first aid stuff, mags, even, he said, a Monopoly board, though some prick once pissed on the money, apparently, and you can still faintly smell it. And a river pool nearby, home to yabbies and eels that come up nicely on a barbie hot plate. But Fink gave the information with increasing reluctance. Fair dinkum, you just don't shop a mate to the cops, do you, even a mate who stole your missus. Fink did.

We flew a fixed-wing high over the area first thing this morning and sure enough, the stolen vehicle is alongside the hut.

Late morning, call it early afternoon, the suspension of our Pajero is being well tested on rutted summer road. Everything's dry as a bone in this big heavily forested world.

A low flock of green rosellas shoots overhead folding their wings between branches. The lead vehicle taps brakes, swerves, so therefore do we, allowing an echidna to waddle on its unhurried way.

Rafe says, '"Anyone can make a mistake" mumbled the echidna as it got off the bristle broom.'

Light mountainside rain begins to fall. Almost at once, a new dampness, making sweet scent from summer dust.

Our tactic, as detailed to Hunt and Walter, is simple enough. By stealth and surveillance, determine that the wanted man is in or in the vicinity of the hut. Surround the place and start negotiating. We're going to bivouac the vehicles well beyond earshot and do a forty minute walk to the hut along the track, which is marked on the forestry map these days as a fire trail.

Senior Sergeant Moxham is the trog in charge of today's business, which officially goes by the name, Operation Sturmer Pippin. He's reliable, efficient and hard as, and on the radio.

'ETA is seventeen hundred, boss. Could be a bit of a damp hike in.'

'I reckon, Moxy. Otherwise it would be too easy for you.'

'Yeah thanks, mate. If I could do the final run through with you, please.'

'Go ahead.'

This is a joint Tactical Response Operations Group and Major Crime South operation and we've signed off on every detail and likely scenario, but should there be need of any unanticipated decision-making it's formally his call. Nothing to do with the fact he's got more guns and they're bigger, eh.

'Me, Matty and Ben are jogging in and will take up surveillance at the ridge overlooking the hut. You, Rafe, Rowan and Steve walk in. You should get my first report when you're about halfway there, that is, twenty minutes in give or take. And the boys in the marked cars stand by to drive in when called.'

'Check all of that, Moxy. Best of luck.'

'And to you guys. Oo-roo.'

We briefly see his tanned hand raised out of his window. Rafe flicks his lights.

In theory, a straightforward operation. Lily is the problem, if things get nasty when Titch is loudhailed to advise him of our presence and that he's surrounded. It's a significant worry. I'm thinking of crossfire, if it comes to that.

The rain closes in, heavier, so that you look up at it cascading down in slanted silver fibres through Gondwana relic forest canopy fifty million years young.

IN THE WAKE OF 9/11, NOT THE BOTTLE SHOP FRANCHISE, THE murder of three thousand people, I took part in an exercise involving police forces from both hemispheres, and one thing I learned was that in the United Kingdom the verb yomp still has some currency. It's a currency I have to say I'm happy to go with, because it stands for your own marching pace. I'm neither huffing nor puffing as we go doggedly in, and the ticker feels tickety-boo, but it's me behind Rafe and in front of him Rowan and Steve, the young troggies bursting at the seams because they'd rather not be hanging back with us plainclothes plods. But they have to because the target has a vehicle and there's a possibility the target in his vehicle could come bouncing along this fiendish track.

Hidden to our right is a creek's energetic burble. The mountainous terrain further in, snowmelt and frequent rainfall make rivers and waterfalls a characteristic of this part of the island. Daylight it is, but up ahead wallabies frequently hop off the track into the thick bush. Long dry summer. They need food.

Settled by the rhythm of steady walking and with heads bowed against the softening rain, we make good progress. No talking, waste of breath. No real rush either, but we want the business done.

Rowan drops back and hands me his radio.

'Go ahead, Moxy.'

Talking softly he says, 'Franz, we're at the ridge looking down on the hut. Vehicle's there, no sign of activity. The hut door's open, but we're at an angle and even with the glasses I can't see in.'

'What's the distance?'

'About two hundred metres. Down through a sloped orchard of feral old apple trees. The hut's facing the apple trees and backed up near the bushline, so we should have no dramas getting up close that way. That's how we'll spring him, from behind. But I'll have two up here in case he makes a run this way. Where are you blokes?'

'Just past the celery top pine with the lightning strike split.'

'Good progress, mate, you'll be here in no time flat. Oo-roo.'

HEAVIER RAIN SWEEPS DOWN, EASES OFF AGAIN. WE'RE IN A BIG green, grey, wet silence, slogging towards the end of a strange and sorry saga. You couldn't make it up. Strange because of the journey of the necklace. Sorry because it wasn't worth a life. Indira Patel was lucky, Dellacroix not so. Titch needs a long spell inside. I'll be pleased to bring him in.

When the skyline starts breaking up ahead we know we're close to the ridge. I'm sweating in my wet weather gear, warm. Jesus, I'll be stiff tomorrow, but that's another day. The rain's reduced to a fine spray barely noticeable after what we've been through. Rowan and Steve speed up, disappear around the bend ahead.

Rafe waits for me.

'Luck, boss.'

'You too, Rafe. Let's get this one ticked off.'

IN FRONT OF US THE TROGGIES ARE LYING PACKED TOGETHER, a black singularity of boot soles and humped heads, hiding behind a sprawling overgrown mound of tree stumps dozered up last century. Moxham's hand waves us down. We crouch, move forward on hands and knees until we're alongside and peer through gaps in the old mound. What chance leeches? My palm skids through a creamy little fungi forest, sharp smell.

The apple orchard slopes away and down, a relatively vast space perfectly angled for cool climate sunshine, which is why it was chosen about when Premier Albert G. Ogilvie ruled the roost and the last thylacine was dying in a small zoo cage in Hobart. Remnant trees, withered but fruiting, make a weird spectacle of it all, verdant, gnarled symbols of this peculiar island.

From here, the hut's small as a matchbox, a classic 1930s itinerant fruit pickers' hut, it'd be ten by twenty feet, raised off the ground on squat stumps, bleached grey-white vertical timbers, small square windows, steeply pitched wood shingle roof, angulated brick chimney buttressing one end, red-rusted water tank the other. In the shittest winter night this island could throw at you, fire ablaze, wallaby steaks, something dark red to drink, you'd be snugger in that hut than a pinstripe in the Henry Jones Art Hotel's millionaire suite.

Moxham and his mates are whispering their plans. Rafe and I wait. Not strictly our business. Then we'll be told what's going down, and our role in it. Should there be a problem, and fallout, we'll need to cover our collective arses and rule number one is an agreed chain of command.

The mobile vibrates against my upper thigh. I roll away, slip it out. Walter.

'Franz you've problems, Fink's king-hit an inmate for his mobile, this is five minutes ago he's barricaded himself in a toilet and using it.'

'Right, I'll tell Mox –'

Too late, no point.

From inside the hut, a bellow of rage, a terrified scream, a gunshot.

Titch springs fiercely into sight, mad in the great slanted space, fires off a shot from a handgun, yells at the moody sky.

'*Come and get me you filthy fucking bastards!*'

And runs straight past the stolen Prado into the thick wet bush.

'Fink called him.'

'Right, let's go! *Go go go!*'

The five trogs sprint into the orchard, the quickest route to the hut and where he disappeared and there's little chance Titch would pick any off them off with so much cover, but even so they weave and use the old apple trees, fanning out.

228

We follow, jogging. Rafe would like to be racing, backing up his mates. It's instinctive, but not practical. We watch two trogs enter the hut. They're in there no time at all, out again, waving us on.

Now the trogs are far more cautious, using the hut and Prado as cover. One by one they sprint the short distance to the bush line where Titch disappeared. No shots. And they, too, vanish into the gloomy wet forest.

THERE'S A SMALL STEP UP INTO THE HUT. THE INTERIOR'S GLOOMY, reeks of old food, alcohol, human bodies, and nauseatingly sweet fresh blood. Titch's tan and ash-grey blue heeler, eye closed as if asleep on the floor, lies in dark red pool spreading steadily away from its head and body across the worn timber floor.

Another dead dog.

Lily's sitting on the lower part of a double bunk bed, one of her arms crudely lashed to its post with a piece of baling twine. She's wearing only knickers and a skimpy tank vest. She's crying, shaking her head, mumbling, woefully drunk. Between her breasts, even in this gloom, Bellyard's diamond necklace sparkles.

'Help him,' she slurs, 'Stop him. *Stop him!*' She tugs against the twine, but Titch made sure she's going nowhere.

WE HURRY THROUGH THE SNAGGING BUSH, RAFE ON THE RADIO getting directions from Moxham, though their tracks are clear enough, they had no trouble following Titch because he used what once would have been a path.

Water noise increases and suddenly we come across two trogs standing in a small clearing, at the edge of a sheer drop. A narrow waterfall splashes about thirty metres into a large pool, the idyllic type you'd expect to find in an ad for the cocktail they drink in paradise. Near the base of the waterfall, a pyramid of debris built up over time into an ungainly sculpture of uprooted trees and other vegetative matter, now also Titch Maguire's final resting place, his prostrate body impaled through the stomach, his head pummelled in a dreadful waterboarding.

The other trogs are carefully picking their way down towards the pool.

'He didn't trip, boss.'

'No, no chance of that. He jumped.'

26

THE BARBECUE AT MY 1960S BRUNY SHACK, UNDER THE TEA-TREE and nearby spread of friendly pigface, is exactly what you'd expect, a cast iron plate the size of a small table over a solid red brick construction to bring it up to waist height, the fire sitting on another plate halfway up the bricks. Willard, the Aborigine who made it many, many years ago, knew what he was doing. You can heat the plate to cook for one or a dozen. On a moonless star-spangled night like this one, it's a pleasure to stoke up this barbie, stand back, stare into the energetic yellow-red flames, think about things, enjoy a decent local red, this one from the Huon Valley, as it happens.

Hedda emerges from the shack, carrying things. Last time I saw her, an hour ago, she was in her cozzie, dripping wet from a late dusk swim off the miniature beach, shook her wet hair at me, laughed at my delayed, stiff-bodied reaction. Earlier she'd kayaked down from Hobart, once she knew I'd found a way to snatch a couple of nights here. Given all that's just happened, it was relatively easy. I advised Walter. Taking a sickie. He hit the roof. So I went upstairs and advised Hunt. Still feeling the effects of the cold or whatever it was I picked up. Twenty-four, forty-eight hours should do the trick. In the matters of Joanna Arundel and the Bellyard necklace, call me if I'm needed. Hunt didn't disagree. He said he hoped I'd get better really soon and congratulations, and he'd talk Walter down from the roof.

'Yo.' Hedda puts two plates down on the rack alongside the barbecue, pecks my cheek.

'Roo steaks for you, in the Red Kelly's pepper marinade you like, eggplant and zucchini for me, though you're welcome to share, heaps of onions, what's a barbie without 'em? Salad inside.'

'Sounds good.' I pour her a cab sav, in a scarred plastic 1998 Taste of Tasmania wine cup. We drink.

'So,' she says. 'He jumped.'

'He jumped. Titch Maguire leaped ignominiously to his death, but you know, Hedda, it was heroic, wasn't it? Even to the point of leaving the gun at the spot from which he leapt, so we could know. Pass it on.'

'To the man.'

'Yes. Fink Mountgarrett's faithful lieutenant stuffed up getting the necklace. Took advantage of Lily. By his death he's apologised to Fink and saved him from the rap for the theft. That's true loyalty, isn't it? Cut your mate's head off rather than satisfy the dogs.'

'Could be, could be. And better than a long life inside.'

We watch the fire.

She says, 'What was the trigger?'

'Lily blubbed it out to us, in that hut surrounded by ancient apple trees. They were both off their scones, by the way, been at the brandy since, well, the night before, and his good water tank weed. The trigger was a tip-off from a bent Melbourne cop.'

She laughs. 'What else is new?'

'That cop alerted the Melbourne blokes who visited Titch in Franklin to talk about buying the necklace, and who we identified and asked the Vics to check. So one of them phoned Titch and said what the fuck's going on, why are your cops onto me? And that's when Titch realised we must be watching him, at his place. Because that's where they met. Hence the pre-dawn escape in his runabout, couldn't risk the noise of his car.'

'Nice drop.' Hedda refills my glass. 'With Lily in tow. Why'd she go along, do you reckon?'

'I asked her that. She said he forced her. Didn't elaborate.'

'Keeping her powder dry, mate. Sounds like she and the Finkster have major housekeeping and relationship repairs to do, once he's out. Then all will be sweet. You might even score an invite to the wedding.'

'Don't fancy my chances.'

Some way off in the intense night, call it a hundred metres, a barely perceptible tent-shaped glow in the forest. I relented. Nora and Jaye. Made her happy. My only condition, no fire. So they're eating marinated Pirates Bay octopus, Mure's smoked trevally, Cold Blow Road baby lettuce leaf mix, Oatlands Companion Bakery sourdough rolls and, I noticed, when I looked in the back of her van while we were in the patient vehicle queue for the Bruny ferry, a few bottles of decent enough Tassie cleanskin rolling around. And I advised them how to do their business in nature, our dunny being out of bounds. Use the spade to dig a small hole, use the hole, fill it, plant the spade upright half a metre along. Easy enough.

We stand there thinking about things. After a while Hedda makes an observation.

'Incest and apples, mate. You wouldn't write home about it.'

'All in a day's work.'

'Funny,' she says, 'that damn hula-hoop song that I can't get out of my mind. Did you know that John Phillips, the founder of The Mamas and Papas, had an incestuous relationship with his daughter Mackenzie? She revealed it in her autobiography not so long ago. People were shocked.'

'Really?'

'Yes, really.'

'Must be catching.'

'Yeah ... hey Puff, what's the definition of a Freudian slip?'

'Don't know.'

'Someone who says one thing and means a mother.'

We chuckle.

Hedda drains her Taste of Tasmania wine cup, stirs a toe at the dark sandy pigface. Sighs.

'Poor bloody Joanna.'

'Yes. Poor bloody Joanna.'

Nothing more to say, really, as we as gaze in our darkness at the cheerfully blazing fire.

A PUFFERFISH MYSTERY

No Weather for a
Burial

DAVID OWEN

SHARK

In peril in the sea

Second Revised Edition

DAVID OWEN